The Paradise That Lurks in Female Smiles

Gary Reilly

The Paradise That Lurks in Female Smiles
Gary Reilly

Running Meter Press
Mancos, CO

Published by Running Meter Press Mancos, Colorado
Publisher@RunningMeterPress.com

Cover photo by Alena Plotnikova on Unsplash
Cover and interior design by Jody Chapel

ISBN: 978-0-9909927-3-8
Library of Congress Control Number: 2022908502
Printed in the United States of America

scene the aggregate of one man's experience. It's a powerful and convincing book, Catch 23 or 24, vivid, considered, and real." - Ron Carlson, author of *Return to Oakpine* and *Five Skies*

The Discharge:

"When I try to describe Gary Reilly's Private Palmer novels, I fail. But I'll try again: The plots are secondary to the writing, which is secondary to the kaleidoscope of self-doubt within Private Palmer's head, which is simultaneously heartbreaking, awe-inspiring, and not-laugh-out-loud funny. *The Discharge* is brilliant in the manner of Richard Ford's Frank Bascombe novels. In a case of life's artful imitations, Reilly's explorative text mirrors Palmer 's busted-rudder search for contentment, and I'm happy to report that both Reilly and Palmer eventually do find their way home." - Gregory Hill, author of *East of Denver*

The Asphalt Warrior:

"Gary Reilly proves himself to be not just a gifted stylist, but a kind of Jedi Master of the understated." - Fred Haefle, Montana Freelance Writer & Author of *Extremeophilia*.

Ticket to Hollywood:

"What if the gloomy 19th century German philosopher Arthur Schopenhauer drove a cab in Denver? What if Schopenhauer, crossed with Maynard G Krebbs (you do know who that is, don't you?) by way of comedian Steven Wright, chased fares in the Mile High City? You'd have this book." - Barry Wightman, author of Pepperland

Also by Gary Reilly

The Asphalt Warrior Series
The Asphalt Warrior
Ticket to Hollywood
The Heart of Darkness Club
Home for the Holidays
Doctor Lovebeads
Dark Night of the Soul
Pickup at Union Station
Devil's Night
Varmint Rumble

The Private Palmer Series
The Enlisted Men's Club
The Detachment
The Discharge

Standalone Novels
The Circumstantial Man
The Legend of Carl Draco
*Jeremy Bannister, or The Ups and Downs of an
Aspiring Novelist*

Introduction

Dear Gary,

Hey, pal. I wish you were here to read this letter. It's my introduction to *The Paradise That Lurks in Female Smiles*. Mike Keefe and I take turns writing these. My number came up.

I found this novel among the dozens of mock paperbacks you left behind. I have a whole big box of your novels, all carefully assembled—by hand—by you.

Remember how you showed me your system for printing out drafts of your novels and then binding the pages like a real paperback, only with a blank cover (often made with a rectangle of manila folder)? Well, I found this story in my box and read it in the summer of 2021. Like the fifteen other novels of yours that we have published, I knew this one needed to see the light of day.

Charley Quinn is right up there with Pete Larkey from *The Circumstantial Man* and, of course, Brendan Murphy from the entire Asphalt Warrior series. Quinn, Larkey, and Murphy all think quite a bit about writing and storytelling. Of course, Private Palmer is in that group, too. And, naturally, Jeremy Bannister, too. It seems to me that Carl Draco might be the lone exception among your protagonists when it comes to main characters who care deeply about writing fiction.

In preparing *The Paradise That Lurks* for publication, however, there was a major problem. We couldn't find an electronic file to go with it. In fact, the mock paperback version was the only one I could find. I was worried, for many months, about somehow losing that lone copy. I didn't feel any relief until after my daughter, Justine Chapel, took the book apart page by page and used a scanner to create an electronic file. And then we shipped the manuscript off to Karen Haverkamp. Karen spent months cleaning up the document and polishing all the prose up to her high, exacting standards.

You might be amazed to know that the team behind you today spans three countries. Karen lives in Niagara Falls, Canada. And now Mike Keefe and his wife, Anita, live in San Miguel de Allende, Mexico. Anita manages your website (yes, you have a website), and Mike and I run the company. I live in Mancos, Colorado, with my wife, Jody Chapel. Jody designs your books, although we occasionally have cover art from other sources. In addition to making decisions for Running Meter Press with Mike, I manage your social media accounts, including Facebook, Twitter (you have a healthy 5,800 followers!), and Instagram (@asphaltwarrior). Justine, who also helped with similar scanning issues with *The Detachment*, lives in Denver.

Yep, this is Book No. 16. There were nine books in The Asphalt Warrior series, there was the Vietnam trilogy, and now this is the fourth standalone following *The Circumstantial Man*, *The Legend of Carl Draco*, and *Jeremy Bannister*, or *The Ups and Downs of an Aspiring Novelist*.

As I write this, you have been nominated for a Colorado Book Award in the category of literary fiction for *Jeremy Bannister*. In fact, this is your sixth nomination! *Ticket to Hollywood*, *Doctor Lovebeads*, and *Pickup at Union Station* (all from The Asphalt Warrior series) were nominated. So were *The Legend of Carl Draco* and *The Circumstantial Man*. These nominations have been a wonderful recognition of your craft and talents, Gary. But you've also had rave reviews in The Denver Post, from Booklist, and even a couple of knockout mentions on National Public Radio. Esteemed writers like Jeffery Deaver, Stewart O'Nan, Ron Carlson, Dan Piraro, David Rea, Larry Barber, Gwen Florio, Keir Graff, Art Taylor, Chris Holm, Brian Kaufman, Mario Acevedo, Wendy J. Fox, Warren Hammond, Brad Newsham, Brendan DuBois, Carter Wilson, Barbara Nickless, Jeffrey Siger, Patricia Abbott, Michael Harvey, LS Hawker, John Mort, and many others have raved about your works in generous blurbs.

It's gratifying. Very, very gratifying. Mike and I were pretty sure that others would recognize your talents. But, in truth, we really had no idea what we were getting into way back in 2011 when we decided to take the plunge and make sure that these stories found their way to readers. Speaking of whom, thank you to all of the loyal readers who have followed Gary's works.

With *Paradise That Lurks*, I'll be very interested to see the reactions and reviews. Charley Quinn's attitudes and ideas, particularly around relationships between men and women, are at times crude and a bit out of step with today's times. If you were still here, we might have had a chat to see if there was anything you wanted to tweak. Maybe. Maybe not. The story flows along beautifully. And I find Charley to be sympathetic—he's smart and self-effacing. Like Brendan Murphy and Larkey and Palmer, he's deeply introspective. Nobody parses moments like your main characters, Gary!

Basically, Charley Quinn recognizes that he doesn't have the fancy job (and money to go with it) that he thinks appeals to most women. And he's okay with that. He teaches writing at a free university and his side gig is working as a janitor. Quinn is three-dimensional and a fully realized character. And so is the volatile, unpredictable, and alluring Linda Hathaway. Some readers might be offended by some of Quinn's crude "awful truth" observations. As Karen Haverkamp pointed out in an email exchange, *The Paradise That Lurks* might make readers feel uncomfortable. But, as she said, that's okay.

"This is what the best literature is supposed to do," she wrote. "Make us think, change us in some way for the better because we have obtained a richer understanding of ourselves."

That's how I feel about our relationship, too, Gary. You always challenged me and my writing. You brought fresh eyes, original insights, and a keen sense of what worked and what did not. Damn do I miss our coffees and long talks at Europa State University.

I miss you, pal. I know I'm not alone. But you live on in the stories you left behind, Gary, and we all have obtained a richer understanding of ourselves as a result.

Mark Stevens
April 2022

Noble are the impulses of opening manhood, where they are not utterly ignoble: at that period, I mean, when the poetic sense begins to blossom, and when boys are first made sensible of the paradise that lurks in female smiles.

—Thomas De Quincey
Confessions of an English Opium-Eater

Part I

Chapter 1

I once invented a game called *Revenge*. This was before I became a teacher, at a time when I was casting around for work, for money. I saw some possibilities in board games. I came up with a concept grounded in malevolence. It would be different from Monopoly, Scrabble, Clue, the fun games that create a bond among members of the family that plays together. This game would satisfy the emotions that also exist between members of said family. Let me be brief: You acquired properties. It was like Monopoly in this sense. But at any moment you might draw a card from the *Revenge* pile. Perhaps the player seated across from you violated one of the Commandments. At that point the dynamic of the game changed. You rolled the dice and headed for his "house." His house contained valuable items. Whatever your opponent had been doing to win the game, he was now required to stop that, roll the dice, and head for his house in order to prevent you from getting *Revenge*!

I bought a used Monopoly board at an ARC store, spray-painted it red, drew some boxes with Magic Marker, wrote some rules, played it with friends, discovered its flaws, put it in the closet, and forgot about it. I was in my twenties. I am now forty years old. When I was thirty-nine I got involved in the best sex-and-drugs deal a man could ever hope for. But just as with all good things, like board games, it came to an end. I'm not sure who won. How did she come to live in my apartment? Stupidity? Lust? Ulterior motives? I could make a list of the mistakes that lead man to embrace unpredictably bad decisions. Unless, of course, you consider involvement with all women to be prima facie imbecility.

She was a beautiful woman. An oddity in my life and occupation at the time. When she walked into the classroom she had a look of desperation beneath the false skin of her face. When I say false skin I mean the makeup that was so deftly applied that she seemed to have two faces, the surface face that made me think of actors and actresses—faces modified with powder and paint to take advantage of klieg lights and camera lenses—and the face beneath, the foundation upon which the makeup was applied, the real face, the desperation face. I thought she had come to the wrong place. But no. She was not looking for any of the other classrooms where men and women like myself picked up a few dollars teaching amateurs how to follow a rational path that might lead them to their dreams.

A woman I was attracted to taught pottery classes down the hallway on the same nights that I taught creative writing. On occasion I was able to talk her into going to the Sunset Lounge on East Colfax for a drink, but she had never come home with me. I knew during the first five minutes of our first "drink date" that she would never come home with me, so I resigned myself to making do with the friendship with a woman that men like myself are stuck with when women we are attracted to are looking for something further up the food chain. A man with a real job. A man with a future. A man with money. From the moment that a girl graduates from high school, she begins the search for the man who will support her for the next fifty years. When they are young they can afford to be choosy. When they pass forty—I was to learn—a great number of them are still choosy. This ran counter to the sarcasm that I unleashed whenever I got drunk in the presence of friends, to wit: a woman will marry a telephone pole if it has a penis and a billfold. Was this bitterness? A psychiatrist willing to work for nothing might be able to give me an answer, but I was never interested in the answer. I contented myself with watching the women I was attracted to walk away with the men who had money. There were always unmarried women around who would take one chance on a date with me. The worst part of each date, of course, was the moment when the woman said, "So . . . what do you do for a living?"

"Is this the creative-writing class?" the blonde said after ascertaining that I was the teacher. I was standing by the desk at the front of the room. The students in my class, who ranged in ages from eighteen to seventy, were busy finding their favorite seats. It was the second week of the "semester" and students were expected to hand in their first "efforts" this week. There were only eight sessions, so I had put them on the fast track. I could smell fear in the air.

"Yes it is," I said. "My name is Charles Quinn. I'm the teacher."

"The woman on the phone said you might be willing to take me on as a student since it's still so early in the year." It was mid-May. The year lasted two months. It was like school, college, high school even. It was a free university. It was unlike a real school in that occasionally nobody signed up for certain classes—homeopathic medicine, esoteric subjects of that order—and when this happened the classes were canceled. It was free-form and low rent and I might have hated it except that it blended perfectly with my life, and I liked teaching students how to write. I do not care what anybody says. It is possible to teach people how to write novels as long as they are willing to learn.

"The woman on the phone was correct," I said. I knew the woman on the phone. Her name was Becky. She ran the school even though she did not own it. A jerk owned the school. But Becky ran the place, made it work. The jerk raked in his percentage. I will call him Hubbard, because that is not his real name. I don't want to get sued. He is the kind of fellow who will sue anyone over anything. I could tell you funny stories about some of his lawsuits. But let's not get sidetracked here. I soundlessly thanked Becky for telling this woman that I would be willing to take her on. She was the most beautiful woman I had ever spoken to in person. I didn't care if it was the illusion of makeup. Her breasts were not illusions, although if I looked at them cross-eyed they were more three-dimensional than was anatomically possible. It's hard to explain optics. I was never any good at science, but at ogling I had been good ever since I saw my first naked tits in a magazine at the age of nine.

"I'll tell you what," I said. "Why don't you take a seat, and we'll get you signed up after class is over. You might as well start now. It's never too early to start writing."

She looked at me intently as I spoke, the golden pupils of her eyes moving with the stuttering quality of a lizard's head. Jerks and tics. She looked at my eyes, my lips, my hairline, as if reading between the wrinkles on my face. I was thirty-nine. Old age was rising like the tide, but I was still young enough to run if I had to. I have a friend who runs marathons, triathlons. He was once chased by a thief who was trying to steal his parked car. The thief had no idea he was trying to catch up with a marathon runner who took his time, paced himself as he dashed up the street. He told me he wasn't afraid. The car thief was probably a druggie, out of shape. "Thank God he didn't have a gun," was all my friend said. Thank God for illegal drugs, I say.

"Okay, thank you, Mr. Quinn," the woman said. This was the first time I noted a character trait that made me feel I ought to be in love with her. It was to happen again and again. She would blink once, and then smile at me, as if her face was waking up. A pause. A blink. An angelic smile. It helped me to understand where cliches came from. They came from Truths. Her eyes glistened when she smiled. The apogee of her bulbous cheeks glistened. The smile would then fade in increments, as if reluctant to leave her face. I would eventually confirm this by performing experiments. I would say something funny, then watch as she blinked, smiled, held the smile until it began to fade in those charming increments. I felt as if she was trying to look inside me, behind the bones of my face, like someone glancing at a closing door to see who had been there. Every smile seemed like the first smile of her life, like the first time a baby smiles. I have two younger sisters and a younger brother, so I am familiar with the milestones of childhood, the first tooth, the first baby steps. My older brother and I taught our younger siblings how to walk, guiding the babies back and forth between us on the living room carpet, our arms outstretched to catch the inevitable fall, usually a quick sit-down. The startled look. The innocent smile as my brother and I roared with laughter. Teaching babies how to do things killed us. From the age of five to the age of twelve my world smelled like a diaper bucket.

"Is this seat taken?" she said, pointing at an empty desk four feet away from me. These were old-fashioned school desks, enter from the left, a hole for an inkwell. Hubbard had bought them at a government surplus warehouse.

"That's fine, take a seat, it's first come, first serve in here," I said, which was only partly true. The elder aspiring writers could become vicious if a young student unwittingly took their favorite seat. I supposed this went back to the days of their youths, school etiquette of the 1940s and '50s. I never delved too deeply into the psyches of the old writers among us. Reading their dreadful stories was adequate for me.

The new student's name was Linda. Spanish for "pretty."

Linda Hathaway. When she removed her coat I noted that she was wearing a little black dress. Black high heels. Pearls. Completely inappropriate for a creative-writing class at a free university in Denver. Even her jacket was inappropriate, in the sense that it did not comport with her dress. It was too large, slightly dowdy looking. It made her appear somewhat childish, the sleeves covering her palms, her well-manicured fingers poking from the cuffs. Aside from that, she looked dressed for an evening at the symphony.

I waited for the rest of the students to settle in. They were a quiet and mature bunch. I had never taught in a classroom prior to this long gig, so other teachers at the free U told me that I didn't know what I was missing. One of them had taught at a high school in Arvada, a suburb northwest of Denver. He told me that the students were ungodly. Forget *The Blackboard Jungle* he said. These were suburban punks who had no discipline at all. He remained for one semester before resigning. I had trouble believing his hair-raising stories of teens giving him, the teach, lip, these offspring of the baby boomers. I attended parochial schools in my youth where discipline was strictly enforced from grade one, so I had no experience to compare with his. "The free university is heaven compared to what I went through," he informed me. I took him at his word.

I had no intention of taking up teaching as a profession. But I had already learned a lesson from the creative-writing classes I had supervised. Policemen say that domestic disturbances are the most dangerous calls they can take off the radio, trying to break up a fight between a husband and a wife. Cops are injured, even killed, in those situations. In my own experience, the most dangerous situation a writing teacher can become involved in has to do with telling a beginning writer that his story is a failure. I have been threatened with physical harm by students of all ages who did not appreciate being told The Truth (by my definition) about their stories. The flash of anger in the eyes, the curled fist forming a knuckle sandwich. I have seen these things. In the early days it had made me wonder about the nature of criticism, of creativity, of ego, of the fabric of words woven into narrative tapestries and presented to the public for judgment. My conclusion? Some people should not aspire to write. But they do. All kinds, all types, all personalities, all temperaments. They have many things in common. Beginners seem to take special pride in announcing that they do not write for money. This is a badge of honor. They talk about it during break time. Of course there is no real break time in a creative-writing class. Students form their cliques and continue to talk about writing while eating donuts and sipping soft drinks or punch provided by volunteers. I do not hang around the classroom during the fifteen-minute break. I step out into the darkness of Denver and have a smoke where no one can see me, not to hide my smoking but to hide myself from students who want special private "mentoring," which consists of asking questions about their prose that they will not ask in class with an audience of equals.

The futility of those questions is painful to behold. "What do you really think of my writing?" they used to say before I learned to hide out from them. They all asked this question. Each aspired to make it in the world as a professional novelist and wanted to be told the microscopic maneuver that might tip them over the line into the big time. How do I get an agent? How do I get an editor? Can I submit half a novel to a publishing company? Oddball questions that had nothing to do with the tedious grind of facing the blank page head-on and producing the words that tell the stories. My speciality in this class is plotting. I care nothing about lyricism or content. This is difficult for the students to digest. How could I not care about the poetry of their prose? How could I not care that they are writing romances or cowboy adventures? I teach the general principles of laying out a storyline. It is Aristotelian. I demand a change of mindset, an attitude adjustment that students are not used to. I have had students resign from my class and ask for their money back when I made it clear to them that I had no interest in the specifics of their stories or the beauty of their sentences. There is something cute about their disdain for plotting. They do not understand that story is everything. They think it is about pretty words. They think "story" is for hacks like Mickey Spillane.

The worst of this lot was a twenty-two-year-old boy named Drew whose brain was infested with the strangest web of reasoning I had ever encountered. He was stupid but in a peculiar way. He wanted to argue virtually every point I taught, but he was not like, for instance, the cretinous draftees I had met in the army whose systems of thought and logic were no more complex than a Number 2 pencil. Why he took my creative-writing classes I will never know. He argued both content and form. My assertion that the use of the comma was rather arbitrary seemed to infuriate him. He wanted steadfast rules in some cases, and in other cases he wanted no rules at all. "John Gardner says there are no rules of writing," he told me during the first class. I was familiar with the text. Gardner was dead by this time, having run a motorcycle directly into a telephone pole. "John Gardner is wrong," I told him. "The first rule of writing is Don't Bore the Reader." Drew argued this assertion. He said it was not a "real" rule.

That was my first glimpse into the strange webwork of his mind. It took willpower not to taunt him. I had known kids like him in college, but he was the most extreme when it came to argumentation. It was as if he wanted to make certain that he could not be blamed for anything once the time came for the public reading of his short stories. This was revealed during the first class he took from me a long time ago. I feared the worst when it came time to critique the student stories out loud. He would be ruthless, of this I was certain, at spotting flaws in the writing of others, while at the same time he would be adamant in the defense of his own writing, either denying the flaws or shifting the blame to others, including his teachers.

During the first class that Linda attended, I could not keep my eyes from drifting toward her. She held a Bic pen in her right hand and steadied a blank sheet of paper with her left as if prepared to take notes, but I did not see her write anything down that evening. I took a moment to introduce her to the class, quickly went over the requirements of which there were not many. They were as follows. Three stories were to be handed in during the eight-week course. The student would provide the xeroxed copies for everyone in class. Revisions would not count as a story. I did not want to force the students to listen to the same story read three times aloud. Not all of the stories would be read aloud, time did not allow for that. But I wanted a mix, both good and bad stories, without labeling them as such. I wanted the students to understand what was being done right and what was being done wrong. If they were going to learn at all, they were going to learn primarily from the bad stories. Linda did not write anything down, but I did catch her nodding when I said this or that. Sometimes she would frown, as though I had said something of particular import. During the class, I decided I would cut it short by five minutes so that I would have time to take down her information and get her set up. I admit it. I was already attracted to her, was already manipulating time, events, responsibilities, as men will do when they go after a woman. You speed things up, you slow things down, depending on the situation. That's just what happens, that's how it's done. I broke rules in order to achieve my goals. But who doesn't do this? Drew brought me his wisdom from another class he had taken: "One of my teachers said you have to know what the rules are before you can break them."

I simply agreed in order to make him feel good about himself and his pedestrian insight. I already sensed that he was going to be trouble. I did express my true feelings, which were "Don't break the rules. They are rules for a reason." But I could tell he wanted to be thought of as a rebel. A rule-breaker. A genius. I had been teaching creative writing for three years, and I still was not able to discern between the writing of people who broke the rules on purpose and those who broke the rules by accident. Geniuses broke the rules on purpose, this was the extent of my knowledge, which made it difficult to grade the papers of the geniuses. But all that aside, I should have obeyed the rules when it came to my relationship with my students. I am speaking specifically of Linda. "Don't break the rules." And most importantly: "They are rules for a reason."

I maneuvered and engineered and sidestepped until the two of us were involved in what the female writers of the world refer to as a "relationship." I broke the rules that said a teacher should not become involved with a student. But you should have seen her. Linda was beautiful. "Leendah," as they say in Spanish. Even stepping out of a shower, her makeup washed down the drain, her hair wet and stringy, Linda was "leendah" in any and all languages of the world. I would have died for her. I almost did. The fact that this is a first-person narrative proves that I did not.

Chapter 2

A class ends, it's time for everyone to leave, and I feel bereft. I enjoy these sessions more than anything I do. I live for them. When I was in college I took all the creative-writing classes that were available. When I was a sophomore I went to the resident novelist and begged him to let me into the E-401 creative-writing class. He was a famous mid-list author who had written one work of mainstream literature and three detective novels. I will not name him. He died recently. He made his mark in the late sixties and now he is dead. His obituary made me feel wistful. The fleeting nature of time, all that. I imagined him as a student in the 1950s going to a school in the Midwest, taking creative-writing classes and dreaming of the day when he would hit it big, which he did. His day came. The novels, the money, the fame, and now he lies six feet under, the sound and fury of his literary achievement neatly folded and tucked into the breast pocket of his shrouded tuxedo. The End. He attended Iowa, as did many of the teachers who stood in front of the classrooms of my youth. "Why do you want to take my creative-writing class?" he asked me after I finished begging. That is hyperbole of course, but I did, at the time, expect to be reduced to begging. "Because I want to be a creative writer," I replied. The truest answer I could come up with impromptu. "That's a *terrible* answer," he said, but he laughed along with two graduate students who were lounging around his office at the time, touching the hem of his robe. I could see through them. They were no different from me. Hanging around with a published author, maybe some of his talent and luck would rub off on them, maybe he would accidentally let slip a secret that would lead to their own literary success, maybe their day would come all the more quickly. But because I did not want to let people like myself see through me, I did not hang around his office after he allowed me to become a student in his class. Toward the end of the semester he called me in and asked if I would like a scholarship in creative writing. "You are the best writer in the class," he told me. I was thrilled. But it led nowhere. I would become a creative-writing teacher in a free university in Denver, the Rocky Mountain Free U, with no published novels to my credit.

When Linda's first class ended I wiggled a vertical finger and told her to hang on a minute while I took down the necessary information to get her properly registered for the class. A complete ruse, of course. But being the teacher, the man in charge, imbues you with a certain amount of power and leeway to bend and reshape reality. I used the time to fend off desperate students who wanted one last important question answered before they went home to stare despondently at their typewriters. This was what most of the students craved. Just a moment or two of private tutoring from the teach, me, which would kick-start their careers. After Linda and I were alone in the room I proceeded to ask her full name, address, telephone number, my God I felt like a kid in a candy store, a junkie trapped in a pharmaceutical factory. What I did not know at the time was that she was lying to me when she told me that she lived in east Denver, that her telephone number was such-and-so-forth. But I took it down with a blank and straight face, the teacher bloated with importance as I recorded the vital stats.

After all this dull stuff was taken care of, she surprised me by handing me a short story that she had written. She said she knew it would be required, and that she had written it a week earlier after being told that she might be able to register for the class. I thought of asking about the history of her interest in writing, but decided not to waste such fertile material while standing erect at the end of a class. The best way I knew of to get to know a woman better was to ask about her own writing, preferably over drinks at the Sunset, and this was not the time or place to shoot that wad.

"I haven't had dinner yet," I said with as much insouciance as I could muster, a casual remark orchestrated to disarm her. "Would you like to join me at the Soup Bowl up on Colfax? You could tell me a little bit about yourself, and I could give you an overview of the class."

If it appears that I was thinking fast on my feet, this was not true. It was a well-practiced ploy that I was laying on her. I had used it on other female students in the past. You do what you can. You learn. You perfect techniques. It's a lonely world out there.

"I'm sorry but I have to get home," she replied. This did not come as a surprise, but only because I was used to it. In most cases it did not come as a disappointment. I knew I had to let time pass, that eventually the woman would join me for an evening meal. I rarely struck out, insofar as the meals went. Women love to eat. But as far as "strike out" as a well-known metaphor, I was not always so lucky. In other words, I did not always "get lucky." Sexual metaphors are legion. But I was disappointed this time. I wanted her now, in the way that beginning writers want to get published *now*. A young writer once said that to me after I told him it had taken me five years before I had published my first short story at the age of twenty-six. "Five *years*!" he exclaimed from his seat on the far side of a big round wooden table in a bar. "I don't want to wait five *years*. I want to get published *now*!" He frequently spoke in italics. He would later go on to get a PhD in English. He teaches in a university in the East. He's had a number of short stories published. His *now* took seven years.

"Some other time then," I said as I casually stuffed papers into my briefcase, short stories waiting to be read aloud in class, or graded, or whatever was expected by the students whose stories had not yet been ripped to shreds.

She seemed apologetic. She frowned as she replied, "Maybe."

I glanced at her dress, her shoes. She looked like she was ready to go dancing but for the shabby coat. A disguise maybe, a means to ward off the type of men whom she had doubtless gotten used to warding off when she was a teenager. A wave of pity and protectiveness passed through me, washing away the disappointment. I wanted to hold this young woman, guard her, possess her. Beauty was a part of the attraction, but not all of it. There was something about her eyes, the impossible thing that poets have difficulty describing. Her eyes begged for me to hug her, to be kind to her, to possess her. This was how I felt. I had never felt this way about any woman, and thus it disturbed me. Was this the beginning of love? I had never been in love, had never had my heart broken, had never experienced the impossible thing that poets write about. That's their job, a fruitless endeavor that has produced immortal lines. Fair exchange. They never quite nail it, but they leave something worthwhile in their wake, like the detritus of a battle. Beautiful lines, titles, imagery scattered across the battlefield of love. There are worse ways for people under the age of thirty to while away their deluded lives.

"May I walk you to your car?" I said.

"I took the bus here," she replied as she gathered herself together in preparation for leaving. This came as a shock to me. It was nearing nine o'clock and this was Capitol Hill, a place where nice girls did not wait for busses in the dark. All cities have such sections of town. My concern for her became more generalized. Who in their right mind would take a number fifteen bus at this time of night? The fifteen was the only bus I knew of that ran near the school.

"Are you certain you don't want an escort?" I said.

"I'll be all right," she said with a note of confidence in her voice that made me think she might have a pistol in her purse. She was a tall woman, almost as tall as me, and I am six foot two. Her blonde hair was cut short and had a kind of "frizzy" look. She had a posture, a way of walking, that seemed boyish to me, but I later realized it was simply athletic. No body fat. I might as well say it now. She would eventually tell me that she had once been bulimic. She got that under control, though, and stuck with exercise and eating right. Other things too. But I do not want to get ahead of myself. She left the classroom, and as I closed up shop, straightening a few desks, picking up scraps of paper, and turning off the lights, I listened to her footsteps going along the hallway, down the stairs, out the door. I checked the snaps on my briefcase, then walked out, closed the classroom door, locked it, and pocketed the keys. I followed in her wake.

It occurred to me to follow her up to Colfax. It was a two-block walk, but I decided not to do it. There was something caddish in the thought. I had every confidence that one night we would eventually make the walk to the Soup Bowl together for a meal. This would take a little longer than a rendezvous with the average woman. She was not average. She was beautiful, so I assumed she was well-practiced in the art of fending off horny dogs, deflecting passes, dodging kisses. I put her out of my mind, although when I stepped outside of the free U building I did look at the sidewalk that led up to Colfax and saw that it was empty. She could not have walked to Colfax that quickly. I set my briefcase down on one of the two low brick walls that border the porch steps and lit a cigarette. Then I heard the sound of an engine starting farther down the block, off to my left, a northerly direction, and I saw a car pull away from the curb. It passed the free U and I recognized Linda's hair as she guided the car south toward Colfax. She had lied to me about taking the bus.

In my youth I would have interpreted this as an obvious rejection. She did not want me to accompany her to her car or anywhere else. As an aging male you quickly get a fix on the complex system of logic that guides a woman through the field of pitfalls that are a necessary part of the landscape of love. Which is to say: the intimacy of a brief walk from the front door of the free U to her car would be wrongly misinterpreted by me as an invitation to take things further. And lying to a man, even getting caught in a lie, well, what is that anyway? Something to be accepted and dismissed as a tactic so simple and old that it would not be worth mentioning at any time for any reason whatsoever. A woman's prerogative. A man foolish enough to say "You lied to me" should be dismissed as an imbecile. But it made me wonder. Had she picked up on some vibe, some aspect of my character that warned her away from me on the same night we had met and after only a few brief words of conversation before and after class? Again, I was so attracted to her that it caused me to give more thought to the situation than I would have given had she merely been a pretty woman, a possibility, a brunette, a redhead with the erotic freckles that enhance the attractiveness of a woman with Scottish background and blood.

I put out my cigarette and walked to my car, which was parked at the curb directly in front of the free U. "The teacher's spot," as I let it be known on the first night of class when the deck was being squared and all the rules were being laid down for the students. "Thou shalt not" park thy rusty Ford in the space perpendicular to the sidewalk that runs from the curb to the front door of the free U. That is my space.

My car was a maroon-colored Plymouth, one of the legendary K-cars that had saved Chrysler the first time it started to go under. It was ancient now, the paint rusted where the salt-strewn streets of winter Denver had eaten away the reddish patina. The bumper had rust spots. One of the rear doors of the sedan was permanently shut and locked. It was one of "those" cars, the kind of car you owned as a teenager or a college student, the kind of car to which you gave a funny nickname in order to cover up your embarrassment for owning such a heap: The Red Behemoth. That sort of thing. A name concocted to countermand the fact that the jalopy belches smoke from the tailpipe. This includes a glove compartment filled with traffic tickets to make your college buddies laugh as they illegally sucked brew while cruising toward a movie theater on a weekend night. The sort of thing that becomes unbearable after you pass the age of thirty, a rolling admission that you cannot afford decent wheels. I would imagine that by the time you reach sixty, you are beyond embarrassment and simply say a prayer of thanks every dawn when the engine starts without a flutter of hesitation. I take good care of my car. I care for it in the way some women demonstrate compassion for stray cats.

I climbed in and started the engine, listened to the purr, then pulled away from the curb and drove home. Home was a house south of Interstate 25 not far from the old Vogue Theatre. I rented it from a man who owned a bar in North Denver. He owned properties all over town, a number of them in the vicinity of the University of Denver, which was farther south. Most of his renters were young people, college students, or entry-level workers. I had been told about the vacancy by a creative-writing student two years earlier and had snatched it up. One hundred and eighty dollars a month for the ground floor of a house. The upstairs apartment, which was accessed by a white wooden stairwell on the north side of the house, was currently vacant. Two sets of renters had already come and gone. The finished basement once had been occupied by a hippie who smoked pot. I could smell it rising from the heating vents at night. It brought back memories. But he was gone now. I lived alone in the house, which pleased me to no end. There was a washer/dryer in the "foyer" of the basement. I occasionally had spoken to the hippie while doing my laundry but we did not become friends, thank goodness. I was thirty-six when I moved in and he was in his late twenties. We were close enough in age that we might have become companion smokers, but it never happened. I took pains not to be present whenever he, or the attic occupants, happened to be around. I have always been a hermit of sorts. My greatest fear at the time of which I am speaking was to come home and hear the drumbeat of rock 'n' roll records coming from the basement or attic apartments, the herald of new tenants.

After I got home I put a TV dinner on to heat, and only then did I dig into my briefcase to retrieve Linda's story, the existence of which had rested at the forefront of my mind ever since she had handed it to me. It was as if she herself was in my apartment, tucked into my briefcase, neatly stacked and held together modestly with a paper clip. Here were fifteen pages of her thoughts, clues, hints, foreshadowings of the things we would talk about when I finally coaxed her into joining me for drinks at either a bar on Colfax, a bar close to my own house, or over drinks mixed in front of my own private bar, a bookcase in my living room containing a wide variety of bottles whose labels could be seen through the tall panes of glass originally designed to display the works of Dickens, Conrad, Twain, et al. Those books were relegated to open shelves on the wall opposite. My apartment was a library stocked with liquor. There were also the books necessary and proper to that of a teacher and unpublished novelist.

The name of her short story was "Mister Eight." I scanned it quickly, as I do with all stories in order to judge whether the student knows how to speak English. Does this sound arrogant? We enter grade school and the first thing a teacher tells the student is "You do not talk right, you do not think right," and eventually, "You do not write right, and I will tell you how to do this." Thus begins the process by which all young people's voices and imaginations are destroyed by the American educational system. Children are taught to speak, write, and think in a banal formulaic mode invented by the sorts of losers who write English grammar books. Homogeneity. We must all speak in the same dull voice. Of course it doesn't matter if the child grows up to be a bank teller or a taxi driver, but it is the children who aspire to write fiction whose potential is destroyed by school. This applies to private schools as well. I attended Catholic schools. As a consequence, my students have to unlearn everything they were taught in grade school and high school. I think of it as stripping away the paint or linoleum that has been plastered over beautiful hardwood flooring. Get back down to the natural wood, the natural voice of these children who come to school filled with a genius that is eroded, painted over, and camouflaged by low-paid teachers.

I see the ruins and wreckage of our education system in the terrible stories that are handed to me each semester. The children are forced by circumstance to imitate Hemingway, or whoever their model might be, because they have been brainwashed by teachers into thinking that their own experiences, voices, and minds are not worth a shit. Take Kerouac for example. His first piece of shit was *The Town and the City*. A pathetic imitation of Thomas Wolfe. He finally found his own voice after reading a letter by a virtually illiterate street kid named Neal Cassady, and suddenly Kerouac saw the light. Write in your own original dynamic voice. *On the Road*. Say what you will, that book was not written by a melodramatist from Asheville.

Linda's story was about a woman who meets a man in a bar. He asks her if she is a virgin, and after she says no, she then tells him that she has had seven lovers in her lifetime. Her age is not mentioned, but I get the feeling that she is in her early twenties. Maybe twenty-three. The point being that he will be Mister Eight in her life. It is a strange story, mostly dialogue that goes like this: (He) "Are you a virgin?" (She) "No." "How many men have you had sexual intercourse with?" "Seven." They might have been discussing a kitchen appliance, a Popeil vagina. It seemed to be a comic story, but I could not really tell. Perhaps it was tragic autobiography. Blithe dialogue. Completely unrealistic. Which is to say, I cannot imagine a man talking like that to a woman he has just met. But I saw that the story was not imitative of anything I had ever read by a student, and so I got the double thrill of reading a piece of fiction where the writer seemed to be drawing upon her own voice, and with luck, her own sexual experiences.

I decided I would have to delve deeper into the creation of this manuscript after the story was discussed in class—or perhaps over drinks at the Sunset Lounge on East Colfax.

Chapter 3

I taught creative writing on Monday nights. Tuesday through Saturday I worked from 6 p.m. to 9 p.m. as a janitor at a medical clinic. I was thirty-nine years old and lived the life of a boy. Early on, for a period of six months, I had picked up an unemployment check even though I was working. I was paid "under the table." My employer was a man named Herb whom I had known when I was younger. He was wealthy, the owner of the janitorial service. He also owned three dry-cleaning establishments in Denver. For a while I drove the truck that picked up and distributed dirty clothing around the metro area, but I did not like hauling gigantic bags of damp clothing like a surreal Santa with burlap slung over one shoulder, so my employer eventually put me to work in the medical clinic—sweeping and mopping and emptying plastic trash containers filled with bloody bandages and used syringes was a step up. I didn't mind the work because I was generally left alone by the rest of the crew, which included two boys in their early twenties who operated the floor-polishing machinery, two nutty kids who reminded me of myself and my friends when we were in college. Janitorial work was how I supplemented my income. Teaching was how I remained sane.

I never gave anybody a grade below B. There are only two kinds of writers in my book, A's and B's. I handed out A's like a mystic passing out loaves and fishes. None of it meant anything. Only the writing counted. I did my best not to guide my students into the telephone pole of literary failure. All of my advice, suggestions, and guidance was sincere. Not all of my students were sincere. For a long time my greatest hope lay with a middle-aged woman who wrote romance novels. She did seem to have the knack, and guess what? She published a Harlequin Romance and I never saw her again. The only feather in my cap. To my knowledge none of my other students ever published any novels, although a number of them did get published in university press magazines. Small feathers. Wine was smuggled illegally into the classroom to celebrate, and my applause was sincere. I considered short-story writing to be the dead end of all dead ends, but it was something anyway. And every one of the writers seemed to believe that the short story was a stepping-stone to the novel. A hop, a skip, and a National Book Award. From the beginning, one thing I vowed never to do was try to dispel anyone's crackpot ideas. All writers are crackpots anyway. It comes with the territory.

After dinner I sat down to write. I practice what I preach. Three hundred words a day minimum. When I told my students that they need not write any more than three hundred words, my statement was met with what I knew were silent scoffs. The noisy provocateur of course was Drew, the boy with the strange brain. "That's not enough words," he said in a smug tone. "You're just getting going when you have to stop." Normally I do not argue with my students. I shrug and tell them that they are free to go their own way. Why they take my course in writing and then argue with everything I say is beyond me, but I take their money and ignore their wisdom. Drew seemed always determined to prove that I was wrong about this or that, but my sense was that he simply didn't want to work hard, or to be told that writing is hard work. "Writing is not like driving a car," I replied to his objection. "It is not a case of getting up to speed and then cruising along, cranking out two or three thousand words before swinging into the driveway and turning off the Selectric." He did not quite grasp that you write a story one sentence at a time. It has nothing to do with velocity, or momentum, or numbers, word counts, dates, a.m. or p.m. It has to do with putting out the work. It is not about writing at a certain time of day, or setting a quota of words and then sticking to it religiously. As I have stated, one thing I learned about students is that they demand either no rules at all or else rigid rules from which one should not diverge, sometimes both. Drew was an example of that sort of person. When he wasn't quoting John Gardner or Raymond Carver ("There are no rules when it comes to writing"), he wanted to know exactly how many words one must write during each session. The three hundred words was merely a guideline to prevent students from being frightened away by such moronic statements as "You should set aside at least two hours a day for writing." I actually read that in a how-to book. What adult has two hours a day to set aside for anything at all? Exercising, hobbies, whatever, Christ, the average hardworking American gets home at six in the evening and goes to bed at ten. Four hours a day to live a life, that is what we are given by the nature of work. You are damned lucky if you have fifteen minutes to set aside each day for something as nebulous as success in the writing game.

I wrote for fifteen minutes. The nature of my work is irrelevant here except to say that I was working on another novel. I did not stare at the blank page. I knew my way around long literature. I knew where the story was headed. Preach and practice. I had worked out the storyline months earlier. I knew what I was going to say long before I said it. When you stare at a blank sheet of paper you should be thinking of how to say something, not what to say. This is what I try to drum into the heads of my students, including the know-it-alls like poor young Drew who "could not seem to get things going," as he had said to me on more than one occasion when he caught me before I could slip out the door for a smoke break. Learn to outline. Plan your story. I will tell you how to do that. You do it like this. The entire semester was devoted to that and that alone. I have faith in the creative imaginations of people who are sincere about wanting to write. Nobody else teaches writing like I do. Nobody in my personal experience anyway. "How to Create Memorable Characters." That is the name of another course taught at the free U. I have managed to successfully avoid running into the teacher of that garbage. Yes. Go ahead and create memorable characters in a vacuum. Give one of them a limp and another a scar on his forehead. But storyline? None of the other teachers know how to plot. This I learned from my little spies who eventually worked their way into my course after trying to become successful by creating memorable characters, or how to fashion prose that resonates with zing. I say give a student a storyline and turn him loose. If he doesn't already know how to write with zing, a course at the free U is not going to set him on the road to stardom. Outlining is the only thing that can be taught, and *must* be taught. Even I speak in *italics* when I get going on the *only* passion I possess, i.e., laying out storylines. It is surprising how well a student writes once he knows where the hell his novel is going. He hasn't got time to create memorable characters or write with zing, he is too busy producing an engaging story.

I finished my three hundred words and closed down my computer. I will try not to speak of it again. I have said too much already but only to clarify and verify that I practice what I preach. I do not worry about getting published, writing with zing, or knocking out a novel in record time as poor Jack Kerouac did (*On the Road*, three weeks). After all, would you want to take a ride in an airplane that took seven minutes to build? Speed has nothing to do with art. Poor dead Jack. Poor dead speedy Jack Kerouac. But he did write with honest fervor about Denver, Colorado, the city that I love.

Having written, having eaten, having taken a shower, I poured myself a glass of red wine and sat down to reread Linda's story with a critical eye, as well as skim the other stories that had been handed in to me. As expected, Drew had not handed in a story on schedule. This was a part of his "act," as I thought of it. Great art was not a product of deadlines, so why should he be held to schedules? I had never spoken with him about this, but I had encountered enough of his type over the years to recognize the danger signs. Great artists come and go as they please. They do not make their trains run on time. After all, if he "acted" like a visionary, perhaps he might be mistaken for one. I played along with his little game. And why not? He was as entertaining as anything I saw on TV. But he had not yet had the opportunity to pull The Big Gun out of the arsenal of his act and accuse me of not understanding his stories because I pretended to understand every one of them, which, in a sense, I did. I recognize faux Barthelme when I see it. Not to mention Barth, Pynchon, Doctorow, Vonnegut, and even Mickey Spillane. It seemed like every month Drew found a new author to idolize and emulate. Did I mention that he had taken five of my classes during the past three years? I occasionally got other recidivists, but he was a steady customer. Faces came and went, but I could usually count on seeing Drew seated at the back of the classroom with a pencil parked behind his ear and an "I-dare-you" scowl on his face, as if he was giving me one last chance to turn him into a writer. I suspected that he thought of us as "old buddies," or that he viewed himself as an "old-timer" in comparison with the new members of each new class. He always managed to mention to the others that he had taken my classes before. For instance, during the middle of an intense discussion about the use of the comma, he might say something along the lines of "In the class I took from you last year you said that . . . ," making certain everybody understood that he had been around the block a few times and knew the ropes. Pardon my cliches, but Drew did that to me.

    (He) "Do you use birth control?"
    (She) "Yes."
    "What kind of birth control?"
    "I have an IUD."
    "Have you ever accidentally gotten pregnant?"
    "No."

Eventually the two characters leave the bar together for what I assume will be a night of mechanical sex in concert with the mechanical dialogue that brought them to a meeting of the minds. What is this stuff? Autobiography or creative writing? I am so damned intrigued that I can barely bring myself to set the pages aside and look at the other stories. But I do. I must. I get paid to do that, so I do it as quickly as possible, as I had done with all of the jobs of my life for which I got paid. Don't let me mislead you into thinking that I am conscientious about work. The fact that I was honing in on the age of forty and still held low-paid dirtbag jobs ought to dispel that misconception, should the misconception exist. As I have said, I lived the life of a boy. In the army they made me live the life of a man. I found that it did not suit me.

One of the stories I perused that night involved a college student who found a magic lamp, rubbed it, and Jesus Christ appeared. Our Savior offered the young man three wishes. That is all you need to know. That is all I wished to know. I often wondered if my students fully understood that, in theory, their stories would one day be read by actual people, the sort who read the *New Yorker, Esquire,* the *Hudson Review.* Or did they understand that, in reality, their stories would be read only by creative-writing teachers and fellow students? Whenever I encountered a story like this I took pains to avoid seeking an answer to those questions. I stuck with the old standbys of grammar and syntax, and let their fellow students pass judgment on the content. I could always count on the students taking seriously this sort of imaginative tale while I wandered on the sidelines like a bemused coach who was willing to let "the kids" run the game. Then I would call for a fifteen-minute break and hope the story was forgotten by the time the class reassembled.

I flipped through the pages of Linda's story again. I could not help but be intrigued. Strange and straightforward dialogue, that's what Linda brought to the table. I looked forward not only to discussing this story with her during a "private tutoring" session in a Colfax Avenue bar, but to reading the two upcoming stories that she was required to hand in to the class.

I drained my wine and set the glass aside. I had the urge to pour another eight ounces and sit up late into the night rereading her story until I squeezed the truth out of her words. Autobiography or fiction? I have a need to know. Obviously she had gotten under my skin for the second time that night. I decided I would live with the assumption that this was a good omen.

I carried the glass into the kitchen and set it in the sink to soak. Time for bed. I would have to wait a week to get the answers to those questions. It was like a TV show, a series that always ended on one of those damned high notes. Tune in again next week. The bastards in Hollywood knew how to do it, and here I was doing it to myself involuntarily. I went to bed.

The rest of the week would be filled with the mundane activities that make up the life of everyone. Working my job, earning the needed money, and doing the chores around the house both inside and out that kept my rent low. That was part of the deal with the landlord from North Denver. I had to keep the vacant apartments tidy and dusted and cleared of any bugs or mice who decided to die lonely deaths in empty rooms. Neither I nor he knew when a new prospect might want to drop by to look the place over and decide whether or not to become my upstairs or basement neighbor. A part of my job was to mow the lawn, pull weeds, check the walls for flaking paint, and cover any graffiti provided by punks who did not live in my neighborhood but who had been making forays throughout the recent years looking for broad wooden or cinder-block canvasses to express their profound visions of urban life and suffering. Most often these were secret gang signs. Occasionally a face, a landscape, a naked body, usually male or female—sometimes a sexless alien being. My job was to pry open a can of paint that I kept in the garage and hide the defacement of private property. The landlord provided the paint and brushes. Twice a week I walked down the alley and examined the garage door to see if any new artwork had been posted in this outdoor exhibition hall. These images usually appeared during the night when the elves emerged from beneath their poverty-stricken rocks to let the world know they existed. They reminded me of unpublished writers, so I did not hold it against them. I found it merely pathetic. It wasn't my property anyway, but I treated it as such. My one dread was to come across a gang of young idiots while they were in the process of spray-painting their way into the consciousness of the middle-class stooges like myself who inhabited the tidy houses in this fine residential block. I had visions of the cast of *West Side Story* dancing at top speed away from me, pirouetting down the alley and leaping over fences, laughing and hooting and using low-hanging tree branches like high bars. Sharks or Jets, it didn't matter. Young hoods bloated with amateur bravado, their giggling gum-chewing chicks in tow, our nation's exuberant youth flexing their worthless little oats. I am as much a film buff as I am a reader.

At any rate, when I turned off my bedroom lamp on the Monday night that I read Linda's first short story, I did not suspect that I was lowering the curtain on what I eventually would come to think of as the last normal week of my life.

Chapter 4

There were fifteen students in my class at the beginning of the semester. By the end there would be eleven. Four dropouts. This was average. Three of the dropouts were female and one was male, although it was not Drew, who spoke up in every class with such scorn and anxiety that he would seem a candidate for quitting, but he never did. I realized during the third creative-writing class, one year previous, that I was probably stuck with him for life, or as long as I stuck with teaching the secret of writing to lost, baffled people.

Yes, I did know the secret of writing. It took me fifteen years to learn it. Therefore, generosity was the genesis of my decision to become a teacher at the free U. Having suffered lostness and bafflement for so many years, I felt an empathetic compulsion to pass my knowledge along to people just like myself. Unfortunately the secret applied only to novels. I did not really care about the short story because there is no real market for it. Television destroyed the market for the short story. Kurt Vonnegut published an essay in which he explained that he got in on the tail end of the era where a man could earn a living publishing three or four short stories per year. This was during the late '40s and early '50s when the *Saturday Evening Post* still paid top dollar.

During the remainder of the week, I read and made comments on the stories by the other students in my class. I could look at only three per night. All bad stories seem to have been written by the same person. I had known this for years, but I did not learn it in creative-writing classes. I was a first reader for two different literary magazines published in Denver before I began generously passing on the secret of novel writing to students. I had read hundreds of short stories that all seemed to be written by the same starry-eyed chump. The stories that did have merit also had a unique voice. I never did read a story that I thought worthy of publication, although I read many that came close. But my only job as first reader was to pass the possibilities up the line to the editors, who would make the final decisions. Had it been up to me, the magazines would have published nothing and would have folded soon after I took over as editor. Ironically, the magazines folded anyway. This is what literary magazines do. They fold. I do not know what makes these publishers think that there is a demand out there for literary magazines. Idealism is more costly than one might expect. The best things in life are not free.

Two of the short stories that emerged from Linda's class briefly held my attention. One was a story about a man who commits suicide by shooting himself in the left wrist with a pistol. He bleeds to death looking through the hole in his arm as he lies on the floor. The last thing he sees is the face of a mouse peering at him through the hole. The name of the story was "Iris Out." The second story was titled "The Dancing Priest Meets the Singing Nun." It took place after World War III and was about a priest dancing on an altar in the ruins of a church while a nun played a guitar and sang to him. That's all you need to know. These two stories exemplify the sorts of things I had to deal with. By "deal with" I mean concoct nice things to say about style and structure, form and content, syntax and imagery. I could go on about how heartbreakingly difficult it is to discuss stories like these in a classroom situation, but I won't.

Throughout the week my mind was on Linda. I felt like a

lovesick teenager who could not wait to get back to school and sit behind the girl whom he wishes to embrace, and to whisper genuinely heartfelt paragraphs in her ear at the drive-in movie. I wondered if teenage girls were truly aware of what romantic idiots boys are. Do girls understand that the mere sight of their sweater-cloaked backs, their necks, their auburn hair flowing down their napes turn boys into squirrel-brained dimwits? And if they do understand it, what is the depth of their understanding? In other words, do girls realize what power they hold over boys? It's hard to say. I have never written a story from the point of view of a female. I would not presume to know how females think. This is the respect that I give to the opposite sex. Maybe girls are too worried about their own looks, their hair, their flesh, their lipstick, their skirts, to give any thought to how boys respond to their presence, to the mere concept of girls in general, women, females. Poor Gloria Steinem. As a liberal I had always been sympathetic to the women's liberation movement, but as I got older I realized how futile it was. As I say, as soon as a girl graduates from high school she starts looking around for the male who will support her lazy ass for the next fifty years. Pardon me if that sounds sexist. The truth always sounds awful. Men want sex and women want security. That is the eternal rule of thumb. My question is as follows: What the hell makes women think they are entitled to security? The answer is obvious: that's just the way things are. I have no other answer. Kudos to anyone who manages to obtain security. I am not a sexist. I just enjoy pondering awful truths. Men want sex. And they want money. Not all men want power. Not all men want to rule the world. But enough do to make it into the history books. I personally would be happy with an old-fashioned girl who would be satisfied to cook for me, clean my house, do my laundry, and generally make me a happy man. No nagging please. In exchange for no nagging, I will do my best to give you the security that you feel entitled to in your hubristic female self-centeredness.

These are the sorts of thoughts that I have when I am mowing my lawn. I find it interesting that the brain has the ability to work like a parallel processor when a person is engaged in manual labor. Painting over graffiti, mowing a lawn, digging a posthole, I find that my hand-eye coordination takes over the job competently, leaving my mind free to think awful thoughts. I assume that most people are this way. A woman doing the laundry or mopping a kitchen floor surely thinks about other things than diapers and dirt. That is as far as I am willing to take my assumption. I will not pretend to know what women think about. I usually think about the plot of the novel I am working on. Any sort of occupation that requires manual dexterity frees my mind for thinking. Most serious writers would probably agree with that. Some of your best ideas come when you are driving along the interstate or taking a shower. But on the last normal Saturday of my life I found myself thinking about Linda as I mowed the lawn.

I felt like a foolish boy as I maneuvered the power mower around the base of a small

tree growing in the backyard. Not since high school had I found myself so obsessed with the image of a member of the opposite sex. Linda. I had felt a sparkle of electricity flit between our faces the moment she had looked me in the eye on that previous Monday. This was kid's stuff. I was thirty-nine years old. There was no question that she was old enough to understand the power that women have over men. I would guess her age at twenty-seven. On the night she showed up for the first class, she was dressed as if she had intended to go out dancing in a hotel ballroom but for the strange shabby coat that she wore. I assumed that she wore it to diminish her attractiveness. I see ulterior motives behind everything, so that assumption should not be taken too seriously. Maybe she had no taste. Maybe somebody else dressed her. This was the first time I considered the notion that she might have a husband or a boyfriend. I shut off the lawn mower at that point and waited for the sound of the engine to fade, for the whirlwind of disturbed grass to settle, for the refreshing odor of hacked chlorophyll to permeate the air around me as I tried to envision her left hand.

Had she been wearing a ring? I could not remember. This surprised me. I usually make a note of the jewelry on a new woman's hand. But this served only to underscore the fact that I was so taken by her beauty that I was aware of nothing else. I had "lost my touch" in the sense that I had failed to assess her potential. Was she married? Engaged? Was there an indentation on the third finger of her left hand where a ring might once have been worn? I simply could not remember. But the thought that she might be unavailable brought a pall upon the scene. The lawn was only half-mowed. I had the sudden urge to give up, step inside the house, pour a glass of red wine, and pout. How could I possibly go on seeing her week after week knowing that she was married, had kids, was "taken" by some lucky sonofabitch. I had to be honest with myself. A woman that attractive could not possibly be free. Absolutely gorgeous women do not remain in the open marketplace for very long, not even women of discriminating taste who are on the lookout for a millionaire.

This started me thinking about how fortunate the truly beautiful women of the world are. Kids in a candy store. A woman graduates from high school, then looks around for a job that will place her in the immediate vicinity of men with money. Business executives. The world is filled with beautiful secretaries. This in turn made me think of Ann-Margret in *Carnal Knowledge*. As a chronic film buff I find myself constantly comparing and contrasting the real world with the false worlds of film. Ann-Margret was stunning in that film. She hooks up with Jack Nicholson, who plays the role of one of the biggest bastards ever conceived of by a screenwriter. I then wondered if that movie had been based on a book. I would have to check into that. It might be worth reading the story in the original Greek. This is how my mind works when I am engaged in manual labor. By then I had the lawn mower running again. It was not in me to leave a lawn half-mowed. Not even as a lazy, worthless teenage boy had it ever occurred to me to walk away from a lawn job half-finished. A good quirk in a personality filled with quirks of every stripe, good and bad, fruitful and fruitless.

I finished the lawn thinking about Linda's face. I imagined kissing her cheeks. I imagined the two of us "making out" on a couch. Do kids today still say "making out"? My mother referred to it as "necking." The word "necking" made me think of giraffes with their necks braided. I was perhaps eight years old the first time I heard her use that word. She had to explain it to me. "Hugging and kissing," I now imagine her saying. Is there anything quite as embarrassing to a boy than to have his mother making reference to that sort of thing? Yes. Here is a joke that I overheard my mother tell in mixed company. It was during a party that took place in our backyard, possibly a Fourth-of-July celebration. "If you goose a ghost, you get a handful of sheet," my mother said. The female guests squealed with laughter. The men chortled good-naturedly. I was mortified. I ran into the house and dove under my bed covers, pulled the pillow over my face, and shrieked with embarrassed agony. How could my mother make such a detestable joke? Was she some sort of trollop from the gutters of London? My mother also once told me that if I ever suffered a broken heart, I should read the poetry of Dorothy Parker. I was eleven years old, so of course I did not know who Dorothy Parker was. It would be years before I read the works of Dorothy Parker. When I finally became familiar with her writing and her point of view, I recalled what my mother had said, and only then did it occur to me to wonder how many men my mother had dated before she met my father. I had never given that a moment's thought in my entire life. After my mother died I realized that I knew virtually nothing about her youth, her experiences growing up. I was an adult by then, out of the army and on my own in the world. This became the first heartbreak I was ever to know. I had never asked my mother to sit down and tell me the story of her life. Where did she go to grade school? What were her parents like, my grandparents? Where did she go to high school? Did she date a lot of boys before she met my father? What sort of jobs did she hold? What sort of ambitions did she have? My mother was an artist. She took drawing classes in high school. When I was growing up, my mother kept all of her sketchbooks on a shelf in a closet in her bedroom where we children could not get at them. But occasionally she did allow us to leaf through them under her supervision. She could render lifelike portraits, the faces of friends reproduced in chalk and charcoal with photographic accuracy. She could have been a fine artist, or perhaps an illustrator for a top ad agency in New York City. She was that good. But instead she got married and had children. When my mother died, I did not even know her.

I stood in the silence of the backyard watching flecks of grass and weed swirling around me in a slight breeze accompanied by that chlorophyll odor, and I pondered the fact that my mother was the first person to explain death to me. I was five years old. I remembered the moment vividly. I went to her one afternoon and asked how long people stayed dead before they woke up again. She was ironing at the time. Raising and lowering a shirt and adjusting it to lay flat on the board. The odor of steam-heated fabric was in the air of the little back room where she took care of that sort of business, along with sewing. My motive for asking came from a TV western where a character named Dick West was shot out of the saddle by cattle rustlers. He was somebody's sidekick. He wore all black. He fell to the ground and lay there dead. The rustlers rode up on their stallions and took a look at the body, smiled with smug outlaw satisfaction, and galloped away. After they were gone, Dick West rose from the dead. He grabbed his cowboy hat off the ground, slapped the dust away on his thigh, mounted his horse, and sped to town. I began to speculate. How long did you remain dead before you got up again? For some reason, I concluded that it was fifteen minutes. I understood the concept of time, of clocks, when I was five. But I wanted confirmation. I went to my mother, the fountainhead of all knowledge. Mothers teach children everything. Fathers are worthless, as we all come to learn by the age of ten.

"You don't get up again," my mother said, creasing the arms of a shirt and laying it down on the ironing board.

"What do you mean?" I said.

"When you die, you're dead forever," my mother replied.

This did not jibe with the facts as I knew them to be. Dick West had been shot out of the saddle. He had been killed by outlaw bullets. But I had also seen death in person, i.e., parakeets died, cats, dogs. A neighbor boy's bulldog had been struck by a car, and the boy showed me the body in his garage. It was covered by a blanket. His worthless father had not yet disposed of the body. The boy peeled the blanket away. The dog looked like it was sleeping.

"He's dead," my friend said. The boy did not seem morose. He was facing up to and communicating a hard fact of life. His little dog was dead, but his mom had told him that they would get another dog. The two of us stood in the garage and stared at the dead dog for a while. Then he placed the blanket back over the corpse and we left.

"Forever?" I said.

I imagine myself twisting my neck, frowning, trying to piece together the contradictory facts. My mother said that after a person died he never got up again, yet Dick West had gotten up. Another baffling mystery in a long line of life-and-death mysteries awaiting me at the door of the parochial school where I would be enrolled the following September. That was where the nuns would teach me that Jesus rose from the dead. The world of grown-ups was contradictory and incomprehensible.

Then I heard the faraway sound of bells. I was getting ready to pull-start the mower, and the ringing of tiny bells seemed to emerge from the air itself. I recognized the tune. I was not certain of the title: "Slide down my rain barrel. Something my cellar door." It was the universal tune of a popsicle truck traveling along the street in front of my house. The street I lived on was named Pearl. The sound of bells shimmered into existence, reached their peak of loudness as they passed my front door, and faded into the northern distance. The bells of my childhood. The bells of summer. I heard the ring, I tasted cherry ice on my tongue. Big business meets Pavlov. I wanted to hurry out to the street and flag down the driver, buy a popsicle. But I merely stood behind the silent lawn mower listening to the bells fading from the warm sunlit air on the last normal Saturday of my life.

Chapter 5

Time began to drag. The lovesick know what I'm talking about. Sunday took forever. After watching the Broncos win again, I found myself walking around the house carrying Linda's short story, leafing through it, concocting questions that I might ask in the formal setting of the schoolroom and the informal setting of a bar on East Colfax. Eventually, I slipped the story into my briefcase and went upstairs to dust the vacant apartment, making certain that it would be in the spotless order expected by a potential tenant. The landlord had told me that he brought people around at all hours of the day and evening, and he wanted the place to be perpetually ready for inspection. Yes, it reminded me a little bit of the army where bullshit inspections destroyed morale and drove men to put in transfers for places like Turkey and Panama. Stateside duty is an ineffective joke. There was a time when I considered putting in twenty years and retiring with a nice pension. Looking back on my life as I wiped dust from the windowsills and shoved a push broom around the hardwood floor, I saw that I might as well have stayed in the army, since I would have been eligible for that pension in less than two years from this very date. What had I done with my life that I could not have done as a supply sergeant ticking off the years in an obscure army base, of which there are many in America? Let the corporals and privates do all the heavy lifting while I gave well-rehearsed orders. *No Time for Sergeants* has always been one of my favorite movies, and the portrayal of Sergeant King is right on the mark. Take it easy for twenty years and then quietly slip away with the monthly check and the blessing of Uncle Sam and a grateful citizenry. Well, it was too late for that, but it is never too late to wallow in regret.

I sometimes wondered if I had ever learned any lessons and successfully applied them on the next go-round. "A lesson learned," I used to say after an egregious error was fully comprehended. I eventually gave up saying that. It did not seem to forestall future mistakes nor put money in my pocket. But an inability to absorb lessons could account for the boyish nervousness I experienced as I swept and dusted both the upstairs and the basement apartments before returning to my own digs and seeing with disappointment that it was not quite five in the afternoon. I was desperate for my Monday evening creative-writing class to begin. I berated myself. This was ludicrous, foolish. The woman was probably married, or engaged, or had a slew of boyfriends who could afford to court her in a manner to which I'm sure she had grown accustomed.

When I was nineteen, I dated an eighteen-year-old girl named Kelly who wanted to go dining and dancing. I took her to drive-in movies so I could neck with her. She got fed up with that and refused to go out with me anymore. She deserved better than a boy who earned fifty dollars a week hauling furniture around town and wore the same blue jeans on his dates that he wore to the furniture warehouse. A lesson learned.

Throughout Sunday night and the daylight hours of Monday I was anxious and bored. At six thirty on Monday evening I finally climbed into my K-car with my briefcase and drove to the free U feeling like an eighteen-year-old champing at the bit to get to the drive-in movie and start working on those soft, delectable lips. Kelly wore Chanel No. 5 for the first three months of our relationship, then stopped wearing it because she said—and I quote—"You're not worth it." I understood nothing of expensive things at the age of nineteen.

I parked in "my spot" outside the free U and hurried up to the door to prepare the classroom for Linda's arrival. I wondered if she would be wearing the black dress and high heels again. Maybe those were her "work clothes." Maybe she was a secretary in one of the skyscrapers along Seventeenth Street, Denver's financial district. Maybe she was one of those girls who had taken typewriting damned seriously in high school, understanding that if she could crank out ninety words a minute she could get a job anywhere in the world. Our typing teacher in high school emphasized this. She went out of her way more than once to tell the girls in class that if they learned how to type well they could make a living just about anywhere they chose. I used to surreptitiously watch the girls in our typing class, and noted that more than half appeared to take these words seriously. They did not cheat as I did to get that A+. Had I been given a private test at the end of the semester I would have received an F. But the teacher, a lay teacher in a Catholic environment, did not seem to care that most of the boys in her class cheated and did not actually learn how to type. I came to regret that. I type with two fingers, sometimes three when I really get moving. In many ways I am a fool. In other ways I am not, but those seem to be the ways that do not matter. A lesson learned.

I unlocked the door to the classroom and entered, turned on the lights, and went to my desk to empty my briefcase of the student stories and to prepare myself mentally for the discussion of "Mister Eight" by Linda Hathaway. Her address and phone number were not the only things she had lied about when registering for the class. "Linda Hathaway." Looking back on it later, I realized that the cognomen had the phony overtone of a pseudonym. A TV-star name. Linda Hathaway, well-dressed creative-writing starlet hooks up with Lionel Dazzletooth, unpublished writing teacher. But I am being too hard on myself, a penitent whipping himself with a cat-o'-nine-tails because nobody else has the inclination to wear out a right arm with the intention of raising my dimwitted consciousness.

The students began filing into the room at five minutes to seven, taking their self-prescribed seats, the older women near the front, the young rebel boys at the rear. Most of the girls in the class, ages twenty to thirty, wanted to write romances as had the published student that I mentioned earlier. Her success was legend, even among those who aspired to other genres, westerns, science fiction. Someone had made it. Someone had sold a novel. A manuscript had been accepted by a real publisher on the East Coast. Heady stuff.

At five minutes after seven it became clear to me that Linda was not going to show. I feel those things in my gut, but maybe everybody does. I do not want to ascribe mysticism to myself. Experience is the root of all vibes. I futzed around at the front of the room, shuffling through the manuscripts, glancing now and then at the door, giving Linda time to show up in a flurry of apologies. But it looked like she was not coming. One of the students, a man in his late twenties named Brad, who seemed a bit self-deprecating as a writer, had agreed to xerox his story for reading on this night, the first story to be read aloud. The opening sentence of his story went as follows: "Her heart was as cold as a well-digger's ass." It garnered the appropriate laughter. That is what I meant by his inability to take himself seriously as a writer. He handled the English language well enough to write a publishable book, but his stories had an undertone that I interpreted this way: "Do not take me seriously." As I said, my focus in this classroom was on story structure, the laying out of a storyline.

The Paradise That Lurks in Female Smiles

I tried to steer clear of style as much as possible. There were plenty of writing teachers willing to focus on style, since they did not know how to plot anyway. This was also true of most creative-writing books, the how-tos crammed into the shelves at bookstores. My attitude, which I tried to pass along to my students, probably without success, went as follows: if you can speak English, you can write a novel. This was a bit too subtle for most of my students to absorb, but it was my way of telling them to have faith in their own voices. Like it or not, their own voices were all that they possessed after taking creative-writing classes and reading all the how-to books. Their own voices were all that they possessed as they sat in the loneliness of their dens staring at blank sheets of paper or computer screens while sipping wine or brandy. "Don't let the bastards get you down," I said. By bastards I meant all the English teachers who ever told them that they did not speak right, write right, or think right. "Write in your own voice" was the only general principle of style that I knew of or believed in. But the majority of my students registered for my class believing that their only real problem was style and that somehow I would "fix" their voices so that they wrote right. It is terribly difficult to convince people to believe in themselves, but that was my self-imposed mission in life.

"Does anybody here know the whereabouts of Miss Hathaway?" I said after Brad sat down. I make my students stand while reading their stories aloud. I want them to get used to the horror of the spotlight.

Nobody knew where Linda was. We then dove into the dissection of Brad's story of the girl with the cold, cold heart. I let them do all the talking. I had lost interest in that night's class when I realized Linda was not coming. My gut told me that she was never coming back. This had a precedent. People would lose their nerve when finally confronting the cold, cold fact of a creative-writing class, standing while reading aloud, offering up their loved one for public dissection, hearing the negative criticism on a much louder decibel scale than the praise. I knew from my own experience how devastating a negative response to a story can be to a beginning writer. Thick skin is no joke. You cannot let honest criticism eat away at your soul. You cannot scream and pound your fist on a desktop when somebody tells you that your cherished imagery sucks. Whining at your critics will not improve the quality of your story. Some people cannot take it. I have friends who abandoned writing altogether because they could no longer take the rejection slips. I am talking about acquaintances who wrote for ten or twenty years before giving up. It appeared that Linda had given up. Already in my mind her story had gone from peculiar to brilliant, and I wanted desperately to discuss it both in the classroom and in a bar.

(He) "I am going to sexual intercourse you now."

(She) "Be my guest."

Who writes like this? The characters did not have names. My plan was to compare and contrast her writing with that of Robbe-Grillet right in front of the whole classroom. Then I would ask if she was influenced by the Europeans, Sartre, Camus, and anybody else I could think of on the spur of the moment. I've never been able to finish a novel by Robbe-Grillet, but what does that matter to a man on the make? If one of the rebel boys had written this story I would have suggested that he not bet his writing career on himself. But Linda? I had known her for barely twenty seconds when I had decided that she could do no wrong.

During the smoke break I stood outside the free U building in the dark, sucking on a cigarette and staring at the spot farther north along the curb where she had parked her secret car the previous week. I did not know the make or model of the car. It had looked contemporary and expensive. Was she a rich bored housewife searching for a hobby? Had she tired of painting plaster-of-Paris figurines, or wrestling with endless knots of macrame, and had decided to look around for another hobby? I decided that she was the trophy wife of a middle-aged banker who had told her to find an activity to kill the hours while he was at work. Get involved in a goddamn charity or something. Or her husband was an oil billionaire. He was pissed off that a woman who bathed in hundred-dollar bills every night was bored with her marriage.

I was crushing out a butt when I decided to make a run past her house after class. If the lights were on in her place, I would knock on her door and ask if she was ill. I allowed fantasies of this nature to flow freely. My thoughts were a violation of the sacred trust between student and teacher. You do not take advantage of the fact that you know a student's address. You do not make runs past her house like a demented stalker. Not even if she is the most beautiful woman you have ever seen in your life, a woman to whom you have secretly sworn eternal love while mowing a lawn. I grew angry. I wanted to smoke another cigarette, but one of the rebel boys stepped outside and told me that the class was ready for the second hour.

I followed him back into the building filled with disgust and rage at the fact that I taught a two-hour class once a week. If I had taught a one-hour class I would already be cruising slowly past Linda's digs and praying that I would see her silhouette on the shade. But I knew that I would not park my car and approach her house and knock on her door. Things like that happened only in the imagination, the land devoid of rules where anything can happen, the place where writers stake out their postage-stamp-sized patch of earth and start lying. That is Faulkner, of course. Faulkner is one writer whom I quote to all my students. Not his style of writing or subject matter, but his advice. Listen to him. Do what he says. It doesn't matter where you come from. Make that your territory. Twain owns the Mississippi. Chandler the mean streets of LA. Bellow Chicago. Hemingway owns a lot of places, including one place that nobody in his right mind would want: Upper Michigan. That was a part of his genius. Having faith in your roots is the same as having faith in your voice. But I didn't care anymore. I didn't want to teach another hour of creative writing. I wanted to know what had become of Linda Hathaway. Would I ever see her again? Why would a woman register for a writing course, attend one class, and then quit? I wanted to get her alone in a bar "to talk." I wanted to embrace her. I wanted to kiss her. I wanted to sexual intercourse her.

The second hour was devoted to discussing the opening chapter of a romance novel written by a thirty-five-year-old woman who was happily married and had three children. She was deadly serious about her writing. She had asked me at the beginning of the semester if it was all right to hand in three consecutive chapters of a novel rather than three short stories, and I told her yes, definitely. I encouraged my students to start novels so that I could expand on my theories about the secret of novel writing. Her book fell into the category of romance that spills over into R-rated. The heroines were not chaste, but they were good in other ways. I once read a tongue-in-cheek article which stated that romance novels were pornography for women, and her book gave credence to the theory. I found it hard to believe that this writer had three children, that she was married, and that she was happy. The main character of the novel was a buxom pirate, a female freebooter. When confronted by a male counterpart on the high seas, "her cutlass did all the talking."

Classes that feature excerpts from a novel always excite

me. I am filled with a sense of anticipation that has no realistic basis. It is not my novel being discussed, but I treat it like it's my baby. I get excited about mentoring a novel through to the end. I get excited about teaching a student who actually listens to what I have to say. But not that night. It might as well have been a poem for all the interest I took in her book. But the other students seemed to appreciate what she was doing. There was laughter in appropriate places. I took my cues from audience response, I smiled when they smiled, I frowned with serious interest when they frowned, but my thoughts were on Linda. I felt as if I were cheating the romance author out of her tuition payment. I could not concentrate on her words. Yet when she finished reading her chapter aloud I was able to collect myself and fall into a well-practiced role, giving her a positive critique and complimenting her on the characterization of the woman pirate whose name I did not catch. It was not myself but my years of teaching creative writing that spoke to her that night. She blushed with pride. Leave them beaming, that is one of my rules of thumb. Writers are like that, myself included. Fire a well-aimed compliment at the heart of a student and she goes home in a state of bliss.

While my "other" self was speaking, my mind was on the door. I kept listening for the sound of high heels hurrying down the hallway, of Linda Hathaway racing to make the end of class. Even though I knew she was not coming, I had Plan B waiting in the wings. If she showed up, I would play upon the guilt feelings that we all carry inside us and suggest that she join me at a bar on Colfax to discuss her short story, since we were not able to do so during class. Guilt: the secret weapon of the shameless manipulator. But Plan B was destined to remain in the wings gathering dust like most of my plans had done throughout my life. Linda Hathaway did not show up that night. I drove home wondering why.

Chapter 6

I awoke to the sound of footsteps overhead. A disturbing, unnerving sound to hear in a house where you live alone. I did not know what time of night it was. I sleep with a piece of black cotton cloth over my eyes to keep out the ambient light of my digital clock and the light that shines from a pole in the alley, an astonishingly bright white light almost crystalline in its radiance and which effectively penetrates the window shade to the extent that it can wake me if the cloth falls away from my eyes. I do not wear an eye mask as Grandes Dames do in movies and *New Yorker* cartoons. I do not fidget and twitch in bed. The cotton cloth remains on the front of my skull all night, so that even if I open my eyes I see nothing but darkness.

The footsteps moved slowly across the ceiling. I thought immediately of the telephone in my living room. I thought of the sharpened knives in the kitchen. I do not own a gun, but I once thought of buying one. When they passed the "Make My Day" law in Colorado, I considered buying a pistol and applying for a license to carry a concealed weapon. I thought the thoughts of a boy who saw the world in terms of heroics. Perhaps one day I could thwart a crime with my concealed weapon, save an old lady from a mugger, plug an intruder slithering through my bedroom window. I was taught in the army how to use firearms, pistols and rifles. The thought of owning a personal sidearm did not disturb me in any particular way, but then I did not have a household filled with children who might discover the mighty treasure of a .38 in daddy's closet. I never gave any truly serious thought to buying a weapon, but as I listened to the slow, almost tortuous sound of footsteps idly pacing the ceiling, I felt a splinter of regret that I did not have a handy weapon that I could grab. There is no getting around it. The grip of a pistol in a man's hand changes the way he relates to the world. He wears a suit of armor.

Then came the voice. Ten seconds had gone by since the footsteps had awakened me, and the muffled voice overhead had a familiar tenor. The cloth was still across my face, and the moment I dragged it away, I saw that it was daylight. I squinted at my clock, which told me that it was 8:30 a.m. The voice was that of my landlord. He was showing the upstairs apartment to a potential tenant.

I draped the cloth across my eyes again and let gravity take the weight of my arms and legs down into the comforting softness of my mattress and pillow. With the sound of that voice I was transferred from the land of danger and death to the physical world where I experienced the disappointing realization that I would now have a neighbor to contend with. My landlord is a bright man who rents his vacancies to quiet people. Mature adults. No young men in groups of three or four, splitting the difference in the rent as they attend college at nearby DU and throw the occasional beer blast. During all the time I had lived on the ground floor there had been only that young hippie who lived in the basement apartment, but he was a quiet enough fellow who turned up the stereo only on the occasional Saturday night when he was getting blasted on the weed that I smelled with envy as I sat sipping beer in my living room.

Believe me, there were plenty of times when I had to stop myself from going downstairs and inquiring as to whether I could buy a joint from him, or a pinch of ganja to poke into the bowl of one of the meerschaums that I kept around the house. I did not want to become pot buddies with the hippie. I sensed intuitively that it would be a mistake, as a natural born loner and a writer, to give someone the impression that I was available for random visits, especially if my friend lived downstairs. I did not have a set time for writing, but I could think of fewer irritating things than to hear a knock on the door as I was sitting down to write only to find a hippie saying, "Hey man, wanna get wasted?" Then I would have to play the role of bad guy and turn him away. He would eventually catch on to the fact that I wanted him around only for his pot. People always catch on to things like that. Another example might be that I hang around women only because they are female. In other words, I have never been physically attracted to a person who did not have a vagina.

I sat on the edge of my bed pulling on my socks and thinking about the emptiness of my double bed and the backs of women I had known, those who slept facing the far wall. I finished dressing and wondered how it could be that at my age I was still engaging in the fantasies you have as a boy in high school when the reality of male/female relationships is as foreign as a language spoken in Europe. I went to the bedroom window and looked out at the backyard that I had mown. I admired my handiwork. Writers do so little work that any form of manual labor becomes a monumental event. I looked at the light pole in the alley that brightens my window shade at night. The light goes off when the sun hits the electric eye. This always makes me think of the men who worked for cities in the nineteenth century, the lamplighters who strolled the streets making certain that the gaslights were lit and functioning properly. This led me to thinking about Jack the Ripper performing his wicked work in the fog. My mind whirls like this before I have had my coffee. I don't know if it is the imagination of the writer part of me or if everybody's mind flits from one thought to another like a bee trying out available flowers. I do not put any credence into the canard that writers "see" things that other people do not see. It is part of a writer's job to take note of minutiae, to remember it, to put it into his stories to give them verisimilitude, vitality, and insight, but there is nothing mystical about it. Yet I have read articles and stories and novels by writers who try to perpetuate the idea that somehow writers are "special" people who "know" things that the nonliterary dullards of the world do not know. Frankly, that posture makes me sick. I do not hang out with writers or have friends who write. I gave up on that long ago, after college, when I perceived how full of shit most writers are. Their self-aggrandizement made me cringe with embarrassment. I was afraid the attitude would infect me, and who knows, maybe it did, but I tried not to think about it. Part of my becoming a creative-writing teacher was a desire to divest aspirants of the notion that they are "special." Just because some twenty-year-old decides that it would be real nifty to spend his life with his lazy ass planted on a chair typing novels does not make him more perceptive than the average truck-stop waitress or insurance salesman. But try and tell that to a kid with a goatee, a pipe, and a faraway look in his eyes.

Yes, this is how my mind whirls before I have had my coffee—I become highly judgmental, enraged, and pleased with myself. As I stepped into the kitchen I heard the sounds of footsteps on the wooden staircase outside that led up to the vacant apartment. I heard the muffled mumbling of my landlord. I crossed my fingers in the hope that the potential tenant would be dissatisfied with the top-floor rooms and go away. I liked living by myself in this house. Not that I ever interacted to any degree with former tenants, but it was nice to know that my own footsteps could not be heard, my own stereo did not keep virtual strangers awake at night, that I could talk out loud to myself, could bark at moronic newsmakers on TV without tenants wondering what was wrong with the man in the ground-floor apartment.

The hippie downstairs once walked in while I was sorting my laundry and simultaneously crabbing aloud about some video injustice or other. He grinned at me. He understood. I was one of "those" people. But I suppose everybody on earth has been caught talking out loud to himself. Why does this embarrass us? What is it about the overheard word that makes us crumple like tinfoil with faces flushed crimson? Why is talking out loud considered a sign of insanity? And finally, is not writing a form of talking out loud to ourselves? And then, after speaking silently to ourselves for six months or a year, we ship a manuscript to New York and beg publishers to distribute our unheard words. That is a much more credible sign of insanity, but I do not tell this to my students. I back them one hundred percent. There are plenty of louses in the world who will tell them that they are wasting their time, most of them old friends.

Tuesday was a work night for me, the janitorial service at the medical clinic. I was not scheduled to go in until six that evening, along with the rest of the night crew, which consisted of the two college kids, a jolly middle-aged woman of Italian extraction named Joie, who scrubbed the aluminum sinks in all the clinic rooms, and a couple who baffled me because the man was as ugly as a toad and the woman almost rivaled Linda in her beauty. Their job consisted of sweeping and polishing the tile floors of the two-story building. The woman, whose name was Katy, always wore an authentic dress when she came to work, the kind of dress a woman might wear when expecting company for a light dinner on the patio. The toad wore blue jeans and a flannel shirt. His name was Ed. He looked like an Ed. He had receding hair and a bulbous nose and could have passed for sixty, but I believed he was in his early forties, not so much older than myself. Ed and Katy were obviously in love.

He must have been a wonderful man because Katy looked like the sort of woman who could have had her pick of any man in town. But she chose the toad man. I assume this makes me a skewed breed of sexist. Doubtless I was jealous of Ed, who stood a head shorter than Katy. They spoke and joked quietly with each other as they worked. I took note of her gaze whenever she conversed with him. There was adoration in her eyes. Ed must have been a kind and gentle and good-humored gold-hearted man to win the love of this doll. I am simply being honest here. I did not desire Katy, but I was jealous of Ed. Whatever he had going for him, it was hidden somewhere beneath his horrid skin. So I say now as I have always said: I do not understand women. Why are they not as superficial as I am? I have always considered myself to be the touchstone of the ordinary guy, the exemplar of everything that is shallow. I am an American male, so I was raised to value surface appearances. But I also believe in self-examination, in self-knowledge. I don't know how a person can ever hope to be a real writer if he is not honest with himself first and foremost. Writing scathing indictments of the government, the military, the church, big business, and all the targets of self-righteous liberal literati is not enough if you are not willing to open the doors of your own heart and peer into the murk of that fetid mess and report with accuracy the things that cause you shame. This is just a theory of mine and as I have said, I do practice what I preach, but I suppose there have been plenty of successful published writers who lied to themselves from cradle to grave. I see no point in it. Judging yourself harshly is the best way to finesse your loudmouthed friends.

I drove my car to the clinic that night. It took three hours to complete my work. This consisted of going from room to room shoving a large cart into which I dumped refuse collected in large plastic wastebaskets. The refuse consisted primarily of bloody bandages and syringes, plastic devices, rubber gloves, the accouterment of the doctors who worked during the daylight hours. It was filthy and repulsive work, but I didn't mind. I wore gloves, a kind of welder's mitt, which prevented me from being stuck by an errant needle. I walked into each clinic room, picked up the wastebasket, which stood waist-high, and hefted it into the hallway where I dumped it into a massive canvas bag attached to the cart. When the canvas bag was full I would wheel it outside to the rear of the building where I would pour the contents into a giant metal dumpster. It was hard heavy work that a woman would have trouble doing. This was one reason why I was hired. My boss, Herb, did not hire women to do this sort of work. He had tried that once years ago, in a spirit of cooperation with the women's liberation movement, only to discover that the libber was asking the men on the crew to help her empty the bags into the dumpster. Enough said on that subject.

The other part of my job was to polish a long black countertop in the clinic laboratory. This consisted of pouring a liquid blue soapy detergent onto the counter and wiping it slowly until the counter sparkled with an obsidian gleam beneath the overhead fluorescents. It was satisfying work. If I missed a spot, it showed up well against the black patina and allowed me to correct the mistake. Each time I finished polishing the black countertop I stood back and eyeballed it, pleased with my accomplishment. It was not unlike polishing the toes of my boots when I was in the army.

That was my job then. Emptying wastebaskets and polishing a countertop. My boss told me to make certain that each wastebasket in each small room was emptied. The doctors would raise hell if they came to work in the morning to find a wastebasket that had been overlooked. "Check each room twice if you have to," he told me. It was not the sort of job for a married man, or any man of ambition. It was a job for a boy, like the two clowns I worked with who ran the floor-polishing machines, the exuberant kids who always seemed to be laughing. One of them sported a mustache. They both had long hair. They wore buds in their ears and listened to rock stations while they worked, diddy-bopping to melodies as they wended their way down the hallways of the clinic wielding their machines with the spinning brushes. The boys were little different from me except that I was twice their age.

After work that night I went to a 10 p.m. showing of a movie at the Vogue Theatre just down the block from my apartment. The Vogue is one of the last of the small theaters in Denver, an art movie house that features retrospectives. It will probably go under one day soon. Josef von Sternberg's version of *Crime and Punishment* was playing that night, and while I did not know if the movie was considered a classic, it qualified in my mind simply because it starred Peter Lorre. How many starring roles did Peter Lorre ever have? Maybe he wasn't leading man material, maybe his strength lay in secondary characters like Joel Cairo from *The Maltese Falcon*, the shadowy geek who flitted around behind the likes of Humphrey Bogart and Sydney Greenstreet. Maybe that is where he belonged, a character actor whose vaguely homosexual persona was manifested in perfumed handkerchiefs and a charming cowardice to offset his small stature. Who, besides Humphrey Bogart, would take a punch at Peter Lorre? Doubtless he was beaten occasionally by Raymond Massey off-screen in *Arsenic and Old Lace*, as well as by dozens of other venal leading villains, but that is what men of small stature were put here on earth to do: suffer for our sins.

It may have been a mistake to go to the movie that night. Peter Lorre's love interest, so

to speak, was a girl who reminded me of Linda. The pawnbroker, the old woman who was destined to die by Raskolnikov's hand, referred to the girl as a "common little guttersnipe." The girl was a slender wistful waif, and whenever she came on-screen I thought of Linda. As for the movie itself, well, I had given up long ago on the idea that Hollywood had any respect for classic literature, so I took that into account. It had been a while since I had read Dostoyevsky's novel so I did not remember the specifics of the storyline, but I sensed that the screenwriters out in La-La Land had taken as many liberties as they pleased in cutting, twisting, and reshaping the movie into a ninety-minute adaptation that probably was a travesty, but I did not care. Josef von Sternberg's sets, lighting, and photography were a treat for the eyes. Black and white, of course, released in 1935. I nearly fell out of my chair when the credits rolled at the beginning of the movie and I saw that it was produced by B. P. Schulberg. My God. Budd's father! The *What Makes Sammy Run?* guy. Budd Schulberg, the *On the Waterfront* guy. Budd Schulberg, the guy who had been given a job of driving F. Scott Fitzgerald around New England and then wrote a book about it called *The Disenchanted*. The little prick. I wonder what Fitzgerald thought of this Hollywood brat using his alcoholism as subject matter for a novel. Schulberg was a socialist who probably saw a roman à clef about F. Scott Fitzgerald as "money in the bank" when word got around about the real story behind the novel. Old Hollywood socialists crack me up, and I'm as liberal as any run-of-the-mill Democrat.

I sat and watched *Crime and Punishment* and thoroughly enjoyed it by pretending that it was based on an original screenplay. Had this been true, the movie would certainly have been an authentic classic. I feel the same way about the film version of *Catch-22*. If that movie had been based on an original screenplay and had not been forced to stand in the giant shadow of Heller's novel, it too would have been hailed as a classic, a monumental, innovative, brilliant film. Instead, it was rather dull.

I got one big laugh out of *Crime and Punishment*, which came toward the end of the movie. The police inspector flopped down on his chair and said, "Well . . . I didn't expect *that!*"

My bark of laughter was inappropriate. But his remark was a thumbnail sketch of my life. It was a dramatic scene in the film, but at least nobody in the theater turned and hissed at me to stop being gauche. The Vogue was half-filled that night. There are few of us left, film buffs who will go out of our way to give life to authentic theatrical venues by purchasing tickets and sitting on threadbare velvet seats. As I say, the Vogue will probably go the way of all flesh any day now, probably sooner than later.

Chapter 7

After the movie I walked back to my house thinking about the word "guttersnipe." Where did it come from? What exactly was a guttersnipe? This was one of the drawbacks of majoring in English in college, getting sidetracked by etymology. Not that I had anything else to do that night. As soon as I entered my house I headed for my dictionary. "Guttersnipe" was defined as "a common snipe" as well as "a gatherer of rags and paper from street gutters." I did not know precisely what a "common snipe" was, other than the fact that I once went on a snipe hunt when I was in the Boy Scouts. But I said to hell with it and decided not to look up the word "snipe." You can get sidetracked, lost, and die in a dictionary.

I wanted a beer and a smoke. There is something slightly orgasmic about the theater experience, sitting in the darkness with that vast screen that transports you to places you've never been before. You walk out feeling light-headed, satisfied, and for a moment you are not yourself, you are the character in the film that you most identified with. It doesn't last long. As long as it takes you to get to your car, start it, and pull out into the reality of traffic, of red lights and speed-limit signs. In my case it was a two-block walk to my own home, though when it was a tryst with the Vogue Theatre it lasted a bit longer than a trip to one of the multiplexes around town. The Vogue is an ancient theater. The trees that grow nearby are fifty, sixty years old. They provide shade from the moonlight. The street is silent. This is not a particularly well-traveled part of town. The interstate is a few blocks north but out of sight and sound and mind, built below street level, thus the old nomenclature "Valley Highway" destined to become the modern, supersonic, lifeless Interstate 25.

I went to the icebox and pulled out a Bud. I popped it open, then took a moment to extract a cigarette from a pack lying on the kitchen counter where I keep it for moments like this. I leave packs of smokes here and there, a habit I developed when I was in college. Even in the army I kept an open pack of smokes on the top shelf of my wall locker, an adjunct to the pack I kept in my breast pocket. As I lit up I felt the brief guilt that all smokers feel, sensed the unspoken words that all smokers sense before they take that first puff: "I'm going to quit one of these days."

That hollow vow fades when the first scintilla of smoke hits the back of your throat and the tingle of nicotine worms its way quickly into your brain, making you see the world slightly cockeyed for a minuscule measure of time. First smoke of the day. It is rare that I smoke before evening, unlike my youth where I would light up before my first cup of coffee at dawn. I went into the living room to retrieve Linda's story from my briefcase. (He) (She). I was fascinated by this oddball format, and I wondered if she had borrowed it from a university press magazine where all experimental crap goes to die. Maybe she had literally stolen it from a young author who had graduated from Iowa and would remain unknown for his entire life because he did not understand that people who paid hard-earned money for books were not interested in observing innovative methods of expressing pedestrian ideas. Let it be known that I was one of those young turks in college, so I know whereof I speak. I threw away more failed experiments than Tom Edison.

I couldn't find the story in my briefcase. Small failures like this infuriate me. When it comes to certain things I am a highly organized man, and my briefcase is one of those things. What had I done with her story? I thought back to the previous night when I had been champing at the bit to discuss it with Linda page-by-page at a bar. I remembered flipping through it prior to heading for the free U. Had I taken it out after I got home? Had I read it last night before going to bed?

I went into my bedroom and looked around, couldn't find it, then made a methodical search, including the bathroom where I get some of my best work done. The trail led me back to my briefcase. I sat down on my easy chair, placed my briefcase squarely in front of me on the floor, and began going through the scores of papers that I keep in there. Luck be a lady. I found it at what might be termed "the far side" of my briefcase where I keep papers having to do with the free U, the curriculum, old syllabuses. This disconcerted me for a moment. I do not stuff things randomly into my briefcase, but then my mind may have been focused too much on Linda when I placed the story into my bag the previous evening. Since it was at "the far side" I may have simply mistaken that side of the briefcase for the other, if you get what I mean. It's a fat briefcase, brown leather, broad bottomed, symmetrical. It even has a lock and small key that might have been fashioned by an elf. I never use the lock. There is nothing in my briefcase that I worry about being stolen. This put me in mind not only of myself but of countless creative-writing students who asked in class how one might go about protecting an idea for a story, or preventing a short story from being stolen by another author. This made me smile. Students worry about the oddest things. "Mail a copy of the story to yourself" was one answer I heard in class. "Send your story to the copyright office" another student suggested.

The young scribes lived in terror that their stories might appear in a publication with someone else's name on it.

The Paradise That Lurks in Female Smiles

Imagine the years of litigation involved in proving who owned a story about a dog named Missy who saves a drowning child but then loses her own life? I forget the title of that particular story. It might have been called "Tearjerker." It was written by a young woman who wept when she read it aloud in class. I will not dwell on that precious memory.

So this was how my week went. I wrote, I visited libraries and bookstores, I read short stories submitted by students, I went to movies, I drank at bars. I had Sunday night off because the clinic was closed on Sunday. I watched the Broncos win on Sunday. I had Monday night off because it was the second day of my two-day weekend. My boss and I had come to an affable agreement. I taught at the free U on Monday nights, and since I needed a two-day weekend like all honest laborers, he arranged to have other people empty the clinic wastebaskets. Occasionally myself and the jolly Italian woman, Joie, substituted for Katy and Ed when they were not available for work. A vacation maybe, or a sickness. I had learned long ago that to do favors for a harried boss was an invaluable tactical maneuver.

I never complained about anything, and I tried to avoid doing anything that might garner complaints, such as forgetting to empty a wastebasket in one of the twenty rooms in the building. I was rewarded by days off when I needed them. I was rewarded by regular pay raises. I was rewarded by working for a man who was pleased with me. The cleaning-service industry has a notorious turnover rate, and a man like my boss was ecstatic whenever he hired someone who proved to be reliable. I wasn't certain how the college boys rated in his book, but Katy, Ed, Joie, and myself were the A-team. I had been told by Joie that my boss was quick to fire people who screwed up on the job.

Which brings me to Wednesday night. I had just finished

dumping the last of the wastebaskets and had entered the lab to begin polishing the countertop when I found the two college boys goofing around with a device called a "centrifuge." This machine was used by the lab people to mix chemicals in glass test tubes. The chemicals would be poured into a tube, the tube would be placed in a round slot on a metal plate. When the machine was turned on, the plate spun like a record player, effectively combining the chemicals through centrifugal force. The boys had found a spider that they were trying to kill by spinning it to death. They had put the spider inside a test tube and sent it reeling at an incredible velocity. When they turned the machine off, the spider began crawling up the inside of the tube. They tried again and again to kill the spider, letting the machine run for as long as two minutes, but when they turned the machine off, the spider was still alive. I found the behavior of the boys abhorrent, and I told them so. "Why don't you take that spider outside and turn it loose in the grass?" I said. I personally despise spiders and smash them with a shoe whenever I find one in my apartment, but I had never tormented an insect to death, not counting childhood hijinks with ants, magnifying glasses, and sunlight.

The boys had been laughing when I entered the lab, but their failure to kill the beast with the centrifuge had quieted them. They were in awe of its endurance. "I can't believe it's still alive," one of them kept saying. They finally took it outside and turned it loose. I felt I ought to have stopped them when I first found out what they were doing, but it was only an insect and I found it difficult to work up animal-rights outrage over something that I would have crushed with my heel if I had seen it scuttling down a hallway. Spiders are not like kittens, puppies, horses, etc. I would kick anyone I caught torturing any breed of mammal, but insects? Let's be honest. Everybody hates insects. I will not apologize for being normal.

The night crew finished up and left the clinic a few minutes before 9 p.m. I drove home and made a sandwich and watched television. I don't remember what else I did that evening before going to bed, except to reread Linda's short story. I did that every night of that week. I made small marks on the paper, my own private proofreader marks, as reminders of the things I might say about the story should she ever return to class. My scribbles were symbolic of a hopefulness that I embraced with abandon. Had I been a lovesick teenager, a high school freshman, I would have whispered, "Please God, let her return to me." I said prayers like that frequently when I was young. I am embarrassed to admit it, but I will admit it anyway because it is funny. My adolescent years were like a bad melodrama that I switch on like a TV every so often and watch with a cringing in my gut.

It amuses me to remember how I used to be, the way I thought and acted, the internal life of a Catholic boy who read from a script written by two thousand years of theologians. "I long to kiss Valerie Barbinski in a chaste manner," I confessed to God one time in the hope that He would take pity on me and arrange for me to walk Valerie home through the utilization of His supernatural powers. I imagined God pointing a finger at Valerie Barbinski, who sat in front of me in arithmetic class, and shooting electricity from his magic fingers. This would make Valerie speak to me after class and ask if I would carry her books home. God was to me what Jeeves was to Bertie Wooster. I was always imploring Him to make my dreams come true and help me out of fixes. It makes me cringe to reveal all this, but I do find it funny, if not pathetic. Is it pathos or bathos? I get those two words confused.

"Please God, let Linda return to me," I whispered as I

sat sipping a Budweiser. Then I laughed. I am as adept at mocking myself as are my friends. Why I do this, I do not know. I suspect that self-hatred plays a large role in my role-playing.

On Wednesday evening I arrived at the clinic and found my boss waiting outside for the night crew. Herb had a somber expression. He asked me to stay with him until the others had gone inside.

"We've got a problem," he said.

"What's that?"

"I received a complaint this morning from one of the doctors at the clinic. You overlooked a wastebasket in one of the rooms last night."

My impulse was to deny it, but he didn't give me time.

"I drove over here personally this morning to see what was going on," Herb said. "It was a room on the second floor. The wastebasket was full of bandages. The doctor brought up an empty wastebasket from the storage room to replace it. I personally emptied the basket you overlooked, and promised that the situation would be taken care of."

I started to speak but was momentarily put off by the ominous tone of his last seven words. "I don't understand," I said. "After I emptied the wastebaskets I checked all the rooms and made sure every basket was clean."

As I spoke I looked him directly in the eye. His expression did not change.

"I can't believe this happened, Herb," I said.

"Believe it, Charley," he said. "I emptied it myself."

"Can you show me the room?"

"What difference does it make?" he said. "You overlooked it."

"Maybe I did," I said. "But I checked all the baskets and they were all empty. I just don't understand how this could be true. Maybe someone . . ." I stopped.

He took a deep breath. I wondered if he was sniffing the air for the telltale odor of alcohol. A man who drank on the job could easily overlook a wastebasket. But I never drank on the job.

"I have to tell you," he said, "I've let people go for doing this. I can't have the clinic complaining about the mistakes of my workers. I can't afford to lose the contract with this clinic. There are plenty of other cleaning services in town who would love to take over my contract. I have seven clinics around Denver that I service, and if I lose one I could lose them all."

I felt the cold chill of responsibility flooding through me. It's one thing to screw up and get fired, but quite something else to cause a businessman to lose a lucrative contract.

"Can I at least see the room?" I said. "Maybe I can remember what happened. Maybe I got distracted." I said this calmly, but inside I was beginning to seethe. I had not overlooked any of the wastebaskets. I always made a special point to double-check my work. This thing was not possible, but I knew he was not lying, was not mistaken, that he rightfully believed I was guilty.

He nodded and opened the door, held it for me to pass into the lobby of the clinic. He shut and locked the door behind us. We always worked behind locked doors at night. This was part of the security arrangement. There were drugs in this clinic that addicts would literally kill to get their hands on. Two people were always required to be present when the glass double doors were locked. This was usually Katy and Ed. They were in charge of the only keys that I knew of.

As I followed Herb up the stairs to the second floor my mind was racing. How could this thing have happened?

Herb stopped and pointed into a room halfway down the

hall on the north side of the clinic. I stepped into the room and switched on the light. It was a small room reminiscent of a veterinarian clinic. Examination table. Faucet and sink. In one corner stood the wastebasket, four feet high, with a yellow body and a white top, a lid that could be removed. It worked on a pivot, like wings. You could drop a wad of used, bloody bandages into the basket without touching the lid.

I walked to the corner and looked down at it. I had no particular memory of this particular wastebasket. My janitorial job consisted of mindless repetitive labor. I did not remember emptying this wastebasket nor did I remember any incidents or sounds that might have distracted me from entering this room, a dogfight outside, or the two idiot college kids dashing down the hall laughing as they occasionally did. I turned and looked at Herb.

"All I can say is that I double-check the wastebaskets every night, and I don't see how I could have overlooked this one twice."

Herb sighed. "Whenever I have to fire someone I bring my nephew in to substitute until I get a new employee," he said. "But I don't want to do that. You've always been a good worker, Charley. You've always been reliable. I didn't believe it either when they called in the complaint. That's why I drove over personally this morning to take a look. You and I have never had any problems. I don't see how you could have overlooked it either. But I can't have this happen. I can't afford complaints. They'll drop my contract in a second" — snapping his fingers — "if the doctors complain too often. They expect to find their rooms clean and ready to go when they arrive in the morning. You know how doctors are. Little tin gods."

I nodded. I realized he was not going to fire me. It would not have been a calamity, but it would have meant going through the tedious process of finding another low-paying gig.

The Paradise That Lurks in Female Smiles

"It won't happen again, I promise," I said, and as I spoke I began to review the faces of my fellow employees. Could one of them have filled a wastebasket and placed it back in this room after I left on the previous night? Katy and Ed, Joie, the two college kids—could the kids have been trying to get revenge because I had given them a hard time about that spider? Would they sabotage me so that they could go on playing their juvenile torture games without an adult reaming their scatterbrained asses? Of course there remained one last viable explanation: I was incompetent. Perhaps I truly had overlooked this room twice, once when emptying the wastebaskets and again when double-checking all twenty of the rooms. But that explanation, while plausible, did not feel right. This whole scenario was baffling, infuriating.

"Let's forget about it and go to work," Herb said, offering a wistful smile. I imagine that he himself did not relish the idea of firing me, of looking for a replacement. I was a reliable worker. This was my first official fuck-up. A good record for three years of employment.

"It won't happen again," I said, deciding to triple-check my work from then on out. Where else was I going to find a job that allowed me to work three hours a night, with Monday off to teach my writing class? I did not have enough money in the bank to go an entire semester without working two jobs. This was the kind of close call that left a sour taste on my tongue and in my gut. The mystery had no solution. I did not believe that I was guilty, and I found it difficult to believe that any of my co-workers would try to get me fired.

As I set about emptying wastebaskets I ran other scenarios through my mind. Maybe Joie had a cousin who needed my job, a young woman from Sicily newly arrived in America. Or maybe Ed had sabotaged me because he didn't like the way I eyeballed Katy. Or the college kids were touchy bastards who did not like being reprimanded by a thirty-nine-year-old equal. And always at the end of the line was the most unbearable one of all: Charley Quinn was an incompetent idiot frantically looking to blame someone else for his first official fuck-up. I decided to settle on that explanation. Laying the blame on others was something you were supposed to have outgrown by the time you were in your thirties.

I got back to work. What else was there to do? Return my life to that even keel. I shoved the rolling basket from room to room, getting used to the idea that I was officially no longer a virgin. I had fucked myself.

Chapter 8

Istarted to let things go then. On Thursday and Friday I did not bother to check the empty apartments in my house and sweep or dust or look for dead bugs and mice. A pall of melancholy had come over me, ignited by the screwup of Tuesday night. It was like an ever-widening crack in a dam that allowed other irritants to pass through having to do with my state of being.

I finished up reading the stories from my writing class, wondering how it was that I took this job seriously. Most of the students couldn't write, and the one student who had held promise had resigned from class after only one session. Maybe this was a turn of the screw. Maybe she had lasted only long enough to conclude that I could not teach writing. Or, more specifically, I could not teach her anything that she did not already know. Some people returned to my classes again and again for the camaraderie of knowing other writers, of getting together after class for coffee or beer to talk about published writers the way English majors get together to discuss *Madame Bovary*, Salinger, Guggenheim grants, and of course their own ambitions, which always seemed to reside over some horizon, ever visible but unreachable: the first acceptance slip, the day of publication, the carrot on the stick that keeps young writers going. But what keeps old writers going? Everyone I ever knew who aspired to write had given up by the age of thirty-five.

I pondered throwing Linda's story in the trash. Fifteen sheets of paper taking up space in my massive leather briefcase. But I didn't. I had never thrown away any short stories, going all the way back to college. I owned a filing cabinet filled with stories written by old classmates. I once revealed this to a friend of twenty years who had taken a creative-writing class with me. "I still have that story you wrote about the fishing trip where everybody got diarrhea," I said to him one night in a bar.

"I will gladly pay you for the negatives," he said good-naturedly.

He did not want to be reminded of his own ambitions, did not relish the idea that evidence of his youthful efforts still existed. This seems to be a universal reaction, that of being embarrassed by first attempts to produce fiction. At the age of twenty you emulate your favorite author, and by forty you want to hide in a bomb shelter.

I stuffed Linda's story into the section of my briefcase with the other stories and forgot about it. I went to the movies on both Friday and Saturday night. I did not inspect the lawn or make my walk around the house to see that everything was in order. I did not go around to the alley to see if new graffiti had been spray-painted onto the blank canvas of my garage. I considered the fact that I was thirty-nine years old and did not have a girlfriend to hug in bed on a Saturday night. I did not have a paycheck worth looking at before I handed it to a bank teller. I channel surfed without interest and thought about moving to another state. I no longer wanted to teach at the free U or empty another wastebasket. All this, simply because I had forgotten to empty a wastebasket in a room on the second floor of a clinic that I was paid peanuts to clean. It made me feel young and stupid, which is appropriate when you are twenty, but when you are within spitting distance of forty it has the quality of a tiresome wake-up call. Melancholia. It had happened to me before. The thing to do is ride it out. Let all your failures flow across you like flotsam sprung from the broken dam. The waters will recede if you give it time. Your clothes will dry. You will rise from the riverbed and brush the sand off your ass and look around amazed that you did not drown. But each time you survive the deluge, you become less and less amazed at what you know was only good fortune. Survival. But what had survival ever done for me?

I watched the Broncos beat the Oakland Raiders on Sunday afternoon. I went to bed Sunday night without giving any thought to preparing notes for my Monday-night writing class. As I had done during the previous Monday, I would let the students take over while I monitored their sniping and bickering and ludicrous insults. Creative-writing students can be a bitchy bunch. Part of my job is sprinkling oil, usually through the utilization of humor. Only once had I ever been forced to get hard-nosed, and that was toward a student who began hurling personal insults at another student who had given his story an honest and heartfelt negative critique. Calling someone a "fat-ass cretin" does nothing to improve the quality of the boring story you forced everybody to listen to. Personal insults do not belong in a classroom, they belong in the political arena where most fat-ass cretins live.

I drove to the free U Monday night contemplating my options and adding up the number of weeks left of the semester. It came to six, counting this night. Without belaboring that which may be obvious by now, Linda was seated at her desk when I walked into the room. She had returned. The sun came out from behind the clouds, a whiff of ocean breeze passed through the room leaving a tingle of ozone in the air. The heavy plod of my feet grew light. I drifted over to my desk feeling bug-eyed as I tried not to stare at her glorious presence. I was a kid. My face felt hot, flushed, red with desire. I set my briefcase down, my mind racing furiously to find a script not written. What would I say to her? Would I chastise her for missing last week's class? But she finessed me by getting up and walking over to my desk and saying, "I'm sorry I didn't make it to class last week, Mr. Quinn, but I had to go out of town."

I glanced up with those still wide eyes as if to say, "You were not present last week? My goodness, your absence was hardly . . ."

"I wanted to leave a message telling you that I wouldn't be here, but I didn't know how to get in touch with you," she said.

"How to get in touch with you." The most heartwarming words I had ever heard in my life. I was forced to call upon the professionalism that I had practiced and maintained for three years pertaining to teacher/student relationships. I smiled a winsome smile and said, not loudly enough for any of the other students to hear, "I will give you my home phone number. If there is ever any problem, you can leave a message on my answering machine." I said it calmly, almost noncommittally, as if I was talking to a salesman who might want to follow up on a wholesale purchase of three-ring binders.

"I hope you're not mad at me," she said, tilting her head at a flirtatious angle and managing to both smile and frown at the same time.

What an opening. Everything was going my way. I gave up a small shrug and told her that I had intended to discuss her story in class last week, and that we might not now be able to get to it in class this night with so many other stories scheduled to be read. "It was a good story and there were a number of things I wanted to discuss in class, but the time factor might prohibit us from getting around to it in a formal classroom situation."

The Paradise That Lurks in Female Smiles

Is there a word for it, an idiom, a euphemism? A woman hears news that is neither terrible nor pleasing. Resignation sets in. Her upper and lower lips go into action as one. They curl inward against her teeth as if she is holding a mouthful of milk. They balloon slightly. It is a mandibular posture also used to express minor frustration. Those inwardly curled, slightly ballooned lips might be aimed at a child who has done something bad. Anger restrained. Wait till your father gets home.

"If you would like to discuss your story after class, we could go for a cup of coffee," I said as though it was an afterthought and not a desperate measure that had been eating my heart out for two weeks. "There's a nice place up on Colfax where we could get some espresso," I said, glancing at my watch as though time was a relevant and crucial factor that would affect our destinies throughout the coming years. "It's a marvelous short story."

Her face went blank for an instant, then she blinked and produced a sweet smile that finished me off. If she had said no, I would have canceled the semester and moved to Mexico. "Okay," she said. Then she gave an odd little hop, turned away, and went back to her desk.

Now that I had gotten over the shock of seeing and hearing a dream come true, I noted her clothing. The little black dress was back, the high heels. Had she come straight from a job? Was she a salesgirl in a posh boutique down on Larimer Square or at the Cherry Creek mall? Who else dresses like that? I caught a glimpse of knee as she slid into her seat, then I raised my head and watched my class assemble at their posts.

"All right, we have time tonight for three stories. Who wants to read the first one?" I felt as if I was talking with my head inside a bucket. There seemed to be an echo. I was giddy. Linda had returned, and when this class was over we would be seated across from each other in a coffee shop, doing the things men and women do before they do other things.

Drew raised his hand. I could always count on Drew to kick things off, and he probably knew it. He had been attending my classes for years and could intuit my frustrations and anticipate classroom response to my suggestions that someone volunteer to be the first to make a target of himself and his xeroxed visions.

"I'll give it a go," he said, standing up with a shit-eating grin that reminded me of assistant scoutmasters preparing to haze a tenderfoot in the troop. He sometimes comported himself as if he was in fact my assistant, since he was the "oldest" student insofar as none of the other students had been here as long as he. I had to be careful around Drew and make sure he understood that he was not an intern or a teaching assistant of any sort, and was not, God forbid, my friend. In some circles that status is referred to as "teacher's pet," and while it was difficult not to show a deference to Drew, I managed to maintain a discreet distance from him by giving his stories honest appraisals. That usually cooled him down.

He raised his manuscript with his right hand and folded his left arm across his chest. "I love writing," he began, his eyes flitting across the page. "I love getting it out of my system and putting it down on paper. It gives me the same pleasure as blowing my nose, farting, sneezing, burping, vomiting, or the more crude forms of removing stuff from your body, including weeping. Does an orgasm fit into the category of 'crude'?"

Drew's primary problem as a writer was that he did not seem to be able to discern between a story and an essay. Every story he had ever produced for my classes had the quality of a lecture. It usually took one page before the narrator got around to telling the actual story, whatever it was. In this case it was a story about a writer writing a story. You get a lot of these in creative-writing classes. I had never tried to dissuade students from writing these or any other sorts of stories, beyond obvious and gratuitous porn. Accept the story on its own merits and then critique the execution, that was my general approach. I didn't care what any of my students wrote about, I cared only that they wrote it well, and that each story maintained an internal logic and was grounded in dramatic structure. That gave me enough problems to deal with without adding "content" to the imbroglio. My heart always sank when I encountered a writer-writing-about-writing story, but I tried not to let it show. Leave that to the fiction editors at the *New Yorker*, *Esquire*, *Harper's*, *Playboy*, and *Redbook*. I forget the precise statistic, but I believe the editor of *Redbook* once stated in an interview that her magazine received approximately four thousand stories per year—or was it per month? It was the kind of statistic that I chose to forget when I abandoned short-story writing in favor of the novel. This was fifteen years previous, so things may have changed. I dealt with an average of fifty mediocre stories per semester, with five stories that showed promise, but I had never read a student story that I myself would publish. If I had a conscience I would probably drink myself to death every night—except nobody forces these students to shove money into my pockets, they do it of their own volition, although writing could be viewed as an addiction. But I was not put here on earth to teach people to wise up, I was put here to teach story structure.

"So fuck the editors and their rejection slips," Drew said, bringing his story to a conclusion. "I will continue to fart, sneeze, burp, vomit, weep, and write, and the slush pile be damned. The end."

I didn't know how serious Drew was about a writing

career, but this sort of nonsense always got a laugh out of his audience. And Drew did understand his audience. Drew once told the room that he belonged to the NRA and that he wanted to write action-adventure-suspense-detective novels someday. When he also mentioned the fact that he worked in an auto-body repair shop, I cannot tell you how relieved I was to hear it. This boy was not going places, and I couldn't have been happier for him.

Chapter 9

I have no memory of the details of the other two stories that were read and discussed that night beyond the fact that they were written by women and were the kind of stories published in romance magazines, although I had no idea whether romance magazines still existed. This is one of the problems with creative-writing classes. The short stories that are produced are like

vestiges of a beast that died in the early 1950s. There simply is no market for the short story anymore, and yet people like myself go on teaching it as though our students are writers-in-training for jobs that open up every time an old writer dies. When I was in the army I was told that they needed five hundred new recruits each week to replace the five hundred soldiers who were being discharged that same week. It seemed an incredible waste of money and training to replace five hundred men a week, but that was the army, and probably still is.

The only thing that returns to mind with clarity is the sound of shuffling as the students arose from their desks. I could almost hear the ticking of the clock as it neared 9 p.m. and the moment when Linda and myself would begin a sojourn to the coffee shop to lay the foundation of whatever was to come. Like a beginning writer, I was making things up as I went along. I had no idea where this was going, yet I hoped that the climax would be tremendously successful. This usually meant publication in the *New Yorker*, but tonight I would be happy if it merely arrived at a flirtatious dalliance. "Flirtatious dalliance" is the equivalent of getting published in a nonpaying university press. I do not think I need to carry the physiological analogy to "self-publication." I had spent too many lonely nights lately engaging in self-publication. It was time to get on with serious literature.

"Would you like to walk up to the coffee shop, or would you rather take my car?" I said. I was holding my open briefcase and pretending to leaf through the papers as a reminder, in case she had forgotten our date.

She looked south in the direction of Colfax Avenue, then turned to me and said, "It's awfully late for coffee."

My heart began to sink at these words. The fickleness of women is understood and feared by men. I once knew a virgin who promised me that I would be her first. As it turned out, I was not.

"Coffee keeps me awake," she said. "I would rather have a vodka tonic."

I almost dropped my briefcase. I quickly snapped it closed and told her the Sunset Lounge was just up the block.

"Maybe we should take my car," she said. "I could drop you back here when we're finished."

"You drove tonight?" I said.

She nodded.

I quickly analyzed this scenario. If we walked we would be together longer, but if we took her car she would be obligated to drive me back here. In my mind this would further increase the intimacy of the situation.

"Why don't we do that," I said, raising the briefcase. "I hate lugging this around anyway."

She reached into her purse and withdrew her car key with such quickness and efficiency that there might have been an elf waiting to hand it to her.

"Let's go," she said with a smile and a lilting laugh like the ringing of a chime.

The Paradise That Lurks in Female Smiles

As soon as we got into her car she dug into her purse and pulled out a joint. I recognized the limp twisted hand-roll. She did not ask if I minded whether she smoked and drove, she simply flicked a Bic and lit up, then looked over at me. "I just need a few puffs to straighten me out," she said. "Would you like some?"

My mind began racing in an entirely different direction. I wasn't certain I wanted to ride in a car with a stoned driver. But as I have made clear, this was not any stoned driver. And besides, it was only a couple blocks up to Colfax.

"No thank you," I said. "I've always pretty much been a juicer," which was partially true. I would have liked to smoke pot because it had been so long since my last toke, already the odor was hauling me back to my early twenties, but I declined because the peculiarity of this situation was dislodging me in a way that pot normally did, and I wanted to stay on an even keel until I got a fix on the nature of our burgeoning relationship.

As soon as I said no she pinched the ember dead and twiddled the ash off her fingers. She placed the roach back into her purse.

I had not ridden shotgun with a woman driver in so long that I felt uncomfortable on the bucket seat as we pulled away. I could not decide whether to face straight ahead like a good passenger or twist to my left and lean back against the door in order to facilitate our conversation. But we were already at Colfax and her right blinker was on. "There's a space," she said. It was directly across the street from the Sunset Lounge. She wheeled the car into the slot with an expertise I did not expect from a woman. I chauvinistically decided her father had been a stock-car racer.

She reached again into her purse, then looked at me and said, "There's no charge for the parking meter at this time of night is there?"

"No," I said, then I pulled the door handle and began the cumbersome process of climbing out, and as I did so I thought I saw her withdraw a small white pill from her purse and deftly slip it between her lips. Speed? Pain pill? It was very tiny, and I may have been only imagining it. This was what I told myself because I was immediately concerned about the mixing of alcohol and drugs—as well as the ride back. It occurred to me as I shut the door and adjusted my coat that I should offer to walk back to my car at the free U when this was over. That way I would not be in her car when she piled it against a tree. All this zipped through my mind. I dismissed it quickly. I have a tendency to fabricate worst-case scenarios that never come to anything. Based on nothing at all I had a sense that she knew exactly what she was doing, and that losing control of her car was not high on her agenda of things to worry about. This was probably how she normally drove. Again, I dismissed it quickly.

We walked a few paces over to the intersection and waited for the green light, then hurried across the four-lane asphalt. The hurrying part made me feel young. "Hello young lovers wherever you are." A WWII song that I heard occasionally on the radio. Eat, drink, and dive into that sack because tomorrow we bomb Heidelberg, and Calvinism be damned. Worst-case scenarios are not the only things that flit through my mind.

There was no Monday-night-football crowd to contend with, so Linda and I found a nice table flush against the large window that gave us a view of Colfax, not the most scenic of streets, but viewed through glass it might have been a diorama in a museum of natural history. The occasional panhandler staggered past. Newspapers scuttled in the gutter. Linda was seated on the opposite side of our booth. A jukebox on the far side of the room was playing a rock tune quietly. An empty bandstand was hidden in shadow. Pool balls clacked. This was not a rowdy joint. That's one of the reasons I liked it. You could converse in this bar without rupturing your vocal cords. We ordered vodka tonics, then I opened my briefcase and withdrew her story.

"I had a chance to glance at this," I lied, having reread it dozens of times during the past two weeks, "and I have to say that you are one of the best writers in my class. I've never read a story quite like this before."

"I wrote it the night before I came to class," she replied, slipping her shabby coat off and letting it fall behind her back. "I wanted to have something to show you right away. I was afraid you might not let me enroll."

This did not jibe with what she had first told me, but I let it pass. After all, she did have a vagina. I started to say that I would have let her enroll anyway. In truth, the deciding factor in these situations was always cold cash. But I let it pass, then wondered if I ought to ask where she had gone the previous Monday when she broke my heart by not showing up. But I decided that I would discuss her story first, worm my way into her heart, and then inquire as to her whereabouts. Had she gone somewhere with a boyfriend? I noted that there was no ring on her engagement finger. Things were going my way.

Down to business. Build the facade quickly. Let the ulterior motive reveal itself as time went by. This might be advice to a beginning short-story writer, but no, it was just the rule of thumb that I worked by when seducing women. You had to build the facade as quickly as possible so that they could have something to "see right through," which I did not doubt most women did. I could not imagine women being anything other than suspicious when going out with a man. I may be wrong about that, and I'm not sure whether or not to doubt myself.

"This is an intriguing story," I said.

She smiled.

"It's like a scene in a play. It has a beginning, a middle, and an end. Very good. What happens after they leave the bar is not relevant given the context. It is the story about a man picking up a woman in a bar."

She frowned. My crude radar picked up on this. "That is how I interpret it; however, as I said on the first day of class . . . oh, that's right, you were not present to hear my little introductory speech. Let me sum it up quickly. I do not have all the answers, and for the most part students teach themselves. Basically, we learn from each other. I have learned a lot of things from my students over the years. One never stops learning when it comes to writing." She was looking directly into my eyes, but I suddenly got the feeling that I was losing her. She did not want to hear my bullshit first-day speech. She wanted to talk about her story, and if she was anything like most beginning writers, I assumed she wanted to talk about herself. I could not have been more wrong about that.

The drinks arrived at this point. I took full advantage of this by canning my lecture.

"Do you want to run a tab?" the waitress said.

"No thank you," I said, reaching for my billfold. I had learned that it was a mistake to begin a seduction by running a tab. It had the quality of effrontery to indicate to my "dates" that I intended to keep pouring drinks down their throats all evening. Take it drink-by-drink. This approach afforded its own advantages in that it could make you look like a good guy while leaving open the possibility of pouring drink number two and any number thereafter. Save the tabs for the full-blown affair, not to mention the excruciating breakup. There was nothing quite as annoying as trying to break up with a woman with a waitress dropping by every five minutes demanding that I pay for the drinks immediately—i.e., keep 'em coming because I'll probably be lucky to get out of this date alive.

"So . . . why did you decide to take my class?" I said to Linda after she drained half her vodka tonic. I wondered how it would mix with the pill that I may or may not have seen her swallow in the car.

She shrugged. "I thought it would be fun to take a creative-writing class," she said. "I've taken other classes at the free university."

"What other courses have you taken?" I said, trying to recall whether I had seen her around the school after all.

"Photography," she said. "Pottery. That was fun. I liked baking the clay bowls and painting them. Last winter I took a course in macrame, but I had to quit because tying all those knots ruined my fingernails."

She showed me the back of her right hand, spreading her fingers wide. Her nails were long, red, polished. I debated asking whether or not she was a secretary/typist. Thanks to modern technology typists could perform their work without hammering the keys like John Henry. It must have been exhausting to be a typist in 1915.

Adjusting my posture in the booth with a glass of vodka gripped in my left fist like a gun, I arranged the pages of her short story in front of me. Since she was seated on the opposite side of the booth I had to twist a given page like a record on a turntable so she could examine her own words as I spoke of them, of her story, of her plot, of her handling of character, and of the strange dialogue.

"This line here," I said, tapping the paper after spinning it around, "where it says, 'I am going to sexual intercourse you.'"

She looked at it and nodded.

"I've never read a sentence like that, and I wondered why your character speaks that way."

"Is it wrong?" she said with an almost childlike expression of wonder on her face.

"No, there's nothing wrong with it at all. It's just unusual. I've never heard . . . well . . . I've never read a manuscript where someone talked like that."

"I can change it," she said. She began moving her arms and shoulders as if she was about to begin a search for a pencil to draw a quick line through the sentence.

"No, no, that's not what I'm getting at," I said. "I think you should keep it. It's very original and displays an unusual sense of humor. Am I wrong in assuming that you meant this to be funny?"

Linda raised her head and looked off toward the bar. Every stool was occupied. Smoking had not yet been outlawed in bars. Red and blue puffs rose from the patrons, passed in front of neon signs, dissipated in colorful horizontal clouds that hovered near the ceiling. I glanced at this mildly psychedelic panorama and then looked back at Linda. Elbow now on the table, her chin rested on one fist as she gazed at the scene. A flush of panic passed through me. Was she bored shitless? Had I made the mistake of asking the wrong question? I again felt that I was losing her.

"On page six here," I said in an attempt to reel her back in, "the male character says, 'The sky has nice tits.' What does he mean by that?"

"He was just joking," she said. "He was flirting. He was trying to be funny."

There was something in her tone which indicated that we were not talking about her story but about a real encounter. If this were true it would not be unusual, since all writers draw upon incidents from their own lives, but I wasn't sure if she had slipped momentarily into reality and had made the mistake of reporting something that had actually happened. If it had happened, I did not want to take the conversation in that direction. I wasn't interested in reality. I had other things on my mind.

"Excuse me," Linda said. She picked up her purse and slid out of the booth, stood up adjusting her skirt at the waist, and disappeared in the general direction of the restrooms.

I sat back in the booth and clenched my teeth. I quickly reviewed our conversation. Had I said something specific that offended her? One thing that I did understand about writers both new and used was that none of them appreciated negative criticism. The problem here was that I had not been damning her story, I had merely been wondering about the peculiarity of the dialogue. "I am going to sexual intercourse you." Who speaks like that? The fact that she had so quickly offered to change the line meant that she had interpreted my question as a hint that her prose sucked. Was she actually that touchy? You never knew how thick- or thin-skinned a writer was until you took up your position in the trenches and got down to the business of targeting a piece line-by-line. I decided I had been coming on too strong. Thank goodness her bladder had come to the rescue.

"Back off, Charley," I muttered beneath the sound of the jukebox and the kaleidoscopic smoke hovering over the heads of the barflies on their stools.

I sipped at my tonic and slowly leafed through the pages, which I had practically memorized by now. The story did read like a script. Very little narrative and lots of dialogue. It could have served as the basis for a one-act play. This put me in mind of one-act plays I had read in high school and college, the standard anthologized plays, *Trifles* by Susan Glaspell, *Sorry, Wrong Number* by Lucille Fletcher, which had been made into a film noir that I had not yet seen and looked forward to catching someday, probably on TMC. I glanced into the gloom. I expected Linda to emerge like a zombie—smoke, darkness, black dress, blonde hair, and a face bleached white by dismal lighting. I looked back at the pages, and as I peeled them I wondered if anyone was watching me. My ego made its presence known. Here is a man leafing through a manuscript in public. Is he a writer? A man of importance? An agent, a publisher? I had felt this way about reading in bars going back all the way to the saloons of college. I once brought a copy of a paperback titled "How to Write Short Stories" and the waitress noticed it, asked me if I was a writer, told me she was a journalism major, and we became friends. This was wonderful. I had accidentally learned a way to break the ice with women. Flash that how-to book around. It was less awkward than bringing a puppy into a bar, a surefire chick-magnet. I once walked a puppy around a Washington Park lake for a friend and was accosted by two girls wearing bikinis who squatted down and oohed and awwed and nuzzled the puppy. Life is a learning process.

Ten minutes later Linda still had not returned, and a familiar sinking feeling was sprouting in my gut. I finally stopped a waitress and explained that my friend had gone to the ladies' room, and I asked if she could go check to see if Linda was still in there. I handed the waitress a buck. She smiled and disappeared into the gloom. She returned a minute later and told me the ladies' room was empty.

Great. I looked at Linda's shabby coat lying on the far seat and wondered if she had abandoned it as she had apparently abandoned me. I quickly surveyed the scope of the calamity. I had pissed her off and she had walked. I would never see her again. Class was over. This was not an unprecedented experience for me. I could tell you horror stories about women I had inadvertently offended and never saw again, but I won't. They are legion. This was shaping up as simply the latest episode.

I slid out of the booth and made a slow walk around the crowded bar looking at the men and women in other booths, at other tables, at the barstools, and I did not see her. I went back to my booth and peered through the picture window at the tableau across the street. Her car was still parked by the meter.

"Excuse me," someone said, touching my lower back with a fingertip. It was like an electric shock. My gut tightened, I stood an inch taller than normal and looked around. "Sorry I was gone so long," Linda said in a loud whisper.

We both slid into the booth, opposite of course, and I picked up my drink and drained it. Despair and adrenaline were battling for dominance. Where the hell had she gone?

"I was talking with a friend over by the pool tables," she said, waving her fingertips vaguely in the direction of the pool room. I had not looked for her in there. Logic was to blame. Why would she be hanging out with hustlers? A classic blunder, deliberately avoiding the one place where the lost object was to be found. Keys, glasses, women, they pop up in unexpected places. I once found a roll of toilet paper in my freezer and had a difficult time remembering when or why I had put it there. Maybe I had been distracted by a dogfight.

Linda picked up her drink and took a sip. I kept my eyes on her face for a brief period of time to see if she might reach up and give her nose a twisted pinch, the sign of the coke user. But her hands remained at the table, touching the drink.

I realized I had done what I frequently do around beautiful women, which was to build things up to disastrous proportions in my mind. What she herself had done struck me as slightly rude, but she had apologized and was with me here and now, and her car was parked across the street and everything was fine. She had not dropped my class, and in all probability had not been offended by my approach to literary criticism. I decided to start anew, and zero in on her ego.

"I've been teaching creative writing for three years, and this is the best short story I've ever read from a new student."

I threw in the word "new" to keep my statement from being a total lie. I had read better stories, but it was nevertheless true that this was one of the most interesting stories I had ever read. I wanted to make her feel good about herself. I still had a dark vision of Linda putting on her coat, thanking me for my critique, and walking out of my life forever. But instead, she laughed.

"Really?" she said.

I nodded and tapped a page with a fingertip. "There is something slightly European about the quality of your style. Are you influenced by the French existentialists?"

She frowned, she shrugged, she reached into her purse and began digging around, pulled out a slightly crumpled pack, and withdrew a 101mm Benson & Hedges. I yanked my Bic lighter from my shirt pocket and held the flame toward her lips. "I wrote it real fast," she said. "I just wanted to have something to show you."

She sucked on the teardrop of fire and sat back. "Thanks," she said.

I decided there was no use taking the critique any further. If she was on drugs harder than pot they would have affected her by now. Half of her vodka was gone. I doubted her ability to focus on homework, to learn or be taught, to analyze the manuscript that rested between us. I decided to take the opposite tack of most creative-writing teachers and go from the specific to the general.

"Do you have aspirations to become a professional writer?"

I said. "In other words, do you want to write novels?"

"No," she said. "I'm taking this class just for fun."

That was the precise moment when I was demoted from a demigod to a man verging on middle age. If she was doing this just for fun, I would never hold any sway over her. My secret hole card in situations like this had always been the fact that I was the man, in the eyes of a given student, who held the keys to success. I had found that young beginning writers tended to idolize their teachers, and even older aspiring writers exuded an aura of anxiety, the desperation to be published, the need to divine my secrets. How do I find an agent? How do I find a publisher? How do I sell a book? How do I join that exclusive club whose membership consists of authors who actually earn a living writing novels?

Linda blew smoke and smiled. "The free university is a good place to meet people."

"You have met the only person you need to meet," I wanted to bark. "Me!"

But I did not articulate this ludicrous notion, which was born of the irrational jealousy that resided always in my heart and awakened like a sleeping tiger at the slightest provocation. She was the most beautiful woman I had ever met, and I did not want her to meet any other men ever again.

Chapter 10

I asked Linda if she wanted another vodka. She shrugged. I might as well have asked if she cared deeply about fishing. I signaled the waitress and ordered the drinks. Linda's statement about "fun" had gotten under my skin in an unexpected way. I knew from experience that a certain percentage of students came to class "for fun" and their lack of talent reflected it. I had never minded before. They paid me to talk, that was how I viewed it, and there were plenty of deadly serious students who compensated for those who would never go on to tackle a novel or even send out a short story. But my ego interpreted her lack of interest in my class as a lack of interest in me. It was plausible that she would drop out before the semester was over, I also knew this from past experience. No refunds though, which was my palliative for those who made me eat their dust.

My immediate inclination was to make a note to myself to give some thought to making this the most fun free U class she had taken since learning how to bake pottery. One way to do this was to make her the center of attention, the star student, the teacher's pet. Cull brilliant phrases from her strange stories and compare and contrast them with the works of Albert Camus, Sartre, Gide. Make the other students jealous, thus making Linda feel special. Something akin to an emotional fever blister was now sprouting inside me, in the sense that I was afraid that I might, in the end, lose her. Christ but I loved to look at her face. This was the perquisite of the intimacy of a one-on-one tutoring session—a reason to stare boldly at a woman's cheeks and lips, the fall of hair across a forehead devoid of flaws, the rise of lean shoulders punctuating her remarks. Something delightful happens to a woman's eyes when you tell her what a wonderful writer she is. I would make this the most fun class that she had ever taken in her life.

"Do you want to have some fun?" Linda said, holding up her left hand and forming the "OK" sign.

Caught off guard, I did the awkward things that men do when women offer to make their dreams come true. The hard swallow, the confused blink. Again I now wonder—do women have any *idea*!

"How so?" I said.

She moved her hand an inch toward my face and I saw that she was, in fact, holding a tiny white pill between fingertip and thumb. She dropped it straight down into her drink. "Would you like one?" she said.

Dumbfounded, I modulated my voice. "What is it?"

"Do you want one?"

I glanced at her car on the far side of Colfax, then looked her in the eye. "It depends," I said. "What is it?"

She smiled. It was coy. Playful. "I'll tell you if you drink one."

Good God, it could be LSD for all I knew. It could be a prescription drug to which I might be allergic. The risks were too great.

"I can't," I said. "I once had a drunk-driving accident, so I never mix drugs with alcohol." This was true. I'd had the accident in my twenties. But that was not the real reason I refused the pill. I was afraid of the pill itself, and if she was not going to tell me what it was until I swallowed it, all bets were off. If it was merely speed I probably would have said yes. Speed is without a doubt the most boring drug I have ever taken. It keeps me awake. It makes me clean my apartment.

I always refuse speed when offered, but in this case I would have made an exception.

She nodded, snapped her purse closed, and lifted her drink. The offer was withdrawn.

"Why are you a schoolteacher?" she said.

This was the turn the conversation took. I will not go into detail. I teach writing because I am an altruist who wishes to pass along my knowledge in order to save students the twenty years they waste figuring out how to write novels. If I had known how to structure novels in my twenties I would have been published by now. This I truly believe. I believe that all beginners waste half their lives just figuring out how it's done. I wanted to save them half their lives. That would be my contribution to the mental health of people crazy enough to think they could earn a living as storytellers.

"Have you lived in Denver all your life?" I eventually said. The seduction had begun. Get the woman talking about herself. Women—and writers—love to talk about themselves. Thus a woman writer is a double whammy. There was a small part of me that believed Linda was lying, that she in fact did wish to be a writer. There is a defensive reflex that resides in many writers who deny that they actually have any interest in getting published. I will cut to the chase. They say this to deflect the possibility of failure. If they do fail, they can always claim they never really cared whether they made it or not. It's a sad state of sour grapes. It applies to many vocations in life, but I had seen it refined to the width of a hair in my line of work. I wrote it off as a fear of being laughed at.

"No," she said.

"Where are you from originally?" I said.

She raised her left wrist and looked at her watch. It was a beautiful thing, silver banded and studded with tiny diamonds.

The Paradise That Lurks in Female Smiles

She peered out the picture window. The only thing worth seeing was her car. When she turned back to me, I saw "the look" that addicts have when the drug of choice is approaching high gear. This made me uncomfortable. Would she be able to drive?

She picked up her glass and tilted it back like a dockworker polishing off a beer. The ice rattled against her teeth. She set it down on the table with a click and smiled at me with her lips closed, which made the smile stretch like taffy from cheek to cheek, thin, pink, delicious. I have noticed that women's mouths seem larger than men's in general, which makes me wonder what genetic process was involved here. Of what use is a woman's mouth in the bag of tricks that evolution has devised to keep men interested? Wide hips, large breasts, seductive eyes, there is no mystery to the biological design, but I have seen women with jaws like jackasses, teeth elongated to an extraordinary degree, and what is this business with the massive upper lip that curves like a half-moon from the septum to the bee-stung rim of the kisser? Seemingly pointless questions are the lifeblood of horny dogs.

"I should probably get going," she said.

I glanced at my watch and saw that we had been here almost an hour. It was nearing 10 p.m. on a Monday night in Denver, and my heart was sinking fast. I wanted to ask if she would like another drink, but those pills got in my way.

"I suppose so," I said, gathering the pages of her story together and tapping them on the table, tucking them into my briefcase. I felt like a child who has just been told that the carnival is closing down. I wanted her so badly. Why did I not look like a movie star, Gable, Tab, Cruise, Rock, Redford, a celluloid hunk irresistible to women? Why did I look like a character actor whose name nobody knows but who appears in every picture that needs a sidekick, a chump, a loser, a bum, or a henpecked hubby? "Do you have another story in the hopper for next week?" I said, making the polite futile small talk that impedes the heartbreaking pace of time. I wanted her so very badly.

She began nodding as she policed up her own area, tucking the cigarettes into her purse, thrusting out her chest as she worked her arms into the coat that lay crumpled behind her. "I have lots of stories," she said. "I write all the time."

"You do?" I said, a banal response that did not reflect my innermost feelings of astonishment. Then an alarming thought intruded. "Do you write poetry?" I said, fully expecting her to say yes. My astonishment increased when she crinkled her nose and shook her head no. Every creative woman I had ever met wrote poetry.

"Poetry bores me," she said, sliding out of the booth and standing up as I hurriedly finished packing. I got out of the booth, reached for my billfold, laid down some cash with an estimated five-dollar tip, and picked up my briefcase. This woman not only attracted and fascinated me, she baffled me. I wanted to know more, why did she write all the time, why did she not write poetry? With the denial of that particular muse it seemed like the evening had only just begun. I could have interrogated her for hours.

She stumbled as we exited the bar. She giggled and grabbed hold of my arm that was not weighted down with short stories. She pulled me close and hung on like a tipsy cartoon celebrant clinging to a lamppost.

"Can you drive?" I said.

"We'll see," she replied. Everything she said was now accompanied by a giggle. The street was empty and she tugged me across it, got to the driver's door, and pulled out her keys. I expected them to drop to the asphalt but she unlocked her door, climbed in, and settled herself behind the steering wheel. Before I was halfway around the rear of the car she had the engine started. I experienced a dread that she would pull away from the curb without me. I patted the roof hard as I moved toward my door. I leaned down and knuckled the window. She put her hand on the gearshift as she looked over at me. She raced the engine. A new dread sprouted. She was going to play games with me. I cursed those pills. Silliness is an insurmountable obstacle, and there was a one-ton machine involved. I regretted the entire evening. I felt responsible. The engine died, and she leaned across the seat and yanked the door handle.

I opened it, and she fell flat-out across the seat. Again with the giggles. "I can't drive," she said.

New scenarios strafed my mind. What would we do with two cars? Taxis might be involved. I envisioned myself arriving at home two hours from now, exhausted, pissed, and making religious vows.

Linda eased herself up to a sitting position, and I slipped into the shotgun seat.

"I should leave my car here," she said. "Can you call me a taxi?"

"I'll drive you home."

"No," she said abruptly, and the silliness went out of her voice.

"Listen, Linda, why don't I drive you back down to the school. We can park your car in the back lot. That way you won't be ticketed when the meter maids go to work. I can call you a taxi from inside the school."

It wasn't until I parked her car in the towering darkness made blacker by streetlamps on the far side of the building that Linda leaned close to me and said, "Why don't I spend the night at your place? It's closer than mine."

"Okay," I said with an expertise that almost startled me. I

had been too long in the game to become one of the lost who hesitate. No schoolboy stuttering and shyness here. I heard The Word, and the word was "Go."

I helped her out of the shotgun seat and made certain all her doors were locked. This was a safe enough neighborhood to leave a car unattended. It was apartment/residential, there were tenant cars parked in spaces farther down the alleyway that gave access to the free U lot. Again she took up her tipsy stance against my arm as I led her around to the front of the building and helped her into my car, ignoring the moaning ghosts inside the university reciting the rules and regulations pertaining to the proper relationship between a teacher and a student. Linda was an adult, and while the jury was still out on me, I did have a Colorado driver's license that proved I was paddling around the shores of middle age.

When I got seated behind my own steering wheel, Linda leaned toward me and said, "You were wrong about my short story."

"How so?" I said, plunging the key into the ignition.

"The man in my story didn't pick up the woman. The woman picked up the man."

I started the car and pulled away from the curb attended by Linda's giggling and a singsong chant that sent chills up and down my spine with each refrain: "I'm going to lay my *writ*-ing teacher, I'm going to lay my *writ*-ing teacher . . ."

Chapter 11

What is the joke—don't go away angry, just go away? I felt like a punch line when it was all over, but it was no joking matter. Stupidity. Lust. Ulterior motives. They all can play a critical role in the outcome of unpredictably bad decisions. By then one would have a hard time convincing me that involvement with all women was not prima facie imbecility. Take a step back and ponder the ludicrous biological nature of sexual intercourse. What a ridiculous thing for two people to do. I do not wish to sound perverse, but I imagine this is what must pass through the minds of pubescent girls when they hear for the very first time the facts of life. Stick what where? Huh? He does *what* with *what*? You have got to be *kidding* me!

He does the thing that historically has driven men to acts of madness. That's one way of looking at it. Everything from petty jealousy to violent revenge. And let us not overlook the strange power of simple sadness. Why did he leave me? Why did she leave me? As a man who up to the point in time of which I speak had never had his heart broken, I had nothing to contrast it with. I am talking about devastating emotion. Poets write about it, novelists turn the concept into bestsellers, but until it happened I had no idea that the loss of love truly did feel like the dropping of a chandelier. My experience gave me a whole new appreciation for the word "bereft," which up until that point was merely an interesting word with a humorous connotation. Pagliacci was bereft. A cartoon man holding the stems of a wilted bouquet is bereft. I had never before been bereft, yet when it happened I could not think of a word that better described my inner turmoil. Sometimes words can be absolutely amazing.

We were in bed within ten minutes of arriving at my place. After I unlocked the front door and let her in, the first words out of my mouth were, "Are you absolutely certain you don't want me to call a taxi?"

"For what?" she said, shedding that dowdy coat and letting it land on the floor as if she owned the place, which, let's be honest, she did. She passed through the living room and into the large space that would have been the dining room if I had a large table, six chairs, and a group of close friends to invite for Sunday dinners. I had none of these things, and on purpose too. She stood in front of the liquor shelves and stared at my bottles, then turned and said, "Do you have anything to drink around here?"

This was my second inkling into the nature of her sense of humor. The first was "Mister Eight."

"I could phone the liquor store down the block and ask them to deliver something," I said. Not my best quip, but I was determined to do everything I could to keep up, stay on her wavelength, find out exactly what she had in mind. It seemed obvious, but I couldn't be sure. Maybe the drugs were talking. I was serious about the taxi. I didn't want her waking up in the morning and kicking herself for having, quote, "done it again." I had seen enough movies and read enough books to recognize a bad decision in the making. I was playing it by ear, playing it cool, and wondering if a husband or boyfriend were already calling the police and reciting license plate numbers, descriptions of her car, black dress, dowdy coat, and blonde hair. Sometimes it's hard to nail down the point of no return. It can pass in a blink like a telephone pole on a country road.

She asked for a Manhattan, but I talked her into another

vodka tonic. I didn't want her mixing liquors on top of whatever pills she had taken. I poured half a shot of vodka into her glass but made up for it by pouring myself a double.

"Would you like to sit on the couch?" I said.

"No," she said. "I want to look around."

She did it then, wandering around my living room looking at the prints hanging on the walls that I had collected over the years, unframed posters of paintings by the masters. I had never seen a real painting in my life. By that I mean I had never been to a museum where I had bathed in the presence of a Rembrandt, a Picasso, a Van Gogh. This was one minor regret of my life. You can read a book by a master, but there is no THE book by Mark Twain or Hemingway or Fitzgerald, save for a first edition of a large print run. But there is THE *Crows* by Van Gogh. There is THE *Guernica*. I stopped short of making a personal vow to go to Europe one day and visit the Louvre. I had no desire to leave the United States. But if I ever sold a book, I would make a run past the Guggenheim before dropping in at Scribner to sign my contract. I have a friend who had seen a Jackson Pollock in person and stated that he had felt a "power" emanating from the painting. I envied him. But I withheld judgment on the "power" remark. Maybe it was knowing only that this vision on the wall was rated as a "masterpiece" by people who knew about such things. Maybe words were as powerful as paintings.

She stopped at the liquor cabinet to peer at my books. As she bent to peruse the novels on the lower shelves, she reached out and touched the varnished wood with a single finger. She had her back to me. I kept my eyes on the slight expansion of her ass beneath the tightening black fabric of her dress. This is what men do. Is it a secret? Just how oblivious are women? If they are not oblivious, why are they sometimes affronted? Men are voyeurs and women are exhibitionists—

thus spake Gay Talese.

"Do you want to have some fun?" she said. It could have been her ass talking. She stood up slowly and turned toward me, raised her hand with the OK sign, and smiled.

"All right," I said in a voice softer than I intended. I sounded wary, but my mind was racing. I was inside my own apartment, there would be no more driving tonight, and if her recent actions were any indication of what she had taken, it was not LSD or anything similar that might justify my paranoia. I have always been paranoid around drugs. It comes with the territory. But when I used to do drugs on a regular basis, regular for a college kid, I always ended up taking them anyway. It was as if paranoia was the price I willingly paid for the pleasure I got from stepping onto the carnival ride, the carousel, the Ferris wheel of the mind.

Linda crossed the room and dropped the pill into my drink. I upended it and felt the white pebble flow onto my tongue and slide down my throat. Here we go.

I will not describe in concrete imagery the next hour of my life. I am always amused when I read a sex scene in a novel, as if people who choose to make money sitting on their asses know more about sex than, say, waitresses or porn stars. "He stroked her ivory thighs." A direct quote from a book whose author and title I have forgotten. Young writers tend to get clinical, biological, gynecological, as if demonstrating their defiance of Victorian morality. Pompous writing can be as embarrassing as a detailed description of the ol' in/out. I note that the post-WWII writers seemed determined to get the word "fuck" into their prose. Norman Mailer hedged it with "fug." It would be historically interesting to find out the title of the first mainstream novel to use the word "fuck" in all its banal glory. Salinger did it with *Catcher* in 1951. I suppose it would be possible to close in on a likely candidate if one had nothing better to do with his life. Henry Miller is high on the list of suspects. But it doesn't matter. All I will tell you is that after Linda and I entered my bedroom, we removed our clothes and crawled into bed, where I proceeded to stroke her ivory thighs.

I lost track of time. I estimate that it was forty-five minutes before Linda switched on the light next to my bed and began digging through her purse for a cigarette. She offered me one but I declined. Like all men good and true I was ready for sleep. The odor of the burning tobacco was not pleasant, though not because I find cigarette smoke unpleasant but because it smelled like pillow talk. I knew it was coming. The question was whether I could get away with keeping my eyes closed when I answered the questions. The most dreaded question of all, of course, would be, "What are you thinking?" I doubt if any man in the history of the world has ever said this to a woman five minutes after sexual intercourse, but my personal statistics demonstrate that it is the most common question women ask within that time period. Women love to open closets, and chests of drawers, and nose around, but the one piece of wooden furniture that they cannot pry open and rummage through is the male skull. "What are you thinking?" I have been asked this question in dozens of different tones and decibels, but it all comes down to the same hopeful imaginary answer. "I'm thinking that I want to marry you and have children, but I'm too shy to say it." This is what women want to hear. I doubt if any man in the history of the world has ever said such a thing. I'm willing to bet a week's pay on it. Call me perverse, but I enjoy listening to a woman's tone of voice, the way she tries to state her desperate question as though it is a gentle afterthought, as if it was something that just now occurred to her and was not something she has been dying to know since the moment she first set eyes on you.

"What are you thinking?" So sweet, so quiet, so thoughtful, so mildly inquisitive, as if she was a palsy-walsy helping a troubled friend to recall something. "What are you thinking?" This is what they say. This is what they whisper. These are the exact words spoken in every language on earth instead of "Tell me every goddamn thought going through your fucking mind!!!!!"

"Can you teach me how to write a novel?" Linda said instead.

I opened my eyes and looked at her as she exhaled a stream of smoke. She was staring at the far wall. What did she mean by that? Did she mean that she actually wanted to learn how to write a novel, or was she just curious to know whether I was arrogant enough to believe that I could teach a person how to do it? In other words: "What was she thinking?"

"I can teach you an approach to writing that works for me," I said in a voice that sounded as if it was coming from the bottom of a tin can. Whatever the drug consisted of that she had dropped into my drink, it was affecting my vocal cords. I cleared my throat but it didn't help. "Why do you ask?" I said. "Is that why you signed up for my class? Do you want to learn how to write novels?"

She took another drag, exhaled, and nodded, revoking her previous no.

My mind was loopy with alcohol, drugs, and orgasm, yet a fourth crutch elbowed its way into my general sense of well-being. The relationship between a private tutor and a student would be vastly different from that within a classroom situation. I felt as though Linda had asked me to marry her. In the brief time I had left before exhaustion dragged me to sleep, I foresaw a situation involving weeks of intimate conversation during which I would mentor her efforts to produce a novel according to a syllabus of my own design.

The Paradise That Lurks in Female Smiles

A visceral sense of satisfaction passed through me with the grace of a soft tropical drizzle passing through a rain forest.

"I can do that much," I said as if a priest had asked me if I could bind myself to this woman through good times and bad, in sickness and in health, till death do us part. I instinctively thought of hedging my bet by mentioning the fact that it would take a lot of hard work and an ironclad commitment, but I let it go. I let it go. I let go my inclination to fabricate the escape hatch that comes with all vague promises. This was no time for honesty. This was no time for truth. I had to treat this moment as delicately as a hunter approaching a bluebird's fanned tail with a shaker of salt. Humor her. Placate any doubt. Yes. I can teach you how to write a novel. Tomorrow I will make clear to you the demands that will be made on your time, imagination, and patience, but for now, rest assured that, yes, I can teach you how to write a novel. Whatever your dreams are, I can make them come true.

"We can start tomorrow," I said, tying the knot. She crushed out her butt in an ashtray on the night table and slid down between the sheets. This move generated a fragment of a poem that a girl named Ronnie once recited to me in high school, a bawdy girl liked by everyone, a girl who had been held back one grade, a girl who dated a college boy attending CU Denver, a girl who smoked cigarettes, chewed gum in class, and hated nuns. ". . . When you're lying face-to-face, and there's nothing in between you but a little piece of lace . . ."

That's all I could remember. I was shocked when she recited this filth. I was a Catholic boy still pretending to take it seriously, back in the days when I shyly informed God with a purity of heart that I wanted to kiss Valerie Barbinski in a chaste manner.

"Okay," Linda said just before she switched off the lamp. "Teach me tomorrow."

Chapter 12

Morning came like it always does. Back in the days when I drank like a fish, morning came as soon as I took my first sip of wine. Morning came with the crack of a snap top on a Bud. Morning came with the gentle pop of a scotch cork unplugged. I couldn't control Time back then. This was when I was still in my twenties and everything began to go wrong. I would take a drink at 8 p.m. and the next time I looked at the clock it was 4 a.m. and the carnival was over. That all changed with the drunk-driving accident. I will not go into detail. Jail. Bail. Court. As a first-time offender the judge let me off with a suspended sentence and alcohol rehab. Twenty-six weeks. The first novel I ever wrote that worked the way I wanted it to I wrote sober. I still couldn't sell it, but I was amazed at how different my writing was when I did not underline every sentence with pink Chablis. Enough on that.

Linda was not in bed when I woke up. To this day I do not know what drug she had given me but I did not have a hangover, only a mild headache that I attributed to said drug. I lay in bed like Scarlett O'Hara, enjoying the fine feeling of not experiencing nausea, dizziness, the portents of a wasted day and bad prose. I closed my eyes and listened for the sound of the shower in the bathroom, or the spring pop of toast in the kitchen, but I heard nothing. Not even the soft footsteps of a barefoot woman doing the things women do when they wake for the first time in his apartment weighing the possibilities that this might be THE guy.

It was only when I sat up and looked around at my pants and shirt strewn on the floor that I felt the first tremor of dread in my gut. Her clothes were nowhere to be seen. I got up and put on my clothes and thought of calling her name. But my throat was drug dry and anyway I did not want to start the day shouting like Brando. I peered into the bathroom as I passed by and did not smell the aftermath of a shower. As I approached the kitchen I did not smell eggs, bacon, coffee, the homey odors of a calculating woman. What I smelled was the odor of freshly mown grass. I followed it into the living room and stood stock-still and stared at the front door. It was wide open.

"Linda," I said loudly, but it was not a shout.

I went to the door and peered out at the neighborhood, feeling guilty. I had no idea what time it was. Why was I worried what the neighbors would think? That was the stuff of bad hangovers. I closed the door and went into the kitchen and looked at the clock above the stove. Ten thirty. What did this tell me? How long had she been gone? Was she in the backyard? Why would a woman depart without letting me know, and leave the living room door wide open? My first instinct was to call her apartment. I had her number. But I had learned long ago to sleep on brilliant plans. They tended to shrink to their actual size with the passage of twenty-four hours. In this particular case I would make coffee and scramble some eggs and let the brilliant idea settle to the ground like the soft bristle of a dandelion. It was too early to implement plans.

I made and ate breakfast after looking out the kitchen window to the backyard, thinking that Linda might be sunning herself on the lawn chair that belonged to any tenant who wished to use it. Afterwards I made a circuit of the house, holding a glass of OJ. I climbed the side stairwell and unlocked the door and wandered through the attic apartment. Had I told her the situation? Did she know that the attic and basement were for rent? Had there been pillow talk? I could not remember. I hate pillow talk. My inability to remember made me wary of the drug. I felt foolish. I should not have let a woman drop a white pill into a glass of alcohol, but that was only the latest in a lifelong list of things I should not have done. Once in a while I make a mental list of the things I would have done differently if I had it to do over. Maybe everybody does this. I would not have majored in English. I would not have lived in this town or that town. Things of that nature. Things that cannot be changed. Linda wasn't in the basement either.

"Will you call me?" This is another of the famous sentences that women say, along with its variation: "Why didn't you call me?" I make lists. "Are you married?" A casual hobby, a mental game. To be honest, I had expected her to ask me to call while putting her into a taxi. Then I remembered her car parked behind the free U and suddenly I felt a sense of guilt. Things had gotten complicated last night, but I had handled them with the élan of a horny dog long in the tooth. I would have even volunteered to ride in the taxi to the free U just to make certain that part of the dreadful morning-after obligations went smoothly. Had she phoned a cab company? There are four or five in Denver but statistically she probably would have called Yellow Cab. Should I phone them and ask if someone requested a taxi at my address? Would the taxi company even tell me, or was that the kind of blue-collar state secret that is impossible to throttle from the throat of a minimum wage bastard on phone duty as he floats down the river of shit jobs on his way to lesser glory?

I sat down on my easy chair and thought it over. The one thing that really bothered me was the fact that my front door had been standing open. A mistake? Maybe she was too drugged up to figure out how to lock it first and then pull it shut behind her. Paranoia set in. Had I been robbed? Had this been a setup? Was she in league with someone who stole television sets from idiots? But my TV was in front of me. I had nothing worth stealing. Why would I even think such a terrible thing about Linda? She was my student. I would see her again next Monday. Six days from now. Had I the right to call her today? Or the obligation? "I just called to make sure you got home okay." But she was an adult. I did not doubt for one moment that she had done things like this before. But that door. Had she left it standing wide open on purpose, or did the wind blow it wide because she had failed to shut it properly?

When I looked at the clock again it was 11 a.m. I had spent half an hour asking meaningless questions as if one of the meaningless answers might put everything to rest. She had left without a word, and in seven hours I had to be at my janitor job. Five work nights left, then Broncos and Sunday night off, then classroom Monday. I asked myself one more meaningless question before I let it go and started making preparations to get out of the house. "Would she show up next Monday?" I let it hang in the air. I would have preferred to nail it to the wall like a moose head so I could stop thinking it and as an alternative simply glance at it every day for the next six days. Save my mental energy for writing.

Just before I went into the bathroom to shower I wondered if she would call me. Did that qualify as a meaningless question? I pondered this as I soaped up, then let it all go down the drain. The pleasant gurgling of the floor pipes helped: the real world acting as a palliative. There goes my last meaningless question. Freud might have loved it. Hard to say. Time to towel dry and go to a coffee shop.

I promised myself I wouldn't do it, which was my way of denying that it was at the forefront of my mind. I kept telling myself that I had an obligation to try to get in touch with Linda for the sake of personal safety. I was the last person to see her alive and therefore it fell to me to make certain she actually was still alive. This was how I framed the argument. She had spent the night with me and then disappeared, and even though she was an adult she was one of my students and I had to make certain she had gotten home safely from a morally illegal tryst, meaning I had violated the sanctity of the ancient student/teacher relationship. I felt as if my guilty conscience was talking to a cop. Which would be better? Call her apartment or go there? I promised myself I would not do either. I thought about going to an afternoon movie. I will not tell you the name of the movie because according to a reviewer in a local rag the good guy died at the end, which pissed me off. I was sick and tired of movies where the good guy almost makes it. Hemingway did this in another ridiculous book that I won't mention. I am not a movie spoiler. I do not reveal whodunit so that my dearest friends do not have to suffer from the anxiety of wondering which of Agatha Christie's characters is the killer. Raymond Chandler did such a thing in *The Simple Art of Murder*, which I found unforgivable and is the reason I do not recommend that piece to my students. I had always respected Chandler until I read that essay, and I could only conclude that he was an egomaniac of the first magnitude who held a visceral hatred for Christie's success. I understand he felt a similar competitive hatred for Erle Stanley Gardner, a close friend of his. But Chandler is dead so I will not dwell on that. Attacking dead writers is as unfair as it is fun.

Well, there was nothing to be done about Linda. Pray that she had gotten home all right, and then head for the medical clinic because it was five thirty now and I had to get to work. Thank God for manual labor. Repetitive work serves two functions: the desire to forget and the desire to dwell excessively on problems. It is a beautiful thing. You can go through the motions of emptying wastebaskets like a birdbrain, or you can empty wastebaskets while focused on things that have nothing to do with bloody bandages and deadly syringes. The repetitive motion is the key. You can calculate plots, both real and imaginary, either one having to do with love or murder, or you can replay a favorite football game, i.e., John Elway spinning like a Beany-Copter on his way to the Super Bowl. John Elway firing a ninety-yard pass on the opening play of a Super Bowl. John Elway throwing a pass to himself in the final days of his supernatural glory.

But I spent my three hours thinking about Linda's body. When I left the clinic I headed for a liquor store to replenish my stock of scotch and beer, then headed straight home and checked the answering machine. No calls from Linda. I cracked the label on the Johnnie Walker and drank one-fourth of the bottle while watching movies on TV. I had trouble concentrating on the storylines but this was not unusual. A character in a film might say or do something and my mind floats away with the concept like a passenger in a hot-air balloon, and I find myself rewinding the TiVo function and trying to get reinterested in the plot, but it wasn't working. How could I possibly wait until Monday night to learn the score on Linda? The price I had paid for being a man was waiting for Linda to give me a second look. I decided to play the game by her rules and simply wait until Monday. What else could I do? She wouldn't call. "Why didn't you call me?" Dare I say that to her? Do men say that? I never had. I felt like a hypocrite. It was not an unfamiliar feeling.

Chapter 13

When I arrived at work Wednesday evening, Herb was standing outside the front door of the clinic. This was the second time he had shown up at my job site and it did not bode well. I am not a mystic and neither is anybody else, but we all seem to know when bad news is in the air. I parked at the curb and got out. I forged a smile as I approached Herb on foot, but his face remained as stony as Gutzon Borglum's masterpieces.

"You missed another wastebasket," he said with the simplicity of a Hemingway sentence rife with multiple meanings.

"NOOooo," I said, my voice falling from alto to bass.

He nodded.

I shook my head and said, "Something's going on here, Herb. I did not miss any wastebasket last night. Somebody is fuckin' with me."

"Who?" he said. "Who would do such a thing?"

"The test-tube spider kids," that's what I wanted to say, but having no proof is a time-honored loser's ploy. "What room did I miss?" I said.

"Two rooms," Herb replied. "One on the first floor and one on the second floor."

"Nope. Nope. I did not miss any wastebaskets last night, Herb."

"I called my nephew in," he replied. He was not interested in furthering this conversation.

"Show me," I said.

"I'm sorry, Charley. I already put your paycheck in the

mail. I don't have time for this."

He went inside and locked the double doors, then turned and went away without looking at me. His nephew passed through the lobby shoving the big canvas cart. I wanted to stand with my jaw hanging wide open until the crew came out one by one so I could interrogate them, but I made myself walk back to my car. I climbed in and sat for a moment staring out the front windshield. Thirty-nine years old and fired without a proper hearing. Should I wait for the spider boys to come out so I could throttle the truth out of them, or just go home and forget about it? My sense of embarrassment was ameliorated by the idea that I could now sit by my phone and wait for Linda to call. Then I wondered if she had given her correct address and phone number to the woman who had taught the pottery class.

The fact that I had a potential clue encouraged me. I started the engine and drove back home, wondering whether to call Liza tonight or wait until daylight. Liza was the pottery teacher. We had drunk together a few times at the Sunset, but I had never bedded her. Or maybe she had never bedded me. That's probably how Linda would put it. "The man in my story didn't pick up the woman. The woman picked up the man." Was this Linda's liberated method of getting laid? Sign up for free U classes, fuck the teacher, and then discard him like a condom. I thought of calling the macrame teacher and asking him if he remembered Linda. The rope had ruined her fingernails. Yeah. Or maybe his bloodied *back* ruined them.

It was dark by the time I parked in front of my place, which made it easy to see that my front door was open. The light was on in the living room. Two emotions collided. The first and best was that Linda had come back, and the second and worst was that my house had been broken into. But I would not find out the answer until after I got out unhurriedly. I left the door to my car unlocked in case I had to make a quick mobile exit. I had no argument with paranoia. I learned in the army to stay alert when entering enemy territory. It's simply called "caution." The cemeteries are filled with giant testicles. I walked up to the open door and looked in, then said loudly, "Linda!"

No answer.

I went into the living room and called again, then went back outside and made a circuit of the house, peering into the windows that did not have drawn shades. That's how I noticed that the door to the upstairs apartment was open. Was my landlord there? Had he come and opened my door for some reason? Confusion is the cornucopia of all questions. A baby is drawn from the womb and finds itself seeing things for the first time, doctors, nurses, walls, and has no words to tell itself what it is seeing, has no words to even ask questions. Cavemen must have been like that. What is lightning? What is thunder? He knows what pain is and he knows what running is, but beyond that he is no smarter than a paramecium.

"Linda!" I shouted like Marlon Brando. There were no lights on upstairs, but maybe my landlord was preparing to exit right at that moment. Maybe he had switched the attic lights off and was moving toward the open doorway at the exact second that I looked up at it. Me and coincidences are old friends. You open a dictionary to find a word and there you are on the very page where the word is defined. Kismet. It happens every two or three years. The same is true of paperback movie guides. I waited for thirty seconds, called Linda's name again, then went back to the front of the house. I entered and looked around, called Linda, made obvious noise. Like I said, I was able to make a racket inside my own place without worrying what the tenants might think since there were no other tenants. I climbed the steps and closed the door and made sure it was locked.

I decided that whoever had come into my house and turned on the light had left already. Maybe the graffiti people. I would check in the morning for spray-painted words. My place had been broken into twice during the past three years, but nothing had been taken because I own nothing worth taking. Even the TV is junk. A pawnbroker would not give it a glance. My computer was obsolete, but everybody's computer is obsolete. That might be the genius of Bill Gates. Drive it out of the showroom while the new models are being brought in the back door with a few more glitches worked out of the operating system.

I leaned into the bedroom and slapped the switch. The overhead light came on. I glanced around and started to walk out, then stopped. On the night table next to the bed was a small scattering of white pills.

"Linda!" I barked.

I closed my eyes and tried to make sense of things. She had come back, gotten in somehow, set up a supply of pills, then went out to buy something. I had plenty of liquor, so what would she buy? A DVD? There was a video store down the block from the Vogue that stayed open until midnight. Maybe she would be coming back.

I opened my eyes and decided to go with this baseless scenario until it was proven wrong. At least I knew she had come back, but why hadn't she waited around? Just my luck to not be home when a sex-crazed woman drops by for a drug-enhanced quickie. When was I ever going to get in sync with life? I decided to go into the living room and sit down and do nothing for five minutes. I read in *Anna Karenina* that whenever Russian tourists were setting out on a long journey, they had a custom of sitting down and doing nothing for five minutes. A tradition to ward off bad luck, to not be there when the bridge collapsed or the tree fell across the road crushing the passenger coach. The superstition had its appeal. Sit perfectly still and take hold of the world controls. Make Fate wait. I liked that.

I went into the living room and sat down in the silence. I did not turn on the TV or even look at the clock. I would make Fate wait. I would not start my long journey until life stopped whimpering like an impatient pup and settled down to listen for its master to give the word. I, in this scenario, played the role of "the master." The analogy of fiction, of acting, would prove to be apt. I was in control of nothing.

Linda did not show up that night. This gave me time to dwell on the fact that I had been fired by a friend who would not take time to discuss my fuck-up. During the five minutes that I was doing nothing, I was in fact planning what I would do to absolve myself. I would go to the clinic around five thirty on Thursday and wait until the spider saps showed up, and I would make an accusation. I would be able to tell by their immediate reaction whether they had stabbed me in the back. If they hadn't done it, then Joie or Katy and Ed had conspired to get me fired because goddamnit I did not miss two wastebaskets! I was furious by the time I stopped doing nothing. I got up from the chair and went to my liquor stock and poured a stiff shot, then paused while raising it to my lips. What were in those pills that Linda had left for me? I set the shot glass down and went into the bedroom and picked up one of the pills and peered closely at it. No cross engraved on it, which would have meant it was speed. This was the extent of my knowledge of pills. White crosses. I took them in college to enhance my studies. I knew nothing about the physical appearance of other uppers, or downers, reds, yellows, on and on, the code words of the pharmaceutical young. But this did look like the kind of pill that she had

116

dropped into my drink.

I fought the urge to take the pill. I wanted it, but I set it down and went back into the living room and swallowed the contents of the shot glass. At least I knew what I was getting with scotch. I would hide the pills somewhere, then take them with me to class on Monday and ask her what these were and a dozen other questions that were eating me alive. "Do you love me?" That popped into my mind as one of the many questions women ask as regularly as clockwork. What are you thinking, do you love me, yak yak yak. Women think words are real. I poured another scotch. Scotch is real.

I watched TV until midnight but my mind was not on the movies. I tried to picture Joie putting trash back into the wastebaskets. I pictured Katy and Ed conspiring against me. It was all too ludicrous. And the spider boys? Would they even have the brains to pull off such a stunt? The more I thought about it, the more I thought it would be a bad idea to go to the clinic and start firing accusations like bullets from an Uzi. Was it possible, was it conceivable, that I had in fact missed two wastebaskets? Had I been distracted by memories of my night with Linda to the extent that I had lost track of which clinic room I had entered? Those lips. Those moans. Those ivory thighs. I conceded that it was possible, which instantly shoved the theorem into the realm of the probable. This made me laugh. The scotch was the wind under my chuckles. I was admitting that I might have screwed up. Here is what I decided. I had rolled the canvas bag outside, emptied it while thinking about my tryst with Linda, then returned to the upstairs but failed to return to the room next in line to be emptied. The rooms were all alike. Easy to miss. You get so used to mindless repetition that it becomes truly mindless. This is how soldiers get ambushed in war. They pull the same patrol over and over again until they get careless, forget to lock-and-load, they light a cigarette in the dusk, they fail to watch the trail for the trigger thread of a booby trap and a Bouncing Betty pops up and blows their balls off.

I wondered if Herb would accept an apology. Maybe if I admitted that I was thinking about pussy he would forgive me and let me have my job back. He was a blue-collar guy. Blue-collar workers understood about pussy. It was hypnotic, overpowering. "I got laid Monday night, Herb, and I was still dizzy from all the poontang." Would he buy that? I bought it and I was pretending it wasn't true. Obviously it was true. This was why men historically had oppressed women. Women were like loose cannons. Put veils on them, don't teach them how to read, keep them barefoot, convince them that they are worthless and maybe—just maybe—they won't destroy us.

I capped the scotch and decided to lay off until Monday. I would let it ride. I could find a shit job anywhere, but right now I wanted to make it clear to Linda that she could not treat me this way, leave without a note, walk in and out of my house without locking the door, drop off enticing pills without telling me what they were. Was I a boy toy? You'd better shape up, Linda, if you expect me to give you an A at the end of the semester because from the moment I first set eyes on you I just *knew* you were an A student. Don't make a liar out of my dick.

Chapter 14

The pretense began on Monday night. I couldn't believe I was doing this to myself, if only because I was almost forty years old. I actually was forty years old if you counted the nine months prior to birth. I was conceived around the middle of November and was born in August, so I had been present on Earth for more than forty years, even if the first nine months didn't count on the basis of tradition. Forty years old and pretending that everything was normal. Forty years old and pretending that I was not thinking of Linda as I packed my briefcase and climbed into my car and drove across town to the free U where I parked in my space one half hour before class was scheduled to begin.

"Charley?"

The voice came from behind me. I turned and saw Linda coming toward me. The sight of her was breathtaking because I had not expected to see her, although I did not know this until I saw her. She had come to class.

She was smiling. She was wearing blue jeans, tennis shoes, and the dowdy jacket. She was coming from the direction of the parking space where she had lied about her car on the first night we met. This was the fifth week and there would be only three more sessions, then I would never see the majority of the students again. Drew would return, of course, as would some of the Harlequin women, as I thought of them, the romance writers who were determined to get a stranglehold on love.

"Hi-low Charley." Lilting. Singsong. As simple as that. It was as if not one peculiar event had taken place during the week. This was true only in the sense that in the past I had slept with other students, but none of them had walked out on me in the middle of the night leaving my front door open to the criminal element of Denver, including the jerks who spray-painted my garage walls as if they had proprietary rights to every blank space in the city.

I glanced at my watch. It was twenty-five minutes to seven. Twenty-five minutes to get so many things done, spoken of, resolved. I knew now that I did not want to teach the class that night or any other night. As she came toward me in the light of dusk, I looked at her face and thought of it approaching me as she sat on my bed astraddle, bending down, the bright alley light from my window painting her perfect flesh white, coming closer, her face growing larger until her cheeks filled the indoor sky. I felt her heat.

"Did you get home okay last Monday?" I said.

"Yes," she said as she came right up to me and stood closer than the acceptable student/teacher relationship stipulated.

"Why did you leave my front door open?" I said, and I saw the flicker of incomprehension in her eyes, the facial hesitation, her lips parting to articulate a reply that she had not yet formed.

"I didn't," she said. "I locked it before I went out."

"What time did you leave?" I said. I felt myself growing angry, and I have to say that it was the most irrational emotion I had ever felt. I was demanding explanations from someone who obviously had nothing to explain.

The heat of her face diminished as she backed away. I felt the coolness of the evening breeze between us as she spoke. "I left at nine in the morning," she replied. "I got tired of waiting for you to wake up, but I didn't want to wake you up, so I called for a taxi. I locked the door on my way out."

Nine a.m.? I had imagined her slipping at 3 a.m. with a cape twisting in a solemn wind behind her as she dashed surreptitiously down the street in the direction of foggy midtown. My God. Nine a.m. in the summer in Denver was like twelve noon everywhere else, bright, the city alive with people going to work, horns honking, busses running. I had awakened at ten thirty.

"What's the matter, Charley?" she said.

"I'm sorry," I said, and it took me a moment to figure out what I was apologizing for. This was not the first time I had found myself apologizing to a woman while in a state of confusion. What was I sorry for?

"My door was standing open when I got up at ten thirty," I said.

"How did *that* happen?" she said as if I were the guilty party. Again—conversations with women sometimes stumbled down inexplicable paths.

"Why didn't you leave me a note?" I said, and saw her eyes go wide.

"A note?" she said. "What am I? A little kid? Why would I leave you a note?"

My heart froze. What was I doing? I was making her angry, that's what I was doing. If one more stupid remark emerged from my mouth I would lose her forever. I had lost more than one woman forever, so I was not in uncharted territory. I had drawn that map of terra incognita.

At this point I became conscious of the trembling of my knees. "I thought maybe you had trouble with the door lock," I said, my voice thin and covered with bubbles. She frowned at me. "I guess I didn't understand," I said. Neither of us did. I was blowing this conversation sky-high. I had lost count of the number of times I had gotten along fine with a woman until we had sex and my world subsequently fell apart. I had to regain control if I expected this woman to continue making all of my dreams come true.

"I did something that maybe I should not have done," I said, my voice again sounding like it was coming from inside a tin can. The lie voice. It had a spotlight on it. It had The Big Ear aimed at it. A saucer dish. They use them in football games to hear the opposition. Undercover cops use them. But worst of all, women use them. Women are born with them. "I was worried about you," I said. "I wanted to talk to you all last week."

"What do you mean?" she said, her eyes growing hard, a ragged firmness shaping her lips. I had seen that same look on the faces of Meg Ryan, Sandra Bernhard, and a number of ex-girlfriends. It is the look that appears before hate becomes full-blown. "The reason I wanted to talk to you is that I wrote a letter to the editor of the *New Yorker* recommending 'Mister Eight,'" I said. "I told them I was a creative-writing teacher in Denver, and I had come across a short story that deserved to be considered for publication."

With a blink, the predatory look evaporated from her face.

"They haven't responded yet, but the *New Yorker* must get fifty thousand submissions per year," I said. "I wanted to tell you what I had done, but I couldn't get in touch with you. It was a spur-of-the-moment thing. I should have asked your permission before I dropped the letter in the mailbox."

This entire scenario was fabricated by my dick of course, the most creative organ in the human body. A penis without a billfold is like a guerrilla in the hills. All's fair, and love is truly war.

"You sent my short story to the *New Yorker*?" she said in a faint voice.

"No . . . I sent a recommendation. If the editor replies, then that means . . . you have a contact at the *New Yorker*."

My reproductive organ had done all the damage it was capable of doing and was no longer in the pilot's seat. I was winging it. I had to change the subject before I started making the poorly thought-out promises that are made by stunt pilots.

"I shouldn't have done it," I said, moving toward the safer footing of disingenuous honesty.

The angelic, trusting, childlike smile that I had seen a number of times before spread across her face. "That's all right," she said. "I'm not mad." She tilted her head at an angle as might a dog hearing a baffling sound. "I wanted to talk to you too," she said.

"About what?" I said.

She looked at her wristwatch, then raised her eyes to my face. "Can we go out for a drink after class?" she said.

Good God. Why do women say such things? Do they really think a man will say no to such an invitation? Are they on a wavelength from an alternate universe? Or are questions like that nothing more than rhetorical courtesy? Can we go out for a drink? Good God.

"Yes," I said, and for the next two hours I might as well have been tied to a ship's mast with wax clogging my ears for all the listening I did. Three stories were read aloud in class. I was cheating everybody out of their tuition. Again I let the class run the class. What did this forgiving, lovely, loving blonde want to say to me over drinks?

"'Hey Death, Wait Up!'"

Drew read aloud the title of his second story as if he was a character in the story itself. As if he was a young man with a stuffed suitcase dashing toward a departing train, a stagecoach, a sailing ship, coat tails a-flying, hand raised in desperate supplication. The class responded predictably and appropriately. It occurred to me later that I was relying more and more on Drew to keep things moving along. Maybe he was my assistant after all. Maybe the day would come when Drew would be published by a small outfit that specialized in the avant-garde. "Hey Death" was a short story about a young man who had not merely given up on life but pursued death eagerly after concluding that "everything is bullshit." End quote. End story.

He sat down to the smattering of applause that accompanied all efforts, even the romances. Half the students had attended previous classes, so there was a familiarity, a family feeling that pervaded these sessions. Drew was the precocious nephew. In the movies he would be portrayed by a kid with red hair and freckles, although he himself was tall, thin, and had black hair like a comic-book character, flat and parted as if a well-aimed bullet had skidded across his scalp.

"Why don't we forego the break, and I will let the class out half an hour early?" I said.

This did not go over well. The smokers protested. They wanted to smoke *right now*, so we went ahead with a ten-minute break. I made my way to the rear of the building hoping that Linda would follow me, but she didn't. I stood in the darkness sucking on my Winston and gazing at the place where we had parked her car on Monday night. When I got back inside I found Linda engrossed in a conversation with Drew. A surge of jealousy flared through me. Get away from her, you prick. He was sitting on top of a desk with his feet on the seat. She was standing and holding a manuscript, fanning her face as they laughed about something or other. I felt like telling him to get off the damn desk. I felt like a nun. What did I care about the damn desk? I wanted him as far away from her as possible, but she leaned toward him with every remark she made. Her breasts came dangerously close to his face. Was she teasing me? Who can tell with women? Do they have any idea what the proximity of their bodies does to men, or is that knowledge so old, so ancient, that they forget?

"All right, let's do it," I said. The more wounded my

heart, the more ridiculous my language. I once actually said "Welcome aboard" to a new employee at a small shop where I had worked. Later on, after we got to know one another, I wondered if he thought I was asinine. It was completely out of character for me. But I was young, in my twenties. I think it was one of the last vestiges of myself trying to talk like an adult. I eventually outgrew that.

A middle-aged woman named Barb read a short story titled "The Perfect Wedding." It was a perfect title. The story had no conflict whatsoever. I assumed it was a fantasy. I had never attended a perfect wedding. I once attended a wedding where a bumblebee crawled down the back of a bridesmaid. This was in the days of the wedding-in-the-park syndrome. All the other bridesmaids surrounded her, unbuttoned her top, and dug around until the bee fled. This disrupted the wedding, relieved the tension, and brought everybody closer together. I stopped going to weddings after that.

"It runs all night too, I suppose," the groom said at the end of Barb's story. This was in reference to Niagara Falls. Fortunately Barb gave credit to the anonymous nineteenth-century English tourist who supposedly made the remark. I refrained from admonishing my students not to borrow an old saw to give pep to a sagging story. Write what you know, write in your own voice, and write your own jokes. But that would amount to fighting a losing battle, and I wanted to end the class as soon as possible.

"There are three sessions left and some of you have not yet handed in a second story," I said. Boilerplate. At this point I could not have cared less if everyone dropped out of the class and demanded their money back. I wanted to get to a bar and find out why Linda wanted to talk to me.

To punish the students for not letting me end the class a half hour early I spent thirty minutes discussing novel structure. I would say that less than half of the students were actually interested in the mechanics of the novel. They either had foolish dreams of short-story careers or else did not believe that novels could be constructed: the Muse would take care of that department. Write what you feel like was their philosophy, and Ms. Muse will square the deck and make them less publishable.

"You do not have to plan a novel in detail," I told them. "Nail down the fifteen high points and fill in the rest with imagination and inspiration." It almost made me laugh to see their eyes glaze over. They did not have a clue, and I had been clueing them in since the start of the semester. Then there was Drew, and a few others like him, whose eyes searched my face as I uttered these secrets. They all wanted to make a living writing novels, they couldn't fool me. They were trying hard to understand what I meant by the fifteen high points and the "filler," as I sometimes referred to the engaging action details that kept a story going for two hundred and fifty pages. But as I say, I was at the point of not caring anymore, and anyway I was punishing them by telling them hard truths that had to be experienced to be believed, much less understood. I have never attended a class on playwriting, but I imagine that the form is far more disciplined than that of the novel due to time and location constraints, meaning the area beneath the proscenium arch. The only time I ever saw an automobile in a play was a performance of *Grease* in the 1970s and that was a miniature car on the order of a go-cart. I was dazzled by that musical. It was a Wednesday matinee, yet the actors gave a hundred and ten percent. I had to assume that once a curtain had risen, stage actors didn't care whether it was a Wednesday or a Saturday at eight performance. The play is the thing, not the goddamn calendar. I envy successful actors even more than I envy successful writers. Their brief time onstage must be like an opium dream.

"For those of you who do not want to read your stories out loud, make certain that you bring xeroxed copies for everyone next time," I said. I understood stage fright. Not everyone was like Drew. Some of the romance writers seemed ashamed of their ultimate ambitions, which irritated me. Anybody who can publish any kind of novel ought to be given the Nobel Prize for pluck.

It took an eternity for the students to file out of the classroom. Pretty soon it was just Linda and myself. I went around straightening the desks and trying not to think about the fact that I had been fired. Should I mention this to Linda? I did not want a job search to interfere with our relationship. I was a telephone pole with a penis, but what woman would marry a telephone pole that didn't have a billfold?

"So . . . do you want to walk up to the bar on Colfax?" I said as I switched off the lights.

She had been waiting silently by the door while I closed shop.

"Okay," she said in a voice that was almost a whisper.

This made me nervous. It was a breakup voice. Was she getting ready to tell me that what had happened last week would never happen again and that we would be only friends? Did she want her money back? But these questions were overshadowed by the ones that grew larger as we walked side by side toward Colfax. They had to do with explanations about her peculiar disappearance.

"Two vodka tonics," I said to the waitress after we got settled in the same booth where this had begun. "I was meaning to ask you," I said before she could take control of the conversation. "How come you never showed up for the third session of the semester?" I was backing way the hell up in time to get a running start at the present, but she flabbergasted me by saying, "I already explained that."

"When?" I said.

"You know . . . ," she said, pointing her thumb over her left shoulder as if pointing backwards in Time, which she was. "After we fucked last Monday night."

I nodded. Clueless. Then I remembered the pill she had dropped in my drink, which reminded me of the pills she had left on my nightstand.

"I forgot," I said. Sometimes the truth can disarm a lady. It's a gamble. "That pill you gave me erased my memory banks."

She laughed and nodded as if she knew all about blackouts. "I had to go to Reno," she said.

The fake smile on my face disappeared. I did remember something about Reno. "Why did you go to Reno?" I said.

"I didn't tell you that part," she said.

"Why not?"

"You and me started fucking again."

I stared at her, confused, a little frightened I will admit. I did not like blackouts.

"What's in Reno?" I said.

"Haven't you ever been to Reno?" she said.

"Yes."

"Then you know what's in Reno," she said.

Gambling casinos. That's what's in Reno. "Are you telling me that you would rather go to Reno, Nevada, than to attend one of my creative-writing classes?"

She smiled, which turned into a frown, which turned into a shuffling of her shoulders and a craning of her neck. "I was invited to go to Reno with a friend," she said, looking off toward the pool room.

I almost asked who the friend was, but that was not something you asked a lady, or a potential lay, or a near stranger. If he was anything like me, I did not want to know who her friend was. I assumed it was a he. A date. A wild weekend. If things worked out the way I prayed they would, Linda and I would someday go to Central City—the Atlantic City of Colorado. Gambling was legalized in Colorado a long time ago, and I do not have the slightest idea how that happened. The local Calvinists must have been asleep at the wheel.

Linda reached across the table and took hold of my hand. It felt so odd. This was the first time a woman had ever done such a thing to me in a bar. Her skin was warm, dry, I felt each bone of her fingers pressing the back of my hand. "I have something to ask you," she said.

I nodded.

"I'm being kicked out of my apartment," she said, "and I want to know if I can come stay with you for a few days until I find a place of my own."

I was instantly of two minds. One said yes, and the other said there were two vacant apartments in the house where I lived. I had not mentioned this, apparently, on the night of my blackout. Then a third voice intervened: Do you want this woman living in the same house permanently? A brief stay was more than acceptable, but what if she moved in upstairs or downstairs and we became an item? I understood everything about trouble in paradise. Who among us has not lived with the roommate from Hell, or the neighbor with the loud stereo, or the neighbor who complains, or the neighbor who wants to be your buddy? It was all laid out before me like the options of an exotic game board where the players made up the rules and assigned the powers of each piece and pawn before the contest began. If I told her there were vacancies in my house, would I come to regret it? Linda's head was tilted like the inquisitive, baffled dog, her eyes imploring, her lips small, pursed, smiling. She had not taken off her shabby coat, and she suddenly looked like The Little Match Girl. Kicked out of her apartment? What was that all about?

"I lost my job," I said. It came out like a fourth voice, that of a deluded stooge who believes himself capable of taking control of dropped reins.

Linda's grip relaxed, and the intense expression on her face settled like the surface of a still pond. "Your teaching job?"

"No . . . no . . . ," I said, and as I spoke I deftly twisted my wrist so that now I was holding onto her hand. "My janitorial job," I said. I waited for the stooge to speak up and clarify this irrelevant interjection, this change of subject matter. Why had I said that? But enough seconds passed for me to grasp what was going on. Panic had set in. I was backing out of a commitment that had not yet been made. I knew then that this woman scared me. Maybe all women scare me. Maybe people with definitive plans scare me.

"Yes," I said. "If you need a place to stay you can stay with me."

I avoided saying "as long as you like," but it was implied. It is always implied.

The squeeze returned, accompanied by the frown of gratitude that appears on the faces of the truly relieved. Her worst fear had not come true. She now had a place to stay. But why was she being kicked out? That was the question, the irresistible plum on top of the sweet pudding that I refused to eat. Let her volunteer this juicy tidbit. Did she play her stereo too loud? Was she broke and could not make the rent? Maybe that's why I told her I had lost my job. A subterranean connection that only Freud would understand might have lit up the single brain cell that cared about my inexplicable firing. Were Linda and I two unemployed bums clinging together for survival in a world we never made? I hoped so.

The Paradise That Lurks in Female Smiles

I could not think of anything that brought two people closer together than mutual desperation combined with alcohol and a comfy mattress.

Allow me that bit of melodramatic hyperbole. I could always find a job. And if I had this loving, lovable blonde to come home to every night, I wouldn't care if the job took eight hours five days a week. My years of teaching creative writing were at last paying off. I could quit the free-school gig and tutor this sexual sibyl in private. Did I mention that Linda had the largest breasts I had ever met in person? I have focused on her face, which I carried in my brain the way the light of a camera flashbulb remains implanted on the corneal rods, brother to the persistence of vision that relinquishes images reluctantly and makes movies viable. But her breasts! That was tactile—a manual memory that I will not describe in detail save to say that each was more than a handful.

A Gene Pitney tune started up on the jukebox, "I'm Gonna Be Strong," which begins as delicately as a floating tuft of dandelion and ends with a crescendo of sad thunder. There was a patch of bare flooring in front of the empty bandstand where a few couples were lolling about in the waltz mode. "Let's dance," Linda said in a breathy whisper, as if she wanted to close the deal symbolically: let us now press our bodies together like melted wax with a royal seal of solid gold.

As our bodies swayed on the hardwood floor I pressed the side of my head against hers and stared hard at nothing. Had I done something? If so, what had I done? Her current landlord must be a female because I could not imagine a penis with a billfold kicking this prize tenant out of her apartment. Linda would have to be a deadbeat of the first magnitude to incur the wrath of any but a blind man. Women have it made. This was what I thought as I nuzzled her ear. Women have it made. It was a good thing that men's bodies were not as sexually electric as women's, or nothing would ever get accomplished. I'm not even talking Chippendales studs here, I'm talking about bodies so irresistible that it would make women crazier than they already are, as crazy as men, as crazy as boys seeing their first pussy in a skin rag, first tits, first thighs spread like welcoming arms. Women have no idea. How could they? If they did, their rule of the Earth would be as awesome as the rule of locusts.

Part II

Chapter 15

Two suitcases, a backpack, and a valise. I was impressed. When I was in the army I traveled light too. A duffel bag, a copy of my orders, and a wallet stuffed with your tax dollars. I offered to drive to her apartment to pick her up, but she told me she would take a taxi to my place. I didn't argue. This is how bad relationships get off to a good start: argue about who is the most altruistic. She was the most beautiful woman I had ever known, but I wanted the arrangement to be that which I enjoyed with my college roommates. I had lived in a duplex with three other nuts, and we lived our separate lives agreeably. One of them was studying to be an engineer, one majored in botany, and one was a PE major, a jock. I later learned that he had become a real estate agent. Not much money in jocking. Lots of money in real estate. We had lost touch, but I assumed his wife had talked him into switching careers. The four of us guys had gotten along fine living in our own little academic worlds, and when we graduated we never saw each other again, although we talked occasionally on the phone. It was like the army in that sense. You lose touch with your buddies. Linda was now my buddy. The fact that we slept in the same bed did not alter the fundamental premise. She would stay in my apartment as long as it took to find an apartment of her own.

After she brought her luggage in, I became wracked with an odd kind of guilt. How much time would pass before she found out that I was living in a nest of vacancies? Would she understand the wisdom of not renting the attic or basement? But of course my dick was making all the decisions that day.

This was good because it left my smaller organ—the brain—to concoct strategies, explanations, excuses, plans, lies, and all the other crap a man needs to armor himself with when he hooks up with a woman. This has to be admitted. I knew my relationship with Linda would not be like my relationship with the three party animals that I roomed with in college, but my brain was free to dash around the playing field trying to figure out how to make my moves during the unforeseen future without getting steamrollered by this babe. That is how I framed the dilemma. If she decided to move into one of the vacancies, my mind would have a whole new ball game to referee, but I would take it one careful step at a time like a member of AA, or Edward Teller.

It was eleven in the morning when she walked through the front door. Five minutes after she dropped her baggage on the floor of my living room, our clothes were draped all over the bedroom. The thrill of big life changes, dreams come true, maidens rescued, knights rewarded, chastity belts flung off the parapet. Her landlord had refused to give her back the cleaning deposit. She mentioned this as she yanked off her bra. I barely understood what she was saying. Nor did I care. She was on a free ride now, which more than made up for her seventy-five-dollar rip-off. I stroked her ivory thighs and everything in between: top to bottom, left to right, front to back. She was a geometric wreck by the time I was finished with her. She was laughing all the way. And then the pills came out.

At first it seemed the chronology was backwards. My experience with drugs and sex usually began with drugs. Dr. David Reuben wasn't kidding when he said that marijuana is the only known true aphrodisiac, although that was a long time ago. But I once went a full hour on pot until the woman politely asked me to give her a break. I will stop there. I do not want to sound like an infantile dockworker. This is strictly FYI—if you happen to need the "I."

Linda went into the living room and came back wearing a see-through nightgown and carrying a pink travel case. She sat down primly on the side of the bed and placed the case between us. I got up on one elbow to watch. She raised the lid, revealing a beautiful lacquered box made of parquet rectangles. I thought it was a music box. She pulled it out and set it on her lap and lifted the lid. The first thing that struck my eye were four tampons. There was also a diaphragm. She removed these things, moved the pink case aside, and laid them on the mattress between us. She also pulled out two orange prescription bottles. One bottle was labeled "penicillin." I didn't ask what the second bottle contained. It was scientific jargon, "lopermaxatol" or something. I didn't really want to know because beside it she laid a half-squeezed tube of fungicide. I started getting nervous. There was also a pink seashell-shaped flat plastic item, which I recognized and knew to contain birth control pills. The coup de grâce was a box of condoms. I will not give the brand name, but they were top of the line. There were also a couple of small saddle-stitched pamphlets similar to the type you receive when you buy a cell phone, except these were instructions on how-to some of the sex tools. Who would ever have thought that sex would create such a lucrative spin-off market? Of course cavewomen must have caught on early, sitting around the campfire chatting about the gold mine between their legs and trying to stay one step ahead of the lusty apes who were out killing wild boar for the evening feed. I'm talking about the evolved super-primitive bimbos who invented the concept of monogamy, teaching the younger females of the tribe how to catch and hang onto that muscle-bound moron: "We don't know what the connection is exactly, but this is where pups come from, so unless you want to roam the forest trying not to be killed by the animals you want to eat, use that slit wisely." The big, strong, fast women as a genus died out and ceased to be a factor in the evolutionary loop. The men couldn't catch them. The evolutionists have it backwards. The proper truism is: "Survival of the unfittest."

Linda raised the parquet box and turned it this way and that for me to see, then began sliding rectangles with her thumbs.

"What is it?" I said.

"A Chinese puzzle box."

"Where did you get it?"

"China." She set it down and continued to slide the clever wooden locks. "Hong Kong to be exact."

"What were you doing in Hong Kong?"

"I was once a flight attendant," she said, but almost as soon as she said it I detected a note in her throat that told me she may have wished she hadn't said it.

"See?" she said.

The box had a false bottom. It slid away revealing a nest of multi-shaped wooden containers. The one that caught my eye first was a long rectangle that held a cluster of perfect hand-rolls that had been made with a steel and rubber device that I recognized. All of my college roommates had them, plus the wheat-straw papers. Again—no brand name, but all-night convenience stores stopped selling them long ago during the right-wing government crackdown on things that were none of their business. Anybody who believes pot will ever be legalized is not smart enough to grasp the power of the cigarette and liquor lobbyists, and the DEA.

The rest of Linda's magic Chinese puzzle box contained little wooden squares filled with pills of every size, shape, and color. I recognized the white crosses and pink hearts, but beyond that I was lost in the valley of the dolls. The big black pills intrigued me to no end.

There were also bottles filled with white powder, as well as orange plastic prescription bottles that had no labels at all. She apparently didn't need labels. By this time my brain had its own label: *jackpot*.

Congratulations, Charley Quinn—you are an instant winner.

"What would you like?" she said.

My eyes swept across the wooden compartments. It was like a box of Valentine sweets, all the little pills in various shapes and sizes, none of which I had seen before. A druggie friend of mine once owned a *PDR* (*Physicians' Desk Reference*), which is a medical encyclopedia. It had a red cover and was the size of a large Bible. The druggie Bible. It showed pictures of every pill ever manufactured. Photos, descriptions, side effects. I flipped through it once, but it meant nothing to me. I was a liquor man. Now I wished I had memorized it.

"Is that cocaine?" I said.

She picked up the clear glass bottle and nodded. "Do you want to do some lines?" she said.

"All right."

I would save the question and answer session for later. Or was it show-and-tell? As she went to get a mirror, I recalled a day in kindergarten when I brought a 3-D View-Master toy that showed Walt Disney characters playing around on the celluloid disk. The thing that intrigued me then, and still does, is that the 3-D of the toy was more three-dimensional than anything in real life. When I was in my twenties I thought of marketing a 3-D porn-picture gadget, but like all my great ideas it faded away due to lack of money and motivation.

Linda laid out the lines and we snorted them. When I glanced at the clock it was a little before twelve. High noon.

I no longer cared that I had been fired from my job. I did not know what I had gotten myself into here, but I was ready to empty that puzzle box and watch TV and fuck and drink for the rest of my life. Who wouldn't?

Linda lay down next to me, gave her nose a short twist, and said, "When are you going to teach me how to write a novel?"

I smiled. "Three weeks left in the class."

"I mean for real," she said. "You don't teach novels in that class."

I was impressed by her perspicacity. I did not teach anything in my class. The American education system taught nothing either. I'm still trying to figure out why sentence outlining is taught. Who cares what an ablative subjunctive adverb in the nominative case is? Send me down a foggy street in London town with a bloody knife and a gleeful laugh to the tapping of bobby nightsticks on the cobblestones and the fading screams of my latest victim. Grammar is bullshit.

"What's that?" I said, pointing at a yellow-and-black-striped pill.

She plucked it from the box and held it up. "An upper. You don't want to take it now. It'll keep you awake forever."

"I don't like speed," I said.

"This is more than speed," she said.

"Do you have LSD?"

She pointed at a small box of blue pills. "I got these in San Francisco last time I was there."

"When was that?"

Hesitation.

"Do you remember the class where I didn't show up?"

"Yes."

"I went there too."

I nodded. The cocaine was kicking in and words were suddenly tiresome. It's only a twenty-minute high anyway, unless you have a lifetime supply, but I was just barely old enough not to grill her for information—where did you get the drugs, how do you pay for them, what's this, what's that, can you get more of them? I settled back on the pillow and closed my eyes. For a moment I gave some thought to the stupid hippies who had ruined the drug trade by succeeding in making everything illegal through abuse and the tendency to get caught. Then I thought of the organized crime lords who sold it, the DEA who pretended to control it, the AMA who took over the drug trade from the pharmacists of the nineteenth century, then I gave up. There is no such thing as a free country. Maybe there is for a few years at the beginning of a new government and the end of an idealistic war, but greed and lust for pleasure always takes over. Yet who cares? I have my beautiful woman and a box of pleasure principles lying between us and my brain is floating like an apple in a tin tub at Halloween waiting to be bobbed. Life would bite me soon enough with its plastic teeth and pull me back out of the galvanized tin for the next party game.

The last thing I remember saying was, "I'm about as high as someone can get without a pilot's license." Then the phone rang.

I woke up.

The phone rang again. Oh Christ, I thought, it's probably Herb calling to tell me his nephew could not make it to the clinic and would I come in. "You can have your job back," he would say. Which is worse? Losing a job or getting a job? My plan was to lie back and do nothing until Monday night when I would be forced to rise from bed and go visit my first and only true love, teaching no-talents how to write. As I said, I didn't really "teach" anything, but I didn't know what else to call the thing I did.

"Are you going to answer the phone?" Linda said. I looked

around at the door that led to the bathroom. She was wearing blue jeans and a T-shirt and brushing her teeth.

"The answering machine will get it," I said.

But it kept ringing. I groaned and rolled out of bed, walked naked into the living room, and noted that the answering machine was switched off. When did I do that? I sighed, switched it on, and picked up the receiver.

"Helleck . . . helg . . . ," I cleared my throat. "Hello?"

"Mr. Quinn?"

"Who is this?" I require people to identify themselves immediately whenever I am forced to pick up a receiver.

"This is Drew, Mr. Quinn." He waited as if he expected me to howl with pleasure.

"Drew from my creative-writing class?"

"Yes, Mr. Quinn."

"Why are you calling me at my house?"

"I have some good news," he said.

My mind was foggy from the drug and the nap. There is no such thing as good news.

"What is it, Drew?" I said. I was too mellow to get mad. I don't let students call me at home. But Drew was no longer a student. He had been promoted. That was his good news.

"I received an acceptance slip from the *New Yorker*," he said. This woke me up. A flush of joy, of pride, of true happiness for the kid flooded through me.

"The *New Yorker*!" I said.

"Yes, sir. I'm calling everybody."

I looked around and sat down on my easy chair.

"Why—that's wonderful news, Drew," I said.

"I called my mom and dad and Cynthia and some friends from college."

I was his teacher, but I was way down on the list. I chided myself for this envy. At least you are on the list, I told myself.

The Paradise That Lurks in Female Smiles

Drew could just as easily have waited until Monday night to announce his success to the entire writing class.

"What's the name of your story?" I said.

"'Down to the Wire,'" he said. "Do you remember? You gave me an A. You said it was the best story ever handed in to your class."

Yes, I remembered. It was submitted to my class during the previous semester. The story was so well written that I assumed he had plagiarized it from some obscure literary magazine that published real stories. That had happened to me before. Try to imagine how awkward and embarrassing it is to fire a student. Four times in the past I had caught students who handed in what they thought were obscure stories. One of them was by Saki. I was certain that Drew had stolen the story from the back issue of a rag that had gone out of business. He seemed like the kind of guy who was just smart enough to cover his tracks. The fact that I was wrong did not really say much for either of us.

"I can't tell you how happy I am for you, Drew," I said.

"The reason I called, Mr. Quinn, is that I wanted to know if I could meet with you this afternoon and buy you a cup of espresso. I want to show you the acceptance slip and celebrate."

My sigh was almost ghastly, but I kept it under control. Drew apparently knew nothing about the logistics of writer envy. Why would I want to celebrate his good fortune? Writers are backstabbing, covetous, petulant cads. Think of the most famed tennis players who explode with childish tantrums on the court. You have seen them. I will not name them, but multiply that by ten and you have a pretty good idea of what one writer feels when another writer publishes a story, especially in . . .

"The *New Yorker*! Wow. First publication," I said. And

I meant the "wow." Writers are also very generous. They appreciate another's good fortune even as they writhe with pus-green jealousy. I knew this was a delicate moment in Drew's life. I remembered my own first acceptance slip. It was an opium dream. It appeared in a student magazine in college called *First Impressions*. I got drunk and read the story a hundred times in a row after it appeared on the shelves of the university bookstore. I doubt if another student even looked at it.

"Sure. I'll be glad to meet with you, Drew," I said. For all I knew this would be the only publication celebration of his life. He might never publish another story, might never publish a novel. I was not so different from Drew. I had no published novels, and my short-story success was like that of so many creative-writing teachers who could never break into the slicks. A dozen stories unread by anybody but the other contributors. University presses were made for people like me. "What do you have in mind?"

"How about one o'clock at the Oceania?" he said.

I knew the Oceania. A kind of beat coffee shop on Pennsylvania Avenue a few miles north of where I lived. "Why don't we make it two o'clock, Drew," I said. "I just woke up."

"I'm sorry—did my phone call wake you?" he said.

"Yes," I said, "but it was just a nap. I needed to get up anyway."

"What for?" he said.

I bristled at this. The conversation was veering in a personal direction and I don't allow that. "I missed lunch," I said. "I'll meet you at two."

"All right. Thanks a lot, Mr. Quinn."

He sounded like the kid he was. Young. An initiate. His mind was probably running in three directions, fame, glory, success. His career had begun. We would see.

I hung up the phone and drifted back into the bedroom. Linda was lying on the bed with her eyes closed. I lay on my stomach and nestled my face into the pillow. I felt physically good and I did not want to leave the house, drive to the Oceania, and kill an hour talking to a boy with stars in his eyes.

"Who was that?" Linda said.

I rolled my face toward her and opened one eye. "That was my fiancée," I said. "I'm getting married this afternoon and I have to rent a tuxedo."

"What!"

I pressed my face into the pillow and generated a mumbled laugh that shook the mattress.

"What do you mean getting married?" she said.

I rolled onto my side and looked up at her. "Just kidding. That was Drew."

"From our class?"

"Yes. He sold a short story and he wants me to come celebrate over a cup of espresso."

She was sitting up on the bed now and looking down at me with her pretty lips parted as if about to ask a question. Her eyes had that look too, the look that travels all over a man's face as if the woman is searching for a sign of sanity.

"Are you going?" she said.

I craned my head backwards and raised my arms. "I don't feel like it, but I do feel obligated. It's his first sale. He's no longer a virgin."

She laughed.

"How do you feel?" she said.

"Great," I said. "But lethargic. I could lie here all year."

"I know what you need," she said.

The pills came out again. She picked up one of the black

beauties and placed it into a device that she explained was a pill splitter. I had never seen one before. I had never had cause to split a pill, especially not in college. It was like a tiny guillotine in function though not in design. It closed, and when it opened the pill had been split in two by a razor's edge. She repeated this process, then handed me one-fourth of the pill. "This will keep you revved up," she said. Her voice dropped to a low growl as she spoke. She had performed this mechanical ritual with the efficiency and precision of a nurse. I trusted her. I let her pop a fourth onto my tongue. She leaned across me and picked up a glass of water that was resting on the night table.

"What is it?" I said, looking at the quartered pill.

"Speed," she replied.

Fifteen minutes later I was ready to single-handedly haul sofa beds into the attic. I had never felt so awake in my life. I was waiting for a taxi. I did not want to drive with a drug in my system, and who knew how my body might handle the speed plus residual cocaine? A cab ride would be nice. Look at the scenery. See the things in town that you don't see when you have to guide a car.

Before I left I handed Linda my extra key and reminded myself to get a new extra made, but not today. I had a key hidden in the backyard. My landlady in college had taught me to hide keys.

"I'll be back in an hour or so," I said after I saw the nose of the Yellow Cab edge up to the curb.

Linda had just finished blow-drying her hair. She smiled but said nothing. The look in her eye said she was high. What pill was it this time? Where did she get that stash? How did she replenish it? I was old enough not to ask. I say that because there was a time in my life when I was young enough to inquire about everything. It had the effect of killing the goose that laid the golden egg. People don't like questions. I eventually grew into that sort of person, i.e., "Just shut up and enjoy the blessings, kid. They are few and far between."

Chapter 16

"Third and Pennsylvania," I said after I climbed into the back seat. It would be a short trip, but I would give the driver ten dollars. I rarely took taxis anywhere, but when I did I always rounded the fare up to ten, tip included. I had friends who drove taxis. They taught me to be generous to the knights of the road.

Drew was seated at an outdoor table on the patio of the Oceania. A cup of cappuccino rested below the letter he was holding in his hand. I knew what it was: the acceptance slip. He would read and reread that thing until it had the consistency of a handkerchief washed a thousand times. It would disintegrate in his hands one day, the molecules separating like the bumbershoots of a dry dandelion.

"Hi, Mr. Quinn!" he said, standing up.

People at other tables looked around at this ebullient young writer as I climbed out of the taxi. The Oceania has big windows but they were dark in the afternoon sunlight. Through the doorway I could see a woman seated at a table working at a laptop PC. It was that sort of place. I wondered if women came here with their laptops to be picked up. I could not imagine writing anything of importance at a coffee shop. I had a hard time believing that people wrote novels at cafes in general. Hemingway in Paris, Kerouac in the Village. How could you concentrate? Nor do I buy the idea of the novelist who downs a half quart of scotch and only then can he articulate great visions on his Smith Corona, or better yet, his yellow legal pad. I had read that William Faulkner lay in bed sucking on a bottle of booze while handwriting *A Fable*, the most unreadable Faulkner I ever encountered. But it won him the Pulitzer Prize. It was an allegory about Jesus. "Time to write my Christ book," he reputedly said to someone. I love apocrypha.

"There he is," I sang out, reaching to shake Drew's hand. I knew how to perform this ritual. I had congratulated newly published writers going all the way back to college. Those were the days when the congratulatory smiles were false. Nothing had changed.

"I'm buying!" Drew said as I dragged a heavy metal chair out from under the round wooden tabletop. "What can I get you, Mr. Quinn?"

"No, no, I'm buying," I said, pulling a ten-dollar bill from my coat pocket. I wear tweed at congratulatory parties. Khaki pants. Hush Puppies. Do they still call them that? "I'll let you go inside though," and stand at the counter. I ordered an iced latte.

He was sparkling like a diamond. The *New Yorker*. There was nowhere to go but down. Although technically he might move sideways if he could make it into *Esquire*, *Playboy*, *Harper's*, and the remaining few slicks.

He hurried into the cafe and I sat down, glanced at my wristwatch, and sighed. Was I jealous? I want to say no. I was happy for Drew. The prestige was the thing, not the money.

Money never lasts but prestige is forever. Ten years from now he would be writing to agents and proudly typing the name of the *New Yorker* magazine in his list of credits.

A breeze lifted the paper that Drew had been reading and carried it off the table. I snatched it from the air, saved his acceptance slip from spinning to the ground like an autumn leaf.

"Dear Mr. Douglas, [it read] We are pleased to inform you that your short story, DOWN TO THE WIRE, has been accepted for publication by *The New Yorker* magazine."

I turned it over and looked at the back. A human trait. What do we look for on the backs of things? I picked up the envelope and examined it. Drew came out the door gently carrying two grande lattes and set them on the table, sliding one carefully in front of me.

As he sat down I held the acceptance slip out to him, making certain that he got a good hold of it before I let loose. This was a keeper. A framer. Hang it on the wall between your high school diploma and your army discharge. That's where my first acceptance slip hung until I grew embarrassed by the snide and envious remarks of my unpublished friends.

I was impressed by Linda's ability to calculate the amount of speed I would need to get through this visit. I had thought of it as an impending minor ordeal, but in fact I felt so well that the hour I spent with Drew did not have the quality of a chore. The residual cocaine, the quarter-cut of that tiny black monolith, made me feel as if I was raised above everything. It's difficult to describe drug highs and I will not bore you. But I felt fine. The sound of silverware touching glass, the sift of a breeze through tree branches that hung over the north side of the patio like weeping willows, the voices of people at other tables elevated me as if I was seated on a cushion of air. Just as I had told Linda that I could lie in bed all year, I felt as if I could sit at this outdoor patio with these round-topped wooden tables and talk of writing for all eternity. It's the kind of feeling that you hope you are buying when you make the surreptitious deal with a friend or vague connection, which I had not done since my college days. After my drunk-driving accident, which had not involved narcotics, I walked away from that murky middle-class scene. Very rarely I toked or snorted at parties. Drew's voice sounded to me as if it was coming from the bottom of a glass bowl. He himself was buzzed on success and espresso.

"I just can't believe they accepted my story," he said.

Drew had short hair, a high brow, a longish face with teeth that reminded me of equestrian faces I had seen on basketball players in high school, athletic young men whose championship grins made them look as if they could chomp a chunk out of the world apple and swallow it whole, successful young men who posed with trophies in front of stubby gym coaches wearing ill-fitting suits and white socks. His joy was immaculate. But there was something at the edge of things that bothered me. If you have ever taken drugs you may have experienced this yourself. Gremlins seem to scuttle along the parameters of your vision, troublemakers portending imminent difficulties. Almost anything can turn a good rush into a bad trip. Paranoia plays a large role. If the pot is too strong, you begin to think that the whispering people across the room are conspiring against you, that the ropes and ridicule will come out, that they will reveal the evil in their hearts at last and take you some place to do something bad to you, now that your motor skills are useless and you are completely dysfunctional.

It's all in the mind of course. *The Tibetan Book of the Dead* covers that territory. Just remember that all those monsters are merely illusions generated by your recently deceased brain. You will get through it okay. And, of course, you always do. The cannabis effect fades, the whisperers turn into Rolling Stones fans discussing the latest album, and the cold sweat breaking out on your brow indicates that the party is over. If you want to scare yourself again you will have to track down the guy who brought the Maui Wowie to the bash.

But the feeling would not go away as I sat listening to Drew gleefully congratulating himself on his good fortune. It seemed to me that the iced espresso I had drunk was making my ears ring. I had dry mouth, and I had swallowed half the contents of the waxy cup too fast.

"They accepted your story because it's good," I said, holding up my end of the conversation as required by the rules of etiquette in a publication congratulation situation. "Everybody thinks it's all nepotism and you have to be a big name to get into the slicks, but it's not true," I said. "The editors in New York are simply looking for something worthy to be printed. The rules are simple, they are not malevolent. You can imagine the thousands of poorly written short stories their first readers have to plow through."

Drew was nodding as if I was saying something that he had not heard before, but he had heard it all in all my classes. There is no conspiracy among editors to prevent the writers of Podunk from appearing in their magazines. "If you can compete with Oates, Updike, Bellow, and Cheever, it shall be acknowledged."

His grin stretched wider. The ringing in my ears increased in volume. I reached across the table and picked up his acceptance slip and looked at it again, stared at it, because the "e" in "Dear Mr. Douglas" was speaking to me.

"How much are they going to pay you?" I said, setting the piece of typing paper down.

"I have no idea," he said, the words tumbling off his tongue beneath a layer of chortles.

"Do you know when the story is going to appear?" I said.

He shook his head no, looking down at the correspondence. "This is all I know right now. I guess I'll have to write back to them and find out the details."

"Yes," I said, "this is doubtless a heads-up. I'm sure they will contact you later. You might even get a call from an editor. Did you include your phone number in your cover letter?"

"Oh, yessir Mr. Quinn, home phone, cell phone, email

address, blog, everything."

"You have a blog?" I said.

"Yeah," he said modestly. "I've never mentioned it in class."

I nodded thoughtfully and reached out, touched the acceptance slip. "Next Monday you will have to share this with all the other students. I'm sure they would want to visit your blog now that you are an official *New Yorker* writer. I have no doubt you are going to mention this to the world."

"I will, I will," he said, and as he spoke I glanced at my wristwatch. Fifty-five minutes had passed since I had sat down.

"Could you do me a favor, Drew?" I said.

"Sure!"

"Could you make me a xeroxed copy of your acceptance slip? I've never had a student whose work was accepted by one of the New York magazines, and I would like to have a copy as a souvenir."

"Sure!" he said again. "I could bring it next Monday."

"That would be great," I said. I picked up the slip and looked at it one last time. "Dear Mr. Douglas." The familiar "e" still spoke to me.

"I can't tell you how happy I am for you, Drew," I said. "I hope you won't mind me cutting this celebration a bit short, but I do have some things I need to get done today."

"Oh, that's fine, that's all right, Mr. Quinn. I'm just glad you were able to make it over here on such short notice."

"No problem," I said. "Even if I didn't have the time, I would have made the time to get over here. This is a special occasion." I reached out to shake his hand. The shadow of our grips slid back and forth on the acceptance slip lying between us. I let go his hand and stood up. "Do you know something, Drew?" I said.

"What's that, Mr. Quinn?"

"We're just a few blocks from an Albertsons store. I know they have a Xerox machine there. Do you suppose we could run over and make a copy of your slip right now and get that chore out of the way?"

It was only five blocks. He drove, as excited as if we were off to Virginia City with "the good news," whatever that might be: Colonel Custer has been promoted to General. All the prisoners in Andersonville have been turned loose. Robert E. Lee made it to Appomattox in one piece.

I let Drew run into the grocery store while I sat in the parking lot of the Albertsons where I did my weekly shopping when I wasn't at the Safeway down by DU. I gazed at the range of the Rocky Mountains in the distance. There was not a cloud in the Colorado sky, yet I felt a darkness closing in. The gremlin whisper. The paranoia. It's always dark when drugs are involved, but I tried to write it off. There was something more than drugs generating this ghostly maelstrom of the intellect. There was the glare of white paper and the funereal darkness of hammered ink.

Chapter 17

Linda didn't seem to be home when Drew dropped me off at my place. The front door was shut and locked. I walked in and looked around, called her name, but I had other things on my mind. I could feel the frown line on my brow. It tugged me from room to room where I made a listless search of my empty apartment, then I went back into the dining room and walked up to the Smith Corona resting on its pedestal in the corner beneath a spreading large-leafed plant. I was holding the xeroxed copy of the acceptance slip. I raised it and looked at the salutation one more time, then set it aside and went about inserting a sheet of blank paper in the typewriter. I typed "Dear" and pulled it from the machine, lifted it and squinted at it, then raised the acceptance slip and compared the two letters. Yes, they compared well. They were exact duplicates. The letter "e" on my typewriter rested at a molecular tilt in relation to the other letters of my typewriter, the result of years of unsticking jammed keys, the drawback to the typewriter that romantics do not mention when they pontificate on the superiority of the manual typewriter over the word processor. The letters were not a virtual match—they were an exact match.

I raised the sheet of paper that I had typed on, but I could not tell if it matched the sheet of paper upon which was written the bogus acceptance slip from the *New Yorker*. From the first moment I had laid eyes on it, I was certain that the acceptance slip was bogus. I had received a number of rejection slips from the *New Yorker* in my youth, but they were printed on form postcards with a logo. "We are sorry but . . . etc."

The fear I felt within me was as much for Drew as for myself. I knew that someone—possibly me—would have to tell him that he had not received an acceptance slip from the *New Yorker*. There was no logo. This would be a blow from which he would never recover. I wasn't about to kid myself. Forty years from now he would still be talking about it. But what was it? Why would anyone do such a thing? The logistics alone were incomprehensible. How could my typewriter have been used to fabricate a fake acceptance slip? Who knew that Drew was one of my students? Who knew this and that and so on? It would take a laundry list of potential questions to cover all the baffling possibilities, but it came down to the fact that my security had been breached, which was far more unsettling to me than the knowledge that Drew was destined to be cut off at the knees within the next few days. That would be his problem to deal with. My problem had to do with the physical reality of my house. Someone seemingly had been in here while I was gone—unless I was mistaken about the literal "e's." I would spend a lot of time in the next few hours comparing those ink digits again and again, just to make sure, but there was no doubt in my mind that I had proof analogous to that of an irrefutable fingerprint. Someone had made use of my Smith Corona to pull off a prank of ungodly cruelty.

I folded the acceptance slip copy and put it into my briefcase. When would I tell him? Did I have a moral imperative to call him right now and let him know what I knew? Or should I take the easy, simple, coward's way out and never say a word? That was extremely appealing. Let him find out on his own that the *New Yorker* had no interest in publishing "Down to the Wire." Would he simply never bring the subject up at all in class and cross his fingers, hope nobody mentioned the acceptance and ask aloud when his story was going to be published? He had already told me, which meant that he might spend the next three weeks dangling by a thread, hoping I would not mention his good/bad fortune to the class. It then occurred to me that he might drop out. His embarrassment would be so acute that he would not return to class, this semester or ever again. I have to be honest. My heart sank a few millimeters whenever I saw Drew's name on a sign-up sheet. It was the equivalent of seeing the same cashier over and over at the grocery store until you did not know what to say to the person and began going to other cashiers. But this had implications that went beyond the tiresome. Who had sent him that fraudulent acceptance slip?

I went to the front door and absentmindedly opened it. Peering out at the street for no reason was a habit that had begun before I left home as a kid. We had a glass door-front and lace curtains in those days, but peering out a front door gave me a feeling of squaring the deck. If no strangers, salesmen, or Jehovah's Witnesses were trundling up my walk, it meant I was safe for the next few minutes. A meaningless psychological defense mechanism that I never tried to control or give up—like the smoking habit.

There was no one on the street. I closed the door and wondered what had become of Linda. My feelings were now mixed. Had it been wise to let her move in "for a few days"? I must be completely honest here and admit that I had never entertained the notion that it would be for a few days. A few months of unbridled sex was how I envisioned it, but now I was not so enthusiastic. I had not forgotten my lie to her, that I had contacted someone at the *New Yorker*. In a way I felt as trapped as Drew might find himself feeling. I was committed to a foolish lie, and he was committed to a mistaken interpretation of a prank. We were both dupes in our way. As I passed from the living room to the kitchen I wondered with a kind of low-voltage horror whether

Linda was connected with this *New Yorker* business, except it made no sense whatsoever. She did not know that Drew had received an acceptance slip, did not know I had lied to her about my having a connection at that staid rag. I had to dismiss this. She was not involved.

I entered the kitchen and went to the sink, peered out the window at the backyard, and saw Linda lying on the lawn chair. She was wearing a bikini. I was startled. Why had she not answered when I called out her name? The sight of her put me in mind of Stanley Kubrick's *Lolita*. Sue Lyon relaxing in the backyard with her heart-shaped sunglasses. I was too young when that movie came out to know whether it had caused an outrage. How did Kubrick get away with it? How did Nabokov for that matter? But maybe nobody cared. Maybe we only think people care.

"Linda!"

I rapped on the glass with a knuckle. She did not move. Sleep would explain it. Sleep explained a lot of things.

I left by the kitchen door and went into the backyard. Not a cloud in the sky. The pale blue dome of Colorado. I had never seen a dark blue sky in Denver. Maybe the thin air had something to do with it. One mile above sea level. It was difficult to envision living on top of a mile's worth of dirt. A mile closer to the sun than almost everyone else in America. Did that extra mile of dirt add to or subtract from the effect of gravity? Why was I thinking about gravity? Did the sight of Linda's breasts make me think of the Rockies? Like Poe's Inspector Dupin I tried to trace my train of thought back to the moment when I had stepped into the hot sunlight. But I couldn't make the connection, other than the fact that my environment had always caused me to think of things irrelevant to the things at hand. In grade school the teachers called it "daydreaming." Pipe dream. Reverie. Fucking off. An interesting line of dialogue in a movie can make me lose track of the plot. An apple hits Isaac Newton on the head while he is woolgathering, and gravity is invented.

The lawn chair, a nylon-strapped chaise longue, had been positioned so that the sun would hit Linda's bikini-clad body full on. The darkness of her tan was accentuated by the bright sunlight. I had not taken much notice of it during our flurries of activity in bed, but I could see that she was the type of sunbather who liked to cultivate the pigment "all over." I imagined her on a tropical beach in Hawaii, Tahiti, a private beach in San Francisco, lying stretched out spread-eagled to give the sunlight equal access to the body parts that are normally hidden by clothing, modesty, shame. The only women I had ever seen with allover tans were go-go dancers and strippers.

I came up behind the lawn chair, which gave me a view of the top of her head, the top of her breasts, the entire length of her legs, which were parted slightly. She was as motionless as a mannequin. Perhaps she was in one of those heat-and-sunlight-induced deep sleeps that minimized the need for breath or heartbeat, like the suspended animation of an Indian fakir. I did not want to disturb her. The city was silent. There was no breeze. The odor of hot grass and dry weed was in the air. The soft buzz of distant bees was the only sound I heard: I could feel the residue of cocaine, of speed, of espresso stretched like a thin sheath beneath my skin. But right at that moment I would have traded all that for the innocent high of childhood, which I was certain Linda was experiencing, assuming she was not loaded with drugs. Heat, silence, sunlight, sleep, peace of mind. Children are born drugged with purity. Then I heard it. The faraway sound of chimes in the air, slide down my rain barrel—the popsicle truck was coming.

Linda stirred, lifted her head, and craned her neck. She gasped when she realized someone was standing behind her. How often do people gasp? I moved quickly around to one side so she could get a good look at me. I was irritated that her drowse had been disrupted not only by the popsicle truck but by my presence.

Linda snapped her sunglasses up with a flick of a finger and looked at me, then lay back, lowered the shades, took a deep breath, and let it out slowly. "Did you have a good time?" she said.

"Not really," I wanted to say. Instead I crossed to the rear of the house where a dusty folding chair was set up near the cellar door. A large flowerpot containing a withered tomato plant was resting on the seat. The hippie had tried to grow tomatoes when he lived here. I wondered if he had ever tried to grow marijuana. I placed the clay pot on the ground, brushed off the seat, and carried it over to the lounge chair. I set it down so that I could sit facing Linda. "Drew got an acceptance slip from the *New Yorker*," I said, and I looked closely at her face as I said this, as closely as I had ever looked at anyone's face, including the students who had plagiarized stories in my class.

"That's wonderful," Linda said. "He beat me to it."

I nodded. I found it difficult to speak. There was nothing in her tone of voice to indicate that she may have already known that Drew had received something resembling a *New Yorker* acceptance. I have always considered myself to be an amateur student of lying, in the way that Nabokov was an amateur lepidopterist. I do not know to what depths he took his studies, or how impressed an expert entomologist would have been by his knowledge of butterflies, but staggering across fields of high weeds with a net seemed to be the passion that took his mind off the grueling labor of producing art in a language

The Paradise That Lurks in Female Smiles

not native to him. Joseph Conrad and Jack Kerouac were two other artists who did not write in their native tongue. I could not imagine learning Russian well enough to write a novel, but I feel that I could detect a liar even if he was dissembling in Swahili. The eyes do the talking, the nervous hand gestures, the beaded forehead. Like music, the lie crosses all language barriers.

"I thought he was lying when he told me he got an acceptance slip from the *New Yorker*," I said.

"Why did you think that?" Linda said, raising her chin to let the sun get at her neck.

"Because it's improbable," I said. "He's not that good a writer. And anyway I've had lying students who tried to get away with handing in plagiarized stories."

A smile broke across her face. She reached up and withdrew her sunglasses. "Are you *kidding me*?"

This remark was made with such astonished innocence, with such lack of guile, that I began to wonder if I was working my way down the wrong bridle path. "I'm not kidding," I said. "One student handed in a short story by Saki. Have you ever heard of 'Filboid Studge'?"

"No."

"Well, apparently she thought nobody else had heard of it either. It's the name of a breakfast food in a short story."

"Why would anybody hand in a plagiarized story to a . . ." She hesitated as if refraining from saying two-bit creative-writing class. "To you?" she finished.

"Laziness," I said. "Or desperation. I don't know why crazy people do things, but I had to drop her from the roster."

Linda put her sunglasses back on.

She clasped her hands together and rested them on the edge of the bikini just below her belly button. I raised my chin and looked at the small hot summer sun overhead. The air of

Colorado is so thin that people sunburn more quickly than they do at sea level. Tourists find this out the hard way.

There were so many things that I wanted to say to Linda, but the pleasantness had gotten to me. Heat, sunlight, drugs, silence, Italian coffee. Everything was so perfect that I did not want to shatter the day by asking if she had typed the fake acceptance slip and mailed it to Drew. How could I do that when I had lied and told her that I had recommended her writing to a *New Yorker* editor? Had she found out that I had lied? And did she know why? Did she know that I was prepared to abandon all morality and sanity just to lie naked on top of her exquisite flesh?

"How long do you think you'll need to stay at my place?" I said.

She shrugged and withdrew her glasses, squinted at me through slitted eyelids. "I plan to start looking tomorrow," she said. "I see for-rent signs all over Capitol Hill. It won't take me long to find a place to live."

Oh God. There were two apartments twenty feet away from us that were vacant. My landlord relied on word of mouth to fill the vacancies, but I always intentionally kept my mouth shut. It worked out well for him. He owned a lot of rentals around town. He was a small-time entrepreneur. He was everything I ought to have been, a man who knew how to make money but also knew he was never going to be a millionaire. A guy who looked out for his own ass and made intelligent business decisions. He didn't teach or practice art. He let the pros make the movies in Hollywood and publish the novels in New York City and build the amusement parks in Anaheim. He was not a dreamer. He took, he did not give.

"Why?" Linda said.

"Why what?"

"Why are you asking?" she said. "Do you want me to leave?"

The Paradise That Lurks in Female Smiles

I looked at her flawless face, looked down the length of her body, and drove the last nail into my coffin by saying, "No."

If she had used my typewriter to send a prank letter to Drew, I didn't care. If she was a lying deceitful backstabbing cruel bitch, I could handle it. I was a man. She was not my enemy. I was my enemy. I could show her the door any time I wanted to say goodbye to the best sex-and-drugs deal I had ever encountered in my lifetime. Women are crazy. They think that men are weak and can be defeated. And men know it. They play women for chumps and take everything they can get. They take it to the edge, and if necessary they let them fall. Men are defeated only by themselves. They say things like "no" when they should be making intelligent decisions.

"You can stay as long as you like," I said. "I'm going to look for a new job, since I was fired from my janitorial job."

She slowly raised her sunglasses and put them on. "Why were you fired anyway?" she said.

A bee appeared in our midst. A tiny thing flying in a vortex. I had never been certain about small bees. Did they sting like bumblebees? Were they like wasps? Did they get irritated and attack? The insect didn't come close enough for me to swat it.

"My boss fired me because he said I did not empty two of the wastebaskets at the medical clinic where I worked as a janitor. He was wrong though. Someone was pulling some kind of cheapshit trick on me. I think it was these college kids who work there. I gave them shit for tormenting a spider that they had captured."

"Tormenting how?"

"Oh . . . they were spinning it around in a test tube. Just a couple of asshole kids bugging a bug, but I think they got mad at me for telling them to stop it. I think they got me fired."

Linda sat motionless, looking in my direction as I told her my tale of woe. But I could not see her eyes. The phone inside my house began ringing. At first I thought it was the popsicle truck. Bells are bells. It rang, paused, rang.

"Your telephone is ringing again," Linda said.

"The answering machine will get it," I said.

She smiled. "I could never use an answering machine," she said.

"Why not?"

"Because I always pick up. I always want to know right away who's calling."

"I never want to know," I said. "I have never once in my life received an important telephone call."

"Maybe it's a friend who needs help," she said.

"If I had any friends, I would be the last person they would call," I said. "I do not have the ability to help anybody do anything."

"Are you saying you can't help me learn to write a novel?"

"I stand corrected," I said. "I do not have the ability to help anybody do anything that might save their life in a pinch."

"Sure you do," she said. "You told me you were a soldier in the army. They must have taught you first aid."

"How did you know I was a soldier?"

"You told me last night when we were fucking each other's brains out."

Oh Christ. Another blackout. I can imagine the things I had told her. In some ways it was probably not good for me to have served in the army. I tended to talk about it in situations involving myself. That's a bad habit to get into.

"I guess I do know how to tie off a tourniquet," I said. "If some friend of mine was bleeding to death, I suppose I could drop my spatula and dash over to his pad."

"The army taught you self-defense, didn't it?"

"Sort of. But you have to practice judo every day for the rest of your life to get any good at it."

The Paradise That Lurks in Female Smiles

The phone stopped ringing. I could not hear the recorded message, mine or the caller's. I thought about going inside and checking. But it could wait. Hurrying to check messages rendered moot the whole point of letting a machine do the talking. Guns. Tape recorders. Mankind was determined to stop doing anything at all. God only knew how long that would take or how much effort it would involve.

The bee flew past my face so closely that I imagined I could feel the breeze of its wings. I jerked my head back and swatted at it. The bee circled away in its vortex pattern and faded into the landscape. It did not attack. I hate insects, ants, spiders, bees, wasps. I've had bug dreams that woke me with terror. I've also had hideous dreams about snakes. I once told this to a man in the army and he said, "Them is sex dreams, buddy." He was from Alabama. He did not elaborate.

"Did you like being in the army?" Linda said.

"Yes and no," I said. "I had a love/hate relationship with the army, like all real soldiers."

"What did you love about it?"

"Soldiering. But that was only about ten percent of the time. The rest of the time we were janitors, maids, and dishwashers. I hated that part of the army. That's why I didn't reenlist."

"Did you want to reenlist?"

I took a deep breath and sighed. "Very few men want to reenlist, but they do it for different reasons. Maybe they just want that re-up bonus to buy a car. It's a funny thing. I haven't done much with my life since I got out of the army, and I sometimes think I ought to have stayed in and been a twenty-year man, a lifer. I could have traveled the world on Uncle Sam's ticket. Could have lived in Germany, Panama, Korea, Turkey, duty stations like that. I could have gone to war occasionally. I could have had an interesting life. But I couldn't take the bullshit inspections, the bullshit officers, the bullshit everything. I wanted to soldier, but I was mostly a janitor. In the end the army wasn't very interesting. Maybe I didn't put enough effort into making it interesting. But it wasn't the life I wanted anyway. The Pentagon wastes millions training men who end up grabbing their discharges after a couple years and running."

"They taught you how to shoot guns, didn't they?"

"Yes. I liked that part. I always figured that if I wanted to be able to protect myself, I could spend the rest of my life practicing judo or I could just go out and buy a thirty-two-caliber pistol."

"That sounds like less work."

"You're right. I suppose guns were invented by lazy people. The mothers of invention."

"Were you a good shot?"

"I was a very good shot. A crack shot. But it seems like everything I learned in the army and in college turned out to be utterly useless."

I didn't want to talk about these things anymore. The uselessness of my past was tiresome and depressing.

"Do you want anything to drink?" I said.

"I'd like a beer," she said.

"I'll go get us a couple."

I arose and went into the house. Before I opened the refrigerator I went into the living room and looked at the digit blinking on the telephone. I had no job and no future, thus I had no reason to pick up the phone. But I did have students, like Drew, and for one awful moment I wondered if everyone in my class was going to call and tell me they had received acceptance slips. To what depths would this prankster sink? And I did have relatives. Always a risk to talk to relatives. But I knew I had to check the message. Linda was right. In the end, you always want to know who called.

The Paradise That Lurks in Female Smiles

The machine spoke: "Charley, this is Herb. Listen, I need to talk to you. It's important. Can you give me a call?" He recited his home phone number.

I wrote it down, but I erased the message on the machine. I had no interest in talking to a man who had fired me unreasonably. His definition of "important" would never match that of mine. I did not define anything that anybody else had to say as important.

I got as far as opening the refrigerator door. Why couldn't the bastard have mentioned the substance of his goddamned important message? I went back into the living room and picked up the telephone, dialed the number, and waited.

"Hello?"

"This is Charley. I'm returning your call, Herb."

"Oh . . . thanks for calling back, Charley. I really mean it. Listen. I have something important to tell you. The police got in touch with me earlier today. Someone broke into the clinic and stole some drugs. They found a window on the second floor jimmied open. What I'm getting at is that it looks like someone could have messed with your work after all."

"What do you mean?"

"I mean someone could have put the trash back into your wastebaskets like you said."

"Why the hell would a druggie break into the clinic and put trash back into my wastebaskets? What the hell are you talking about, Herb?"

"What I'm getting at is that you were right, Charley. I didn't think it was possible that someone could have done that. I thought you had overlooked the wastebaskets."

"I still don't get it. You think someone broke in and filled up my wastebaskets?"

"No. What I mean is I'm sorry that I fired you because I thought there was no way anyone could have done what you said, only I see now that I was wrong."

"So you think someone filled up those wastebaskets."

"What I'm saying is that I was wrong. I don't know what happened, but I was wrong to fire you. I'm just saying it was wrong of me. I want to give you your job back."

I stood slack-jawed for a bit, then said, "What's this about drugs?"

"Someone broke in and stole some drugs. The feds are all over the place because it's felony narcotics. For all anyone knows they could have broken in a week ago because nobody at the clinic noticed that the window had been jimmied open until today. The cops said it was a clean job. A dozen people could have climbed through that window all last week. That's what I'm trying to get at. Maybe someone played a trick on you and climbed in the open window and filled your wastebaskets. It's not impossible. I know you didn't lie to me, Charley. I feel like a shit for firing you."

I took a deep breath and sighed. That's about all I had. I did not want to work for him anymore.

"I don't think so, Herb," I said. "I'm already looking around for a new job."

I heard a similar sigh at his end of the line. "The thing is, Charley, the police are going to want to talk to you about the break-in. I hate to say this, but you are a suspect."

"What the fuck!"

"They told me that because the break-in was discovered after you were fired that you are a suspect."

"Jesus Christ."

"I know you're not a second-story man, Charley. Why don't you come back to work for me, Charley? It'll look good to the police."

I got it. Right off the bat. Herb was a friend after all. We both knew I wasn't a stupid fucking idiot who broke into clinics to . . .

"Are the police coming to my house?" I said.

"I don't know. They didn't tell me. But they did want to talk to you, and they did ask for your address."

"Let me get back to you, Herb," I said. "I have to get rid of all the naked dancing girls in my bedroom before the cops show up."

He laughed. We said goodbye and I hung up. Shit. The best sex-and-drugs deal of my life and the cops were closing in with guns drawn. Goddamn shit and fuck it all. As I walked through the house toward the back door, I felt like I was suspended by wires that kept my feet just barely touching the floor. It was not a good feeling. My mind was racing. Linda knew nothing about the vacant apartments in the house, I had lied to her about contacting a *New Yorker* editor, someone had sent Drew a fake acceptance slip, a criminal had broken into the clinic to steal drugs, and the police were on their way to talk to a bona fide suspect who had a Chinese puzzle box filled to the brim with tickets to Supermax. What the hell was happening in my life? As I stepped out the door I almost tripped and fell facedown on the lawn, which served only to remind me that if I took a blood test right now, I would fail in the worst way possible. For one moment I entertained the crazy idea that I ought to run back to the bathroom and empty my bladder of all that golden evidence, then drink a fast liter of water. As I walked toward the lawn chair where Linda was sunning her flawless flesh, I could feel my hands shaking. The only thing that could have made this moment more perfect was projectile vomiting.

"Linda?" I said, seating myself on the folding chair. "Could I ask a favor of you?"

She looked over at me and removed her sunglasses. "Sure."

"The police are on their way here to question me about a

break-in at the clinic where I used to—"

She was up out of the chair like a shot. She walked toward the nearest doorway quickly, but calmly, like a student during a fire drill. Walk, do not run. Maintain silence. She opened the kitchen door and disappeared inside.

I got up and followed her. By the time I entered the hallway that led to the rooms at the back of the house, she was already tugging on a pair of blue jeans over her bikini bottom. She grabbed a T-shirt and slipped it on, then worked her feet into a pair of pink tennis shoes while saying, "Is there a bar or a coffee shop in this neighborhood?"

"There's a little bookstore on the corner beyond the Vogue Theatre that sells espresso and—"

"I'll be there. When the cops leave, you come and get me."

She opened the closet door, reached to the high shelf, and grabbed the puzzle box. She walked past me out of the bedroom, through the kitchen, and into the backyard. I had never seen anyone move with such proficiency, with such expertise, particularly someone who did not know precisely what was going on. It was as if she had done this before, as if she had generic moves memorized that could be adapted to a specific time and place, like a soldier dropped behind enemy lines who immediately calculates the best spot to set up an observation post with a loaded rifle and a pair of field glasses.

The last I saw of Linda was her blinding white cloth-covered back moving down the alley in a southerly direction, toward the Vogue Theatre and The Solid Muldoon, a bookstore that sold espresso, homemade cakes, and paperback books for a buck each.

I stood in the silence of the kitchen for a moment to get my bearings. All the thoughts of guilt, lies, and strange occurrences that had been spinning through my mind faded. I walked slowly back to the living room and peeked through the curtains toward the street expecting to see patrol units and drawn guns. Who was the asshole who had broken into the clinic and ruined my life, my peace of mind, my sex-and-drugs deal that was heading south right at that moment? I suddenly felt I should have a "story" ready for the cops when they began firing questions at me. It took a moment to comprehend fully that all the drugs, all the incriminating evidence, had been removed from the premises.

This too spoke in favor of Linda's efficiency. Who was this woman? I knew absolutely nothing about her except that she wanted to be a novelist, she was wild in bed, and she knew how to go on the lam.

I stood with my thumb and forefinger pinching the curtain over the picture window, holding the fabric aside so that I had a clear view of the street. I wanted to be psychologically ready when the police pulled up. I tried to imagine the questions they would ask. Drug-related questions. What if they wanted to know if I had ever engaged in recreational drug use? "Do you mean during the last twenty-four hours?" I would say before I trembled uncontrollably, dropped to my knees, ripped up the floorboards, and hoisted into the air a hideous bleeding heart!

I was cooked and I knew it. I could still feel the cocaine residue under my skin. I would be a case study in manifest guilt. My eyes would do all the talking. Furtive eyes. Bloodshot eyes. Evasive eyes. Blinking eyes. Eyes that refused to make contact with the police as they asked if I knew anything about the break-in at the clinic.

I dropped the curtain and crossed the room, sat down on my easy chair, and closed my eyes. I contemplated the fact that I had gone from Heaven to Hell in the space of a single phone call. I felt like ripping the telephone out of the wall—but then I realized that Herb's call had saved Linda and myself from being taken by surprise by the police. She was gone and the drugs were gone. So God bless that telephone after all. A sense of inner tranquility began to sprout beneath my breastbone. I managed to give up a single whimsical chuckle before I heard a knock at the front door.

Chapter 18

They say your life passes before your eyes when you are dying. I found out that the presence of a possible drug bust can do this too. I began clearing my throat and quietly saying "hello hello hello" to myself to get the vocal cords up to speed before I opened the door. I did not want to be coughing and choking down phlegm when they began asking the "tough" questions. I reminded myself to look the detectives right in the eye when I spoke to them. My father had advised me to do the same thing when I went up before a judge on a drag-racing charge when I was seventeen. I was fined twenty dollars for that glitch. I wondered if the crime was still in my record—or my "rap sheet," as they say on cop shows. I reached for the doorknob, wondering what the derivation of the word "rap" was. This is what happens when you have a Bachelor's Degree in Irrelevancy.

"Mister Quinn?" he said.

The detective was alone. He looked like a furniture salesman. He appeared to be in his mid-fifties, the hair going white around the fringes, and he was wearing an ugly rumpled brown suit. Under his left arm was a thin briefcase. It was unzipped and I could see the paper edges of my future peeking out from the fake leather darkness.

"Yes?" I said, setting into motion the process of feigning surprise, bafflement, innocence.

"My name is Detective Morris, I'm with the burglary division of the Denver Police Department."

He held up a badge, just like in the movies. It was shiny and seemed rather well-worn.

"Yes, sir, what can I do for you?" I said, but already I was convinced he could see right through every word I spoke. His head was cocked forward, slightly bowed, so that he seemed to be looking up at me even though we were the same height. His voice was soft-spoken, weary. I wondered for a moment if I was in the presence of a fellow actor. The front of his coat was unbuttoned, but when I gave it a quick scan I could not see a service revolver or even a bulge indicating that he was armed with the authorization to fill me with lead.

"I wonder if I could come in and speak with you about a case I'm investigating?" he said. The barest hint of a smile graced his lips. A good-cop smile as opposed to a bad-cop smile. I wondered if he liked his job. He looked like a man waiting for a pension and trout fishing at Red Feather Lakes in the high country.

"Certainly, sir, come on inside," I said. I held the door open and let him pass. He walked to the middle of the living room before turning around and looking at me. I assumed he was taking mental photographs of everything in sight, including my ridiculous bookshelf full of liquor bottles.

He gave up a larger smile before opening his briefcase and pulling out the paperwork. The smile faded and he looked me in the eye.

"I'm investigating a break-in at the Bayaud Clinic in west Denver. I understand that you were employed there until recently. Is that correct?"

Yep. The games had begun. He would be asking me questions that he already knew the answers to. Feign innocence, I told myself, feign innocence. Do not let him know that you are onto him, that you have seen every cop show produced since 1960. Look stupid. You don't have far to go anyway.

"Yes, sir, I was employed as a janitor at the clinic."

The Paradise That Lurks in Female Smiles

He nodded and looked down at the paperwork. He performed this maneuver many times throughout the inquisition. He looked up at me.

"What were the circumstances that led you to leaving your job?" he said as if he was clueless, as if he was me. I had the urge to start enjoying this duel, except my system contained a residue of drugs that in the worst of all possible worlds might be actual evidence in this investigation. Would this series of events lead me to throttling the neck of Linda Hathaway, either metaphorically or otherwise? Stay cool. Feign innocence. Sit down before you fall down.

"I was fired for incompetence," I said. I did not dislike this man, but I decided not to give any information that he did not specifically ask for. Keep the answers simple. I imagined him saying "It was like pulling teeth" to his detective friends down at DPD. I had to assume I was walking a tightrope here. What if Linda accidentally came back in the middle of this visit and blew everything sky-high?

"How so?" he said.

"My job was to empty all the plastic trash bins in the clinic offices. I was accused of failing to empty some of the bins on a couple of occasions, but that was not true. Somebody refilled them after I left work."

His eyebrows went up. A bit of shine, a sparkle of life, came into his eyes, which were pale blue and slightly watery. He looked like a drinking cop to me.

"Why would somebody do that?" he said.

"I have no idea," I replied. "I told my boss that I never failed to empty a bin, but he didn't believe me. He asked the same question you just did. Then he fired me. I have to assume that he thought I was lying to save my job."

He nodded and kept his eyes fixed on mine.

"Could it have been one of your fellow employees?" he said.

I had to think fast. I had been certain it was the college kids, but that was when I was alone and angry. Now that I was in the presence of the Law, I was not so eager to make an accusation. I didn't want to ruin their young lives even if they were assholes. But I decided that if I did find out that they were responsible for my firing, I would report them to the SPCA. I wondered if bunny-huggers cared as much about spiders as they cared about fur-bearing sweetums.

I shrugged my shoulders, turned my splayed hands palm-upward, and said, "Who knows? I don't have the slightest idea who could have done that or why."

"Did you get along well with your fellow employees?"

"Yes."

"Do you happen to know if any of them abused drugs?"

"No."

He nodded and looked down at his paperwork.

I spoke: "Would you like to sit down?" I said, indicating the couch. He shook his head no. "Do you mind if I sat down?" I said. "I have a slight hangover."

"Go right ahead," he said, and as I lowered myself to the chair it occurred to me that I might have made a tactical error. As soon as he had brought up the subject of drugs, I had asked if I could sit down. Did this make me look guilty? Of course it did. My every word and gesture made me look guilty. I would be posting bail before sunset and I knew it.

Now that I was seated, he was looking down at me, which felt both right and safe. At least I did not have to worry about my knees buckling, and I also felt that it would please him to be in a position of dominance, like a Poe character in Toledo and I do not mean Ohio. When I was a kid I thought Edgar Allan Poe was British. After I learned he was American, it made him seem like a fake. Only the British should write about moody atmospheric mansions.

"When was the clinic broken into?" I said.

"We're not certain. Maybe some time within the past week. The medical personnel didn't notice the open window. It's on the second floor in the northeast corner of the building."

He stopped, examined my eyes. Then he opened his briefcase and pulled out a sheet of photo paper. He handed it to me, a color photo of the window. A tall rectangle with a handle to wind it open and closed. There was a neat slice from top to bottom in the fine wires of the screen mesh on the outside of the window. You wouldn't know it had been breached if you didn't know it already.

"It was a professional job," the cop said. "Whoever did this knew what he was doing."

"I spoke to my former employer," I said, just to cover my ass. Feigning innocence can be a chore if you try to feign everything. I wanted the cop to know that I knew some of the details. "He told me they stole some drugs."

He nodded, then inhaled and looked around my apartment. "We don't know when the window was opened, but we do know that the drugs were taken last night. They keep a tight inventory on narcotics at those clinics."

I nodded and tried to fabricate a quick timeline because I was wondering if this was where Linda had gotten her drugs. I had already convicted her. I would make a good cop in a totalitarian country. But I couldn't do the timeline. I didn't know what kind of drugs were stolen, and I wasn't about to get too inquisitive.

"What do you do for a living now, Mr. Quinn?" he said.

The question that women ask. But they don't really want to know what you do, they want to know how much money you make.

I feigned a sigh—or did I?

"I teach creative writing at a free university on Capitol Hill."

He raised his head, his jaw parted, and something positive came into his expression. I could not help but feel that he suddenly realized I was a dead end as a suspect.

"Is that right?" he said. "So you were holding down two jobs, janitor and teacher."

"That's correct."

He nodded again, kept on nodding, then said, "My daughter attends the free university."

I smiled. "What courses does she take?"

"I don't know. Hippie stuff. She made some pottery. She took a screenwriting course."

He was doing a good-cop bit now. Get me to let my guard down, then ask me where the puzzle box was hidden. I forced myself not to ask if his daughter had ever taken creative writing. There are two other people at the free U who teach what I do, which is nothing. One of them published a book three years earlier that didn't go anywhere. It was a credential. Something to brag about in hopeless letters to agents.

"What do you do at night?" he said.

"Pardon me?"

"Extracurricular activities."

I shrugged. "Watch TV. Go to movies."

"Are you married?"

"No."

"Do you date women?"

I paused, which made me angry at myself. That sentence could be interpreted in any number of ways. Do I date at all? Do I date men? This is the problem of having an English degree. It makes you look guilty.

"I date women," I said. "I don't have a steady girlfriend right now."

"Do you live alone?" he said.

"Yes," I said, and right at that moment my eyes fell on the

pretty pink suitcase and travel case that Linda had set in one corner of the room before our wild sex session. He kept his eyes on me.

"I don't have a roommate," I said. I could feel my throat constricting. Linda wasn't my roommate, yet there stood the evidence of a woman's existence. "I have a friend who is staying with me for a few days."

"Female friend?" he said.

I nodded.

"Is she here right now?"

"No, she's . . . out."

Damn these hesitations, these tells, these giveaways. I was obviously trying to cover up something. Cops must enjoy these off-the-record interrogation sessions. Everybody is hiding something. Their job is to figure out what is worth hiding.

"What's her name?" he said.

"Linda Hathaway," I said, feeling my world beginning to collapse. But it wasn't really my world. It was the fake world I had been living inside ever since the first night I set eyes on Linda.

"Does she know about the break-in?" the detective said.

My heart stopped. Froze. Started up again. "How would she know about that?" I said, my voice withering with wonder.

"You told me you had talked to your employer," he said. "I just wondered if you had mentioned the break-in to her."

Had I? I couldn't remember exactly what I had said to Linda before she grabbed the box full of drugs and hightailed it toward Antarctica.

"I may have mentioned it to her. My ex-boss called earlier today. I may have mentioned it to Linda before she went out."

"Where did she go?"

"She's looking for an apartment," I said disingenuously.

He nodded and looked up at the ceiling. "Do you rent this entire house?" he said.

Aw, crap. "No," I said, ripping up the floorboards. "There's a basement and an attic apartment."

"Vacant?"

"Yes," I said in a small voice.

I was waiting for the other shoe to drop. But he didn't ask me if Linda was going to move into this house. Suddenly he seemed no longer interested.

He took the photograph from my hand and tucked it into his case, zipped it partially closed. He looked at the ceiling again, then looked at the floor. "My daughter is looking for a place to live," he said. He lowered his chin, looked at me, smiled. "You seem like a nice guy," he said. "Mind if I tell her about the vacancies here?"

I got out my hammer and chisel and carved a smile onto the despondent rock of my phiz. "I don't mind," I said. "My landlord mostly finds tenants through word of mouth."

He nodded and began making the subtle moves preparatory to leaving. Tucking the briefcase, clicking a pen, touching his tie.

"Well, thank you for your time, Mr. Quinn. You probably won't be seeing me again, although if I have any more questions I'll get in touch." He asked for my home phone number. When he asked for my cell phone number, I lied and said I didn't have one. I felt like an unreconstructed redneck. The gumment was prying too deeply into the things that were none of its business. But I knew that if Sherlock here ever caught me talking on a cell phone, I could always tell him I had bought it recently. Instant alibi—a mere twenty bucks at Kmart.

He adjusted his briefcase under his left arm, then did a slow pirouette and looked around the interior of my house, leaned a bit to see down the hallway to the kitchen, then looked at me and smiled. "Again, thank you for your time, Mr. Quinn." He headed for the door.

I stood up and followed. The back of his brown suit needed pressing, coat and pants both. He needed a haircut. He smelled of Old Spice. I said goodbye and told him I hoped I had been of some help, but as he turned and looked back at me he did not say anything. Just smiled. Cards close to the vest. God only knew what I had told him in actuality. I felt as if I had been a sample of vermin in a petri dish being examined by an objective scientist searching for answers. What did he see in me that I—a self-analytical unpublished semi-autobiographical novelist—had never seen before in my lifetime? Big lies, little lies, big guilts, little guilts. I had to assume that experienced detectives could separate chaff from wheat. I had to assume that he did not believe that I had broken into the clinic, but that I was lying about various small things, which I was. I had to assume that he had discerned the unimportant truths.

"Detective Morris," I said before he went outside. "Can I ask you something?"

"Certainly," he said, turning to face me.

"Am I a suspect in this break-in?"

He smiled. "We are talking to everybody connected with the clinic. You apparently worked at the clinic at the time of the break-in, so I have to ask you these questions. But no, you are not a suspect. We're just talking to everybody we can find who was associated with the clinic."

That damned Herb. He had filled my mind with Kojak crap where everybody is a suspect. This cop was obviously a member of the real world. He was just a guy doing an ordinary job.

"I didn't break into the clinic," I said. It came out with a nervous chortle. I wanted to say I don't do hard drugs, but I wasn't about to start ripping up floorboards at this point in my exoneration. Maybe Poe had more to do with this than Herb.

For the first time a smile broke across his face that I would label as "truly friendly."

"You don't have anything to worry about, Mr. Quinn. If you were going to commit a felony and burglarize the narcotics drawer of the clinic where you worked, you would not have broken into a second-story window. You probably would have arranged to leave the window open for easy access."

I was both shocked and embarrassed by this revelation. He was not only stating the obvious, he may have been crossing the line and telling me something that detectives in the ordinary course of their investigations do not reveal to civilians. My guess is that he was trying to calm down a nitwit by bending the rules.

Then he did something that floored me. He winked, and turned toward the door. The interview with the nitwit was over. Detectives must encounter a lot of nitwits in their line of work.

I almost said "Have a nice day," but somehow managed not to. My heart was pounding as I closed the door. Was I sweating? Only then did I sense the cessation of an adrenaline pump. I went back to my chair and sat down and took deep breaths. My God. The cops. Worse than parents. Then I started thinking about Linda. Yes. I would put on a light coat and dash out of the house, run to the bookstore while the detective surreptitiously follows me in his car, nabs the two of us whispering frantically among the shelves of The Solid Muldoon, and finally asks Linda to open that peculiar-looking box that she has been embracing in her arms like a favorite housecat. "Do you have prescriptions for the *legal* drugs?" he says as he pulls out the cuffs.

I thought of calling The Solid Muldoon. I knew the owner fairly well. Booksellers are a part of the network that writers like myself cultivate. The owner is named Troxel. Elgie Troxel. He's a poet. I know a lot of poets. Too many poets.

Chapter 19

Instead of walking surreptitiously down the alley, which was my first instinct and inclination, I decided to act like an innocent man and leave my house by the front door. I knew I would be paranoid for the rest of my life, or until this nonsense came to a close. Whether he was watching from a discreet distance, I assumed the detective was tailing me, was curious as to what I would do after being grilled. I put on a light coat and left by the front, locking the door like a normal person and heading down to the sidewalk without glancing around the neighborhood like the paranoiac that I was. They say that this is a giveaway for shoplifters, glancing around the department store to make sure no clerks are watching before you steal a sweater. It all comes out on the security tapes anyway. Thieves are crazy.

I walked down the block past the Vogue Theatre and slowed to look at the one-sheets posted in the windows, but after I passed by I could not remember what was showing. *Crime and Punishment*? My mind was distracted by the thought of drug busts, prison, remorse, regret, self-flagellation. I again began to think that it had been a mistake to let Linda into my house, much less my life.

When I got to The Solid Muldoon I stopped to look at the used books displayed in the window, but I was really peering through the glass to see where Linda was lurking. I couldn't see her. I went on down to the front door, which is set at an angle at the corner of the building. The Muldoon used to be a grocery store. That part of town was filled with great old storefronts. Denver is dotted with these charming little neighborhood business districts that were destroyed by the malls of the suburbs.

I walked in and nodded at Elgie T., who was seated behind the desk reading a paperback. He nodded but didn't say anything. It was one of those shops where the clerks leave you alone to browse and do not frantically ask if they can help you find something. People don't go to used bookstores to find something. The art of browsing is a corpse in this country.

I walked up and down the narrow high-stacked aisles, of which there were only three, and did not see Linda anywhere. It was obvious that she was not in the store. Had Detective Morris already busted her? I thought of asking Elgie if he had seen her but decided to keep as many people out of this mess as possible. I imagined the detective stepping in here later and asking Elgie to reveal the substance of our conversation. "He was looking for a woman named Linda," Elgie says in his bookish innocence, thus cracking the case wide open.

I picked up a copy of *The Time Machine* by H. G. Wells that I did not need and paid Elgie a buck just to make it appear to the man watching me through a telescope two blocks away that I had come here looking for something specific. I would put it on my shelves along with all the other books I will never read, like *The Magic Mountain* by Thomas Mann. I got through almost ten pages of that book before I fell over dead.

I left the bookstore thumbing through my Wells like an avid reader eager to get home and dive into the treasure he had found. I then stuffed it into my back pocket and looked up the block wondering where the hell Linda was. Had she gotten lost? I hoped so. Maybe she would not come back. Maybe she would disappear forever. Best sex-and-drugs deal I ever got involved in and a cop shows up like a nun wanting to know if I was entertaining the near occasion of sin.

I expected the front door to be wide open when I got home,

but it wasn't. I unlocked the door, stepped inside, and walked through the house saying nothing. For all I knew Sherlock had placed a bug in a potted plant and someone in a van would hear me singing, "Linda? Where are you?" No, it was not a good idea to allow paranoia into my house. Maybe I should tell her about the vacancies just to get her out of my place so that when the SWAT team arrived I could direct them upstairs. As I inspected each empty room it occurred to me that it was simply the combo of espresso, cocaine, and speed that was making me paranoid. Maybe it would fade. Maybe I should not be so quick to evict Linda. If things worked out the way I had imagined, we would be in bed soon. Endless sex, lots of drugs. I could feel the Iron Claw reaching out to clutch me. I'm talking about the hand that drags you to a bar three days after you have sworn off drinking. In the case of Linda it was the Iron Claw of Sex.

She was not in my place. I took off my coat and tossed it over the back of a chair and departed by the front door. I went around to the side of the house and climbed the wooden staircase to make my daily inspection for mice, vermin, and dust. Of course it was at the back of my mind that she had somehow slipped up to the attic room, just as I assumed she had slipped down to the basement room in her efforts to conceal both herself and her drugs from the Law.

I wandered around the upstairs apartment, then made my way down to the basement and searched from one end to the other. Linda was not in the house. I couldn't decide whether this was good or bad. I kept thinking about her naked body. Even that thought did not sway me one way or another. Part of me wanted her to be there and part of me wanted her to be gone from my life. Good. I was now schizophrenic. But this is what women do to men. They begin their man search at the age of eighteen, target their victim, and spend the rest of their lives tearing us in two and rifling our billfolds. And we love every minute of it. Who is more insane, the chicks or the dicks?

I went back up to the ground floor. The basement apartment was accessed by a door near the cellar door. I stood in the backyard looking at the lawn chair, at the alley where I had last seen Linda, and I wondered if she had been scooped up in a net like a butterfly. Did the police engineer daring daylight drug busts? Where did Linda get her drugs? Did she have anything to do with the break-in at the clinic? There were parts missing from this puzzle, assuming it was a puzzle. I decided that I had to sit down in the quiet of my living room and sort things out, analyze the coincidences, and discern whether or not there were connections between the dots or if I was just rattled because a cop had interviewed me. The thought of going to jail for any length of time at all can really rattle me. It's like going to the ER at the hospital and being told you cannot go home. I try to avoid emergency rooms. Let the pain go away as it had come—unexpected, on its own, without warning. Isn't that the history of pain? Pearl Harbor. Hiroshima. Pregnancy. This is why I do not ski or bungee jump. Two years in the army had taught me that sometimes pain can be a matter of choice. This might very well be the derivation of that famous phrase: *never volunteer*.

I walked into the kitchen, went down the hallway, and saw someone in the bedroom. "Christ!" I barked. It was Linda changing out of her jeans.

She stopped dead with her bikini bottom dragged down to her knees. She had no top. Her blonde pubic hair drew my eyes like a magnet.

"What's the matter?" she said, as if picking up in the middle of a casual conversation.

I could feel my blood pressure rising. I stared at her

nakedness, then looked at her eyes. "Where the hell did you come from?"

"The bookstore," she said, continuing her striptease. She stood erect and went to the chest of drawers, opened it, deposited her bikini.

"When?" I said.

"Just now," she said, withdrawing a pair of pink panties and slipping them on.

"Through the front door?" I said.

"Yes. Why?"

Oh God. She was not this kind of woman, was she? It was like pulling teeth. I was losing control of this conversation. I had to direct it away from the whimsical back-and-forth of misunderstanding—although right at that moment I would have been glad to get a grip on anything at all, not just the conversation. My life did not seem a likely candidate at this juncture. I entered the room and sat down on the bed, took a deep breath, and exhaled. I waited a good fifteen seconds, as though I was waiting for something to catch up with me and run concurrent with my inner clock, my metabolism, my sanity.

"We need to talk," I said. I will admit it. I never in my wildest dreams thought I would ever utter that sentence. It was a woman sentence, a sentence of foreboding. But I wanted to establish a solid parameter. We need to talk. To clarify. To make sense out of the past hour.

"Okeee," she said, picking through the clothing that she had stored when I was not around, primarily colorful bras.

"I went down to the bookstore to get you . . . like you told me to do," I said while trying not to sound judgmental, accusative, censorious, pissed. "But you weren't there."

She turned to face me and went about the business of strapping on a see-through pink bra with her arms winged behind her back. "I know," she said.

Ignoring this non sequitur, I drove onward. "Why did you leave the store before I showed up?"

"Because the cop left," she said.

"How did you know?"

"Because I saw his car go by the store, so I left by the rear exit and came back up the alley."

"How did you know it was him?"

"Because I looked at his car before I went into the bookstore. I saw him get out and go up to your door."

"How did you see all this?"

"I went out to the sidewalk and watched, Charley. What's the matter with you? What's the problem?"

As I spoke a trickle of phlegm entered my throat. This was like the pus of a sore, of two warring factions, one that wanted to get laid *now* and one that wanted to know if Linda knew anything about the break-in. If I got the answer I didn't want, I might lose the best sex-and-drugs deal I ever floundered into. See? I admit it. I am weak. Men are weak. Lenny Bruce said it best: you can be at the point of near death and you will hit on the nurse bandaging your broken body. Should I tell her that the cop was asking questions about the drug robbery? What if she packed up and fled the state? I would not only lose that red-hot body of hers, I would lose a hatful of interesting drugs whose allure could not be denied.

And then there was the business of Drew and the fake slip.

And then there was my lie.

Why did I do that?

Ask Lenny Bruce.

"The detective seemed to think I might know something about the break-in at the clinic," I said, watching her carefully, drawing upon all my years as a student of lying.

"Really?" she said. "Why is that? Did you break into the

clinic?"

This was exasperating.

"No, I didn't break into the goddamn . . . I mean he told me I wasn't really a suspect, he is interviewing everybody connected with the case. I used to work there, so he had to talk to me."

"Did you convince him that you were innocent?"

"He never suspected me in the first place," I said with a note of irritation in my voice. Why is it so hard to connect with people through language? Talking is such a crude medium. Mental telepathy would be the ideal, provided you wanted every woman in the goddamned world to know what you were thinking at all times. I'm sure they would love it. It would be the end of men as we know us. "The detective told me that if I was going to rob the clinic, I would not have cut a hole in the screen and jimmied the lock, I would have left the window open."

Instead of reacting as I expected—raised eyebrows and a bit of "Ah-haa" with a finger pointed at the ceiling—she got a glazed look in her eyes and began staring at the puzzle box on the night table.

This was disconcerting. I waited a few moments, then tried to calculate a way to broach a subject that I did not want to broach. Now I was Detective Quinn and Linda was the prime suspect. Did she know anything about the break-in? Where the hell did she get her drugs? Did she send that despicable letter to Drew? And for that matter, who was this woman? Where did she come from? Why was she taking creative writing? Why did she want me to teach her how to write a novel? Suddenly I felt like a woman. I wanted to know everything that was going on inside the head I was talking to. Perhaps I should say I now "understood" women. I did not actually feel like one. I was starting to get a boner. I didn't know if it was sex in general or Linda in particular, but something was clouding my mind with the insidious subtlety of The Shadow. Maybe it was just that I had been exonerated by the cop and was experiencing a form of relief that was being intensified to an almost uncontrollable degree by the presence of a beautiful woman in my bedroom and a hatful of kick-ass drugs.

As far as my "student of lying" moment—the "built-in bullshit detector" that Ernest Hemingway speaks of—I had not yet detected anything in Linda's demeanor that indicated she knew something about the break-in at the clinic. She continued putting her clothes on, half listening to me and half dressing, so to speak. She seemed mildly amused by the whole business. Was she a master of deceit? Was she hiding something at this very moment? Everybody is hiding something during every moment of their waking lives, so that was a worthless line of inquiry.

Linda was fully clothed, her erogenous zones hidden from my sight, when the chimes of the popsicle truck began trickling through the neighborhood trees.

"Oh Charley, buy me a popsicle!" she said with the piping squeal of a child.

I sat on the bed staring at her while all my doubts and questions riffled past like file cards. The sound of the bells grew louder.

"You want a popsicle?" I said.

"No—a fudgsicle!" she said, clasping her fingers together. "I haven't had a fudgsicle in years!"

I just stared at her. Was she being evasive? I couldn't tell. It was as if my powers of observation had been damaged by everything that had taken place during the past twenty-four hours. Did she want me to leave the house so she could pull some new shit on me?

"Hurry," she said, "before he gets away!"

She dragged me up off the bed and pushed my backbone, giggling like a child. The electricity of her enthusiasm passed through her fingers and traveled up my spine. I hurried toward the rolling sound of bells, yanked the door open, and rushed outside to see the truck casually creeping along the street in search of children, the velocity of the white van out of sync with the dynamics of that haunting song—slide down my rain barrel, crawl in my cellar door . . .

It reminded me of my mother. She was a toper. When I was growing up I knew where my mother was in the house based on the tinkling sound of ice in a glass full of scotch and soda. It was like the faint chiming of popsicle bells. I always knew where my mother was because I could follow the elfin music of her ice cubes as she moved from room to room.

Feeling like an idiot, I walked out to the asphalt and waited for the truck to pull adjacent. I raised my hand. I made eye contact with the driver. I was taken back thirty-five years to another part of Denver where I had lived as a boy and where the daily arrival of the summer truck was a momentous event in the lives of the neighborhood kids, the gang, the bullies, the leaders, and the followers like me who stood clutching hot sweaty dimes in our sticky fingers.

Here comes the popsicle man!

The driver was in his twenties. Tennis shoes, blue jeans, T-shirt, baseball cap, the uniform of the young American loser. My first thought, of course, was how much did he earn? Was he married, did he support himself with this job, was it part-time? I had the ridiculous urge to ask him these things. After all, I too was a member of the losers' club. I had just been fired from my job as a part-time janitor, and until this moment I did not think I could sink any lower. But maybe I could become a demigod to children with sticky coinage.

"Can I get two fudgsicles?" I said.

The Paradise That Lurks in Female Smiles

"Yessir," he said, and he hopped off his seat and disappeared into the rear of the vehicle. He came back out and stood in the doorway.

"Two fifty," he said as he held the items expertly out to me like fanned cards. An authentic job skill. I handed him three bucks and told him to keep the change, then used both hands to take them from his talented fist.

As I walked back to the curb I looked up and down the street in search of both cops and kids. Where were all the children? I had never seen the popsicle truck stop on this block. I glanced back at the truck and saw the man seated behind the steering wheel. He was looking at me. What was he thinking? Was he judging me? Was he writing me off as a buffoon? When your intellect has been artificially expanded to the size of a pumpkin, you tend to think the sort of thoughts you might expect from a pumpkin.

I hurried up to the front door and entered, shut the door behind me, and leaned back against it.

"Before I give you your fudgsicle," I wanted to shout, "tell me where you were on the night of the twenty-third at 10 p.m.!"

"I have your fudgsicle!" I called out firmly but gently.

"In here!" she hollered from the bedroom.

I walked down the hallway. Linda was seated in the middle of the bed with the sheet over her head like a Halloween ghost. She was perfectly still. She was playing with me. I could hardly stand it.

I carefully held the two fudgsicles in my left hand, plucked at the sheet with my right hand, and raised the tent to see underneath. Men had been doing this since the invention of the fig leaf. "Peekaboo," I said, then almost choked. She was bare-ass naked and grinning at me.

"Oh goody," she said, limning the very thought passing

through my mind. "Gimme!" she squealed, reaching for a fudgsicle.

Was I going to pick up the interrogation where I had left off and jeopardize the best sex-and-drugs deal I had ever latched onto in my life? Ha! Fuck that flatfoot. I would never let him step inside my house again as long as I lived. Cooperating with the authorities is a fool's ploy.

"Quick—before it melts," I said. That was a Tony Curtis movie. The odds of her getting the joke were zero. The odds of her knowing who Tony Curtis was were even zeroer. I was now living with a woman who was probably too young to have heard of Lenny Bruce, Tony Curtis, or for that matter, Benny Hill. It was a dream come true.

Chapter 20

After the calming fudgsicle moment I joined her under the tent, where she sorted through the little wooden compartments of drugs and explained their effects. Some I was familiar with from personal experience, some from word of mouth, and some not at all. Uppers and downers. Prescription and illegal. There was no LSD. I have to say thank God for that. I know I would have succumbed to the temptation. I had never used acid, had wanted to when I was young, had a few "almost" moments but never made it. Ken Kesey's plague remains to this day a mystery to me. I will not bore you with a *PDR* of her stash. We did lines, then she gave me a pill. It mixed well with the fudge. The inside of the tent became a warm snow cave where we huddled for the reasons men and women huddle. I will not tick them off. The air got thick under the sheet and when we threw it off, it was like breathing air on Everest. This was not an uncommon drug reaction. When I first smoked pot I had those "I can't breathe" moments that everybody gets. You think there is no air inflating your lungs, and just when you start to panic you become distracted by a delightful riff on the stereo played by George Harrison. You keep telling yourself it's all in the mind. You are your own guru. Then the pizza guy shows up and you forgot to remember that you ordered a large sausage and green pepper. You stand shirtless in your blue jeans trying hard not to giggle while you tip the kid five dollars and usher him back out the door. You feel foolish and hungry. Then you chow down and forget to wipe the sauce off your face. You notice that the TV is off and you wonder why anyone invented

TV when the mind is so much more fun. You become deep and profound. Drugs are truly an idiot's delight.

"Will you teach me how to write novels now?" Linda said as she cleaned my face with a washcloth. We were back in the tropical snow cave with a fan blowing the white sheet into grand Arctic swells. God but I love illusions.

"Sure. But tell me . . . why do you want to write novels?" I said, even though I knew the answer. It was the universal answer: money.

She smiled at me, a compressed simper that stretched across her face in a thin line. "Because I want to write murder mysteries," she said.

I began nodding and gave this some thought, then said, "I probably can't help you there."

"Why not?" she said.

"Because murder mysteries have an added layer of complexity that I am no good at. You have to be able to create a puzzle that works, like the puzzles Agatha Christie created, and Conan Doyle with Sherlock Holmes. I don't know how to teach someone to create puzzles. Besides, I generally don't read murder mysteries. They don't interest me, and you should write only what interests you. You know the drill—write what you know about. Write what you care about."

She was lying on her side as we were speaking, but she made a slow roll like a log in water until she was resting on her back gazing at the ceiling. I waited for her to speak, but she did not.

"I can teach you basic story structure, but that is all," I said, watching her left eye as it probed the ceiling. Her profile was perfect. She could have been a model. How do you describe a woman's nose? It is probably best not to. Women are touchy about their body parts. I don't blame them. Their bodies are flowers that draw bees—they like to imagine they are petal perfect. I once knew a woman who was embarrassed because her breasts were, as she said, too small. I somehow managed to refrain from saying anything. I smiled, cupped one breast, and kissed it. I knew I was on dangerous ground if I spoke. This was rare insight for me, especially when I was drunk and naked in bed. I wanted to tell her that men do not give a flying fuck about the size of a woman's breasts. Maybe Las Vegas swinging assface jerk Hollywood morons do, but the only thing men want to know is whether or not she has a vagina. I simply am not certain that women understand that the only body part men are interested in resides between their legs.

Suddenly I sensed that I had said the wrong thing. Forget tits. Linda's were magnificent and made partially of silicone. But by stating that I could not help her to write murder mysteries, I realized that I may have been the fly in the ointment of our relationship. Which is to say, if I had nothing to teach her, why should she hang around? She wanted something from me. I wanted red-hot sex and she wanted to know how to write. If I played my cards wrong, if I played them the way I usually do, she might find an apartment on the far side of Denver, quit my creative-writing class, and I would never see her again.

"You could write suspense novels," I said. "They don't have clues that have to be uncovered. Like in an Alfred Hitchcock movie where you already know who the murderer is."

Her head rolled slowly like that damp log until she was looking me in the eye. "I love Alfred Hitchcock movies," she said. "When I saw *Psycho* I carried a nightstick with me for a week to protect me from Anthony Perkins."

"Where the hell did you get a nightstick?" I said.

"In an army surplus store."

This made me laugh, which fomented a round of giggles that neither of us tried to suppress. It might have gone on for days. Drug giggles do that. You have to take the bull by the horns and stop it deliberately. It's like trying to pull a car out of a dangerous skid on ice. It takes concentration, skill, and determination, the three things that drugs destroy.

"You went to an army surplus store here in Denver?" I said. I was fascinated by the image of a beautiful woman walking into an army surplus store on Twenty-Third Street and asking the clerk for a head-bashing stick.

"In Reno," she said. "I was living there when I saw *Psycho*."

"What were you doing in Reno?" I said.

"I lived there. I had a job."

"Doing what?"

"I was a stripper in a crappy dive next door in Sparks."

For some reason this revelation was like a pleasant punch in my lower abdomen. I envisioned Linda onstage, clinging to a silver pole and performing those athletic moves that are expected of women who have perfect bodies, plastic tits, and the determination to make men stuff large tips into G-strings. This idea made me forget all about creative writing.

I will pause to let you use your imagination, then we will move on. I rolled off that heated moist log and lay breathing heavily while she hummed a delightful tune, her eyes closed, her body cooling from exertion. After her revelation, our lovemaking sessions were never again the same. I will be honest here. When I first met Linda I had a subconscious assumption that she was like the majority of the naive young women who take my creative-writing classes. A dull-witted, deluded woman who had illusions of literary success. But she was not stupid. If I sound sexist, the dull-witted and deluded part also applies to men. Is it wrong of me to be honest about my own tribe of starry-eyed telephone poles? After all, writers attack big business, the military, the church, the hypocrisy of the complacent middle class—why should we not attack ourselves? Are we—speaking as pundits and philosophers—immune to criticism, sarcasm, satire, and condemnation? You rarely see writers making fun of themselves. Nossir. Nope. Verboten. Don't go down that road. Everybody knows that writers are supreme beings.

But back to the issue at hand. Linda was a former stripper who had moved to Denver and began attending classes at the free university because she was bored. Why was she bored? Because she had nothing to do. She did not have a job. Which led to the ultimate question, the question that women invariably ask men . . . what do you do for a living? How much money do you have, and how do you acquire it? And in the case of Linda, how can you afford a hatful of drugs?

"Don't ask me about that part of my life," she said as she lit a cigarette and blew rings at the ceiling. I knew instantly that I was going down the wrong road. I did not want to know where she got her money. What if she was a hooker? What if she was having sex with dozens of men every month so she could score drugs, stay unemployed, and live with me? What if. What if. What if. The heart of storytelling.

After I finished my smoke I sat up and crushed it out in an ashtray, lay back down, and decided that I would not say a thing in the presence of Linda. I would treat Linda the way a birdwatcher treats a rare fowl that settles on a branch within grabbing distance. Stand perfectly still. Bask in the honor of wallowing in the glory of something breathtaking to behold. Cherish the moment. It will soon fly away.

Part III

Chapter 21

"Let's go to Central City."

"Central City?" I said. After she told me not to question the Reno part of her life, I had written off my notion of visiting the gambling center of Colorado. The fact that she had brought it up was a miracle of dictionary Kismet.

"It'll be like Reno," she said. "I want to gamble."

Although I had occasionally visited Central City with friends, gambling was one of the few vices that had never burrowed itself under my skin—except, perhaps, in the sense of "salt in the wound." I once dropped five hundred dollars at a blackjack table in Las Vegas. It took twenty minutes. When I walked out I felt light-headed, dizzy, enraged. I felt as if I had been robbed. My billfold was empty. That was the largest amount of money I had ever thrown away out of greed.

"Okay," I said. Aside from gambling, Central City is where Coloradans used to go to get a glimpse of how people lived in the olden days. There is an opera house in Central City. Oscar Wilde visited Central City. He even read poetry to sourdoughs in Leadville. "The Face on the Barroom Floor" was immortalized in Central City. Jack Kerouac writes of Central City in *On the Road*. But that was then and this is the new Central City, bright-lights/big-city mountain valley of unalloyed commercial enterprise. But they did maintain the historic flavor of Victorian architecture.

We would make a Sunday of it. The only caveat was that I would not take drugs of any sort, and that included alcohol. I was not about to risk even a minor fender bender that might ultimately lead to cops entering my house with a search warrant while I cooled my heels in a mountain lockup. In spite of its cleverness, I did not actually have any faith in the Chinese puzzle box. I did accept the fact that nobody but Linda could open that wily vault with its sliding wooden locks—unless they had a clawhammer. However, Linda was so certain of its security that she kept it on top of the dresser drawer among bottles of perfume. If a cop opened the lid and saw the birth control pills, the condoms, the douche bag, the diaphragm, the IUD, the tampons, and that delightful pinched tube of fungicide, the search would cease. I took her word for it. I did not ask if her confidence was born of experience. I would let her lead the way. I would—to paraphrase Gale Garnett's poetic ditty—"take what she would give me, and give but what I can."

But I insisted that she bring drugs. My insistence was purely altruistic. I did not want her sneaking drugs into her purse and slipping them into her mouth surreptitiously. I wanted her to know that I not only approved but I looked forward to the contact high that comes from partying closely with an activated druggie. I wanted to enjoy through her the thrill of going to timberline with a narcotic buzz on, of hunkering down in cheesy slot-walled gambling rooms and watching spinning numbers click click click with the sound of coins spilling like ice cubes into trays.

We drove away from my house at high noon. I left a radio playing loudly in the kitchen to ward off back-door men. My house had been invaded once by a thief who did not take anything because, I assumed, he had broken in, heard the sound of a radio I had accidentally left on, and split.

I drank an ice-cold Coke on the way and was pleased when Linda, on her own, decided to bring a beer to sip like a rebel teen when no cops were looking. We made our

The Paradise That Lurks in Female Smiles

way to Sixth Avenue and sped out of the city toward the foothills. Just the thought of going to the mountains gave me a high that flatlanders do not comprehend. There is something exhilarating about driving up into the mountains on a fast asphalt road. It makes you feel wild and humble. The evergreen-riddled mountainsides loom over your head like gods. Authentic tragedies have occurred on those roads. Boulders sometimes fall from the heights and crush cars. It is no joke. Tom Jones sang it best: "Tomorrow is promised to no one . . ." Just to arrive in Central City safely made me feel as if I had survived a launch to the moon.

The rustic metropolis comes up fast. It is really only a small town, but you round a few curves and suddenly there it is, new and old buildings dotting the stair-stepped landscape and generating surplus for the taxman. In some ways the legalization of gambling recreated not only the look but the milieu of the nineteenth century. Central City was once known as the "Richest Square Mile on Earth." There had been a gold rush. Some people got rich, some didn't.

Next to surviving a moon launch, there is nothing quite as exhilarating as strolling toward a gambling casino with a beautiful woman on your arm. Except for Linda's one beer, neither of us would be drinking alcohol, an anomaly in my life, but who needs alcohol when you are eight thousand feet above sea level, inhaling rarefied air, and sucking on a Percodan? Linda's happiness became my happiness. We entered the first casino we saw and bought a bucket of tokens.

Slot machines. Poker slots. Blackjack slots. Slots with unfamiliar complicated rules that required a gambler to drop ten quarters to win big. One quarter won small. I didn't understand most of the rules and didn't care. The liquid sound of spilling tokens made me feel good as the machines swallowed our stash coin by coin. But that was okay. Anybody who goes to a gambling hall to win needs a psychotherapist, a priest, Ann Landers, someone with their feet solidly planted on the earth, or with the case of Ann, in the earth. It reminded me of writing for money. It was the possibility of hitting the jackpot that made it intriguing. We sat side by side at two separate slots and giggled and fed those one-armed many-buttoned dinging electric bandits. We left the casino with half a bucket of quarters stuffed into our pockets. Tourists in Central City jingle when they walk.

Then we came to The Phone Booth. A crowd of smiling people were gathered on the sidewalk, blocking it, making it impassable, the lesser cousin of impossible. What's the attraction? Look? Up in the sky? It's a bird? No. It's a young blushing woman stepping into the booth, an arcade game. Linda and I eased our way to the front of the crowd. No pushing, no shoving, everybody is affable in a gambling town. The show began. An overhead fan was turned on. Money began swirling inside the phone booth. There was no phone. A tall glass case containing a woman laughing as dollar bills, fives, then twenties, maybe fifties, maybe one-hundred-dollar bills, began swirling around her from top to bottom like a green tornado. The crowd went wild. The woman was clumsy, laughing, bending over and trying to pick up bills from the floor that fled her fingers. She stood erect and snatched at money in flight. She could not catch anything. "Face into the wind! Slap the bills when they land on your body and hold on tight!" Advice as old as mankind. A good-looking young guy shouted this from outside the glass. Probably her boyfriend. She caught one! She folded it into a rectangle like a stick of gum and shoved it through a tight slot in the glass. Her boyfriend grabbed and unfolded it. Merely a one-dollar bill. My God, what a cruel set of rules. She had no chance to get rich. "How long does this go on?" I said to a man standing next to me. "Three minutes!" he hollered, pointing at a sign that explained the obvious. I squinted at the words. The game was played every fifteen minutes. The crowd was howling. The girl's hair wrapped itself around her head, blinding her eyes as she grabbed at empty air. "Slap your body! Slap the money and hold on tight!"

The fan stopped. The money swirled down the drain—down, down, down—she continued to grab. She had corralled six bills before the game was over. Folding them ate up half the allotted time. Truly cruel rules. Linda and I walked away before the body count was finished. Everybody was buzzed and laughing, but I did not want to know how little the girl had won. That she had slapped six green rectangles kissing her torso had satisfied my craving for bizarre human behavior. When I was a child, I referred to money as "fun tickets." My father was not amused.

Central City is built on hills, a little Rome. We puffed along the rising wooden sidewalks. I could not take it. I felt as if I were treading on the deck of a moving ship. I guided Linda through the first door on our right, an ancient hotel with wide sweeping stairs rising to the second floor. I could hear the muted sound of slots at ground level, but no noise on the second floor. Exploration time. Where can you end up in an old building in a tourist town? The second floor wasn't a room anyway but a wide hallway lined with slot machines. There was a single black man seated on a folding chair playing two slots simultaneously. Younger than me. Wearing a blue corduroy cap. A poker floor. Electric bluffing. I had never played video poker before, but I was willing to try anything with a blonde on my arm and cash in my pocket.

"Do you know how to play poker?" I said.

"No," she said.

"Perfect," I said, but when I pulled out a chair to situate

her in front of a machine, I remembered that she had been to Reno. What? Been to Reno and never played poker slots? Or even good old-fashioned slick deck Maverick poker? A dark cloud drifted across the bright sun in my sober brain. How could anybody live in Nevada and not know how to play poker? But then there are those who live in New York and have never visited the Statue of Liberty. Linda was leaning toward the screen reading the rules. Rules. Who reads rules?

She set her purse on the floor beside the chair.

"Put five quarters in the slot and pull the handle," I said.

She complied. She hit a pair. Liquid silver spilled into the tray. I did not like this game. You had to pause and study the hand. I had never been much of a poker player, like most young men. Poker is played by math majors in college. They play chess. They play any game that requires a contestant to think five moves ahead, to bluff, to add, subtract, to measure odds. That is not game playing. Game playing is hitting a ball with a stick. Games that make you think are bloodlust.

"Holy cow," I said. As I said this I heard the sound of footsteps sauntering down the hallway behind me, but I did not take my eyes off the computer screen because Linda had drawn the ace of spades, the king of spades, a four of hearts, the jack of spades, and the ten of spades.

"Wait, wait, wait," I said as her hand crept toward the one-arm.

"Now . . . what you need to do here is select the four of hearts and then draw a card," I said.

"Why?" she said.

"Because you have a royal flush going."

The footsteps stopped behind me. I knew only by the heavy tread that it was a man. Possibly wearing boots. The floor was wooden. It thumped when he walked. He was standing directly behind us.

The Paradise That Lurks in Female Smiles

"If you hit a royal flush you win a big jackpot," I said.

I could feel his eyes on the screen. But I did not glance around. I could not take my eyes off the fact that Linda was about to do something they said should never be done: she was going to draw to an inside straight.

"Okay, okay, now, all right, press that button," I said, my hand hovering over her hand. I did not want her to make a single mistake. This was it. I was about to see a human being draw to an inside straight and subsequently complete a royal flush. I felt drunk. The floor behind me creaked.

Linda pulled the handle and drew a two of diamonds.

"Shit," I mumbled.

The footsteps started up. I glanced around and saw a man wearing a casino vest walking away with the wrinkled edge of a delighted smile disappearing from my view. He must have seen this banal melodrama a dozen times a day.

"Did we win?" Linda said.

I almost laughed. Was she kidding? Was she, in fact, laughing at me on the inside? Or was all this rarefied air, all these mountain breezes combed by evergreen giants, making me paranoid? There was no smoking allowed in the gambling halls of Central City. There was nothing between my blood and my brain but pure oxygen.

"No," I said.

I glanced at the casino employee who was leaning down and talking to the man who had both hands on both handles of the two dream machines he was rowing like a boat.

"Maybe," the black man kept saying. "Maybe. Maybe." They both laughed. The clerk slapped him on the shoulder and moved toward the stairwell. The seated man seemed like he might possibly be a regular customer. The world loves regular customers, until they go broke. I thought of a short skinny young man I had once seen at a bus stop, a manic mustached kid who kept saying to everybody who would look his way, "If you ain't got money in this world, you ain't shit. If you ain't got money in this world, you ain't jack fucking sheeee-it." For some reason I sized him up as a prison parolee. He was smoking a cigarette pinched between thumb and forefinger, one hand jammed into his jeans pocket, grinning and hopping on his toes and gazing about like a man who had not seen a lot of things in a long time.

"Let's go," I said to Linda. The predictable loss, the "feel" of a stranger hovering at my back, the memory of a lonely hyper punk at a bus stop, took the edge off the day. I did not like this casino with its wide sweeping hallway lined with slots where a single black man sat rowing his way to nowhere.

Linda picked up her purse.

"Where do you want to go now?" she said.

"I know a place," I said. "I saw it a long time ago when my family visited Central City, back before gambling was legalized."

We made our way down to the ground floor and out the door. The sky was overcast. A wind was bringing in dark clouds. But that was okay. We had made a day of it. There was still time to look at one last thing, then head on down the hill and beat the sun as it traveled toward Reno, San Francisco, the Pacific Ocean, pausing to tip its hat to the glistening brown bodies laid out on Maui, and moving on to the international date line.

'Twas a balmy summer evening, and a goodly crowd was there,
Which well-nigh filled Joe's barroom, on the corner of the square.

We arrived at the Teller House just as a flash of lightning brightened the sky to the west. No thunder. "Sheet-lightning" as my father used to say. I had no idea what that meant and still don't, except it is lightning that makes no noise. I escorted

The Paradise That Lurks in Female Smiles

Linda inside. The floor was wooden. A painting, framed by the posts and velvet ropes that keep people from entering a theater before showtime, lay on the barroom floor: *Madelaine*. Painted in 1936 by Herndon Davis, and based on a poem by Hugh Antoine d'Arcy, written in 1887.

Who were these two bonded artists? I had no idea. Was it even art? I know only that it got under my skin as deeply as it had when I was a boy. It was dynamic. A girl with the wistful face of a soiled dove glancing backwards—at *him* of course. There is always a him. Who else would she be looking at in the nineteenth century or any other century? The manhunt is exactly the same age as Time itself.

"This is neat," Linda said.

Gertrude Stein could not have said it better.

"We came here a lot when I was growing up," I said. "Every year this girl's face got smaller."

Linda smiled at me. "It's as small as it will ever be now," she said. She understood.

But this gave her the giggles. There are words that make women giggle. I cannot name them all here. Small. Big. Bigger. Long. Longer. Hot. Hard. We are verbal monkeys. I wondered if the Teller House still rented rooms for the night. Or the hour. Or three minutes in my case. Suddenly I wanted to be back in Denver. But there was a long drive ahead of us.

Another drink and with chalk in hand, the vagabond began,
To sketch a face that well might buy the soul of any man.
Then, as he placed another lock upon that shapely head,
With a fearful shriek, he leaped and fell across the picture — dead!

Chapter 22

Linda kept glancing back as I negotiated the winding road down down down from Central City toward the plains and that patch of smog where lungers once came for the revitalizing clean air of the Queen City of the West. Not unlike Hans Castorp, the star of *The Magic Mountain*, the book that would have killed me if I had read the whole thing. In skimming through it I noticed a cluster of pages that were actually written in French. Did Thomas Mann think everybody in America spoke French? What a birdbrain. But I guess he wanted to communicate his boring ideas to intellectuals only. A friend of mine once tried to read *The Magic Mountain* in the hospital. The sturdy stitches saved him from relapse. Thank God for surgeons. They're the best critics around.

"What are you looking at?" I said as Linda sat twisted in her seat.

She did not reply. She faced forward and knocked a Benson & Hedges from her pack and lit up. She sat with one arm akimbo beneath her protuberant breasts and took little bites of

smoke.

I glanced in the rearview mirror and saw nothing. Evening was coming on, and the sky was now completely overcast, but it was not yet raining, not yet dark. In half an hour I would have to switch on my headlights, just about the same time we arrived at my apartment. Interstate 70 to Interstate 25 to Pearl Street. We would be there in no time. Thank God for the highway developers who destroyed the landscapes of our cities so that horny dogs could race home in record time for a quick fuck. That's what speed is all about.

It came up fast, a small car that switched its headlights on when it was three lengths back. I thought he wanted to pass. I tapped the brakes twice, turned my left blinker on, turned it off. The road to Central City is old-fashioned two-lane blacktop, the asphalt hugging the folds of the steep hillsides where rocks drop at random onto cars. But he did not pass. I assumed it was a he. Men love the challenge of winding roads, like steering a boat in rough seas, one false move and you are off the cliff and into the raging whitewaters of the nearest gulch.

Linda glanced back.

The car slowed, gave us leeway, drifted away until it was too small to see. Its headlights went out. Did it fall into the river? I looked at Linda's profile. She lit a new cigarette off the old cigarette and tossed the old one out the window.

"Jesus Christ!" I yelled. "What are you doing?"

Startled, she looked at me wide-eyed. "What?"

"That's how forest fires get started!" I said. I was spluttering. People did not throw cigarettes out of windows in the Rocky Mountains anymore. That was the nasty practice of Tom Brokaw's Greatest Generation, when the world was every smoker's ashtray and nobody wore seatbelts.

"Remember that fire a few years back?" I said. "Practically burned down the whole front range!"

I didn't remember the date or cause, I remembered only the stink in the air of Denver, the falling ash of that remarkable debacle. Linda raised her palm to her lips. "I'm sorry," she said. She turned and looked up the road. "Maybe the rain will put it out."

"Oh, the *raaain* . . . ," I said with disgust. I didn't know what else to say. I didn't know I had it in me. I didn't know I cared about the environment. But it was like seeing a hobo spit in a hospital.

Linda reached for the ashtray, slowly ground out her cigarette, and sat back with her arms folded. I sensed remorse. She was a girl of the city. In cities, people still tossed butts into gutters.

"I'm sorry I snapped at you," I said, reaching over and placing my palm on her thigh. "I was just so surprised. Native Coloradans don't do that."

She nodded. "You were right. I wasn't thinking. I don't want to burn down the mountains."

She again glanced behind us, but I told her I did not think the mountains were going to catch fire. "You're right about the rain," I said, feeling as if I were trying to comfort a child. At that moment a single raindrop appeared in the center of the windshield like a smashed bug. Lightning flashed above us. I listened but did not hear thunder. I raised a finger, touched the spot where the water droplet had exploded. "See? The gods are taking care of us."

We drove in silence for a while. The sharp edge of joy had been completely shaven from the day. Crankiness was setting in. I wished like hell I had not snapped at her. Although I did not know the stats, I calculated that snapping at a woman prior to sex diminished the pleasure factor by a minimum of forty percent. Nothing like lying on top of a woman who is staring out a window. She's there, but she's not there. Which is exactly how I began to feel.

"What are you *looking* at?" I said.

She had turned again to peer out the rear window. The cigarette was far behind us and surely dead by now. She could not possibly be worried that her gauche act would set the world on fire, unless she had an ego bigger than my dick. I wished we were on the interstate. Winding mountain roads are not only slow, they can make me dizzy. That might sound ridiculous but I am talking thin air, abrupt sweeping turns, and a constant descent without surcease. You drive with both hands on the steering wheel. You drive in second gear. Your right foot dances between the brake pedal and the accelerator. Another drop of rain hit the windshield. The headlights behind us came on again.

The road to Central City rolls down out of the mountains and feeds into a small town called Golden. There is a large interchange of different routes connecting Golden to Denver. We were just coming out of the last canyon when Linda said, "Let's don't take the highway."

"What do you mean?" I said.

"Let's take Forty-Fourth."

"If we take Forty-Fourth, it'll take forever to get back to Capitol Hill."

"Come on, Charley, let's take Forty-Fourth," she said, smiling at me. She unloaded another cigarette and lit up.

I was exasperated. This had started out to be a great day and it was now disintegrating, but then I remembered something from my childhood: this was what always happened after trips to the mountains. The days ended with a long dull ride home, wood ticks clinging to flesh, the need for gas station bathrooms, and general exhaustion taking the fun out of the moment. Everybody gets cranky. It's part of the game. It had been so long a time since I had participated in a road trip that I had forgotten the theme of the third act that always accompanies the first two: depression. This made me smile.

Yes. Let's get off the highway and take the long slow road back to Denver. Pass through the old suburbs and into Wheat Ridge, drive east into North Denver, and cross the valley on an old viaduct. By the time we enter the bright lights of the big city, we just might not be cranky anymore. Go with the flow. Take it easy. Take a break. Take a pill.

That occurred to me.

Linda had brought some of those little white pills that had taught me how to laugh again. I was wary about downing a narcotic while driving, but like all aficionados of bad ideas I thought perhaps taking the slow back road would be okay. Play it safe. Maybe. If I ever had another accident involving drugs, I would probably be looking at six months in the county jail. The judges in Denver don't fuck around with recidivists. The first time I was in court charged with drunk driving I saw a woman who tried to get out of going to jail on her third conviction by weeping and telling the judge that she was pregnant.

"The county jail has adequate facilities for pregnant inmates," the judge responded in a kindly voice. The woman's hole card did not work. I recognized the ploy. When everything else fails, claw desperately for unalloyed pity.

This was why I put a cap on it and decided not to take a pill until we got home. I had less than an hour on the road to go, and it gave me something to look forward to. A pill, a naked blonde, a cozy bed. Better than Antabuse, if you looked at it from a strictly rational point of view. Plus, I could use the discipline. My craving for instant gratification needed a towel snapped at its ass every so often.

I negotiated the complex series of white lines on the big intersection just to the north of Golden and guided my car onto the two-lane asphalt of old Forty-Fourth Avenue, which rolled east as straight as a picket fence through the low foothills and out onto the Great Plains that used to be a part of what was once known as Kansas Territory, the most apt description of a landscape that I had ever heard.

We were approximately fifteen miles from the skyscrapers of downtown Denver, and it was not yet dark enough for the sky glow of those buildings to light up the horizon. The rain clouds were coming in fast, but I hoped to be completely out of the low foothills before a downpour began. The drive through the suburbs would not be so bad, but I hated the idea of driving along a rainswept two-lane country blacktop with headlights coming toward me. The rain had not yet really begun, only a sprinkling on the windshield that forced me to hit the wipers every two hundred feet. I was concentrating on the drive, but I kept hearing a sound of Linda turning in her seat. At one point she mumbled, "Shit," and tamped her cigarette out in the ashtray. She slammed the tray shut against the dashboard, looked out the rear window, and said, "Turn left up there at that cemetery."

"What?"

"I want to go into the cemetery."

The boneyard she was referring to was Mount Olivet. It was an old cemetery with historic figures buried there, including Horace Tabor, a silver magnate who is probably more well-known in the West than the East. He was mentioned at least once in *Paint Your Wagon*. I forget who the character actor was.

"Why?" I said.

Linda twisted all the way around in her seat and stared at the road behind us, then her shoulders sagged and she said, "I think he's following us."

"Who is following us?" I said.

"Will you just do what I fucking say!" she snarled. I had never seen this side of my gorgeous affable drug-rich blonde. But then I had gone out of my way to avoid seeing that side of everyone I had ever known. I do not like friction. When people get mad at me I tend to bring such friendships to a close rather quickly. I did not sign onto this long strange journey to become anyone's punching bag, verbal or otherwise.

I slowed the car and turned left into the entryway of Mount Olivet Cemetery.

It was like all cemeteries. Narrow asphalt lanes passed between the gravesites. I took it slow, certain there were speed bumps to stop wild teenagers from acting normal. As I made my way toward the heart of the city of tombstones, Linda turned around and watched the entry.

"Damn," she hissed softly.

"What is it?" I said.

"He followed us in here."

I grabbed the rearview mirror and began adjusting the angle until I could see the entrance and the car that had turned in. It was perhaps fifty yards behind us.

"Who is it?" I said.

"Do you know if this cemetery has a back exit?" Linda said. At this point I pressed the brakes with a controlled force that threw her gently toward the dashboard. She didn't slam into it, but she did look at me with shock in her eyes.

"Linda, who is back there? Are we in some sort of danger? Who is following us?"

She sat back against the seat and closed her eyes. "I think it's my boyfriend."

Good God. I looked in the rearview mirror. The car had stopped near the entry.

"Boyfriend?" I said. "You never told me you had a boyfriend."

She sighed and looked over at me.

"Ex-boyfriend," she said.

I waited, but when she did not elaborate I put the car into park and said, "Would you please tell me what's going on here? If you've got some kind of an angry ex-boyfriend following you around, then I'll go talk to him."

"You don't want to do that," she said.

"Goddamnit, Linda, I'm not afraid of ex-boyfriends or anybody else. We're not children. If that guy isn't man enough to talk to me face-to-face, then I'll approach the sonofabitch myself. I cannot be intimidated, okay? I'm not wired that way. I will not have assholes following me around like macho morons!"

I was furious. There are fewer things in this world that make me go ballistic faster than bullies. I had my share of them in grade school, and that was then and this is now, and if I ended up getting punched in the mouth by an ex-boyfriend, I would let the court system take over, starting with the goddamned police. My paranoia about drugs evaporated. I would not be bullied by anyone—not even the goddamned police.

I looked in the rearview mirror. The car was gone. I twisted around in the seat and scanned the graveyard, then saw the car moving along the far west border. It was a dark green sports car. I did not recognize the make or model, but who can nowadays? He pulled up parallel to my car thirty yards away and stopped. I put my car into gear and pulled forward. So did he.

I turned right and went down a lane, and so did he. I turned right toward the entrance and so did he.

I stopped the car.

"Fasten your seatbelt," I said.

Linda had not worn her seatbelt up to Central City and had not put it on during the ride downhill. I let it pass because it was all part of our fun excursion. It bothered me, but I did not want to hassle her. Why? Because I was afraid I would frighten the unicorn. The Iron Fist of Sex had me in its grip. If I started bossing her around she might get mad and leave me, or at the very least, stop having sex with me. And if she wanted to play Zelda Fitzgerald and sit on the hood, that was okay with me. I wasn't going to wet-blanket the day. But things were different now.

"What are you going to do?" she said.

"Just put on your fucking seatbelt!"

I was already wearing mine. Ever since my drunk-driving accident I had worn a seatbelt. It had kept me from going through a windshield on that bleak night.

Linda snapped her seatbelt on and I placed the gearshift into low, stepped on the gas, and raced toward the first available cemetery lane.

It is difficult to speed in a cemetery. The asphalt paths are narrow and if you are making ninety-degree turns to catch up with someone, you cannot keep it floored long. But it didn't matter. The ex-boyfriend seemed to read my mind. He began evasive action immediately, playing the most infuriating game I had played in memory. He sped up, he slowed, he kept pace with every move I made as I worked my way to the west side. I drove up a lane, he drove down a lane ten plots away. I slowed, he slowed. I turned, he turned like a mirror image. It did not take me long to realize I was not going to catch and confront him in the cemetery. He drove like a professional, like a trained bodyguard, while I made wild moves, frantic stops, sudden accelerations, performing every maneuver I could think of to approach this jerk who had shown his hand. Linda was right. He was following us, but it was more than that. He was shadowing us, dogging us, teasing us. This was the most juvenile horseshit I had ever been involved with in my life.

I made a quick turn and sped toward the main gate. The opening was too wide to block with my car but I nevertheless swung around and parked parallel to Forty-Fourth Avenue. If he was going to exit the cemetery, he would be forced to drive past the front of my sedan.

I undid my seatbelt and climbed out wishing I had that nightstick Linda had bought to ward off Norman Bates. I had no intention of hitting the ex-boyfriend and going to jail for battery, but a tool of intimidation can never be underrated. The only thing better than a nightstick would be a pistol, but I did not own a pistol. Like many men I did not own a gun because I was afraid I might use it in a situation that called for good judgment. Like many men there were times when my rage had gotten the better of me, and I did things I would never have done if my inner barbarian had not been awakened by an ill-advised word or deed. Temporary insanity may be a questionable legal device used by shysters to defend guilty men, but I was not unfamiliar with the phenomenon. The few times in my life when I completely lost control I had felt as if I was a dirigible cut loose from its moorings and floating freely in a hurricane. It gave me a sense of exhilaration that was virtually satanic.

The car slowed at the far end of the cemetery and pulled around facing me with its headlights on. I could have driven straight toward it, but I knew it would move. Whoever was driving that thing was surely laughing at me. My best hope would be to play the game until we both ran out of gas. The game would continue on foot, and if the ex was as young as Linda, I would lose.

I stood and watched the car for a full minute, then I conceded defeat. I got back inside and put the car into gear.

I looked at Linda and was disgusted to see a shine in her eyes. Maybe it was only adrenaline. I might have had that same shine in my eyes, but I was angry and tired and wanted to go home and forget this day that had gone sour. The juvenile nature of the past few minutes engulfed me like a tide. I pulled out onto Forty-Fourth and drove east. At Ward Road I turned left and drove toward Interstate 70. We would be taking the highway back to downtown Denver. I did not speak to Linda. We came to Interstate 25, which took us south toward the Washington exit. This would feed us up onto Pearl Street. I did not speak to Linda because there were many things I wanted to say, and she seemed to know that those things would be said only after we were back inside my house and behind closed doors. It took twenty minutes to get home on the highway.

Chapter 23

"**W**ell?"

I was standing in front of her. She was sitting up straight on the easy chair, her fists clasped in her lap and her thighs pressed tightly together.

"I need a drink," she said.

"You are not mixing drugs with alcohol in my house, now tell me what the hell this is all about."

She did the woman thing, raising her eyes but not her head. All women do this. It must be genetic. It's the move of a spy—or a coward.

"Well?"

They were the eyes of a leery, angry animal. A desperate animal almost trapped but knowing that an exit existed if she could make it across the metaphorical landscape to safety.

"I used to . . . date the guy who was following us. He has a jealous streak."

"But you and he are not dating now?" I said.

"No."

"So this guy broke up with you, but he is . . . what . . . still in love and is following you around because he doesn't like to see you with another man, is that it?"

She started to nod, then paused and said, "Sort of."

"Oh Jesus Christ," I said, going to the front door, yanking it open, and looking outside. If the bastard was out there, the cops would be here in three minutes. Denver cops come fast, I knew this from experience. There isn't much doing in Denver, and when a citizen calls for help, they come running. "Is it going to be like this?" I said. "I'm going to ask you a bunch of fucking questions and you're going to give me a bunch of vague answers? Is that it? Are we going to play games? Who the hell is this fucker? Do I have to call the police? Is he dangerous?"

She frowned so deeply that it must have hurt because she raised her palms and began stroking her face.

When she lowered her hands there were tears streaming down her cheeks. "I should leave," she said in a voice filled with resignation.

Panic set in. She was opting out. The problem was solved. By leaving this place, everything would snap back to the way it had been one second before she entered the house with her pink baggage.

I closed my eyes and rubbed my own face. I felt like a deflating balloon. I had been standing in front of her with my fists on my hips like an obnoxious hall monitor. Now I sank to my knees and took her hands in mine. "I'm sorry I spoke to you that way," I said. "If you want a drink I'll make you a drink. I don't want you to leave. I just want to know if your ex-boyfriend is going to cause any trouble. I'm not worried about him. I'm worried about you."

She tugged at my hands as if she wanted to wipe her eyes, but I held onto them and watched as the drops trickled like ladybugs. It must have tickled. I let loose and she raised her hands, wiped away the tears, then nodded. I did not know what the nod meant.

"Let's do this," I said. "Let's take a shower together. We'll dry each other off and get into bed. We'll go through your puzzle box and you can pick the drug you think best fits this situation. We'll turn off the lights. Then you can tell me anything you want to tell me."

It was a designer question molded to fit a nod. When she nodded I felt a heavy weight rise from my heart. I stood up and led her into the bathroom.

We made love standing in the shower, and now we were heading for a trip to China. When we were dry we moved into the hallway shivering with happiness. The nights in Denver can be cold even in the summer, and while Linda crawled onto the bed and opened Pandora's box I went around the house naked, turning off the lights and closing open windows. Until this night I had never been very concerned about whether the windows were raised a crack for ventilation, even after the few break-ins. This was not a high-crime neighborhood. But I intended never to leave a door or window unlocked again. As each room went black I peered out into the rainy night, looking for the shape of a man standing on the lawn, diving behind bushes, lurking beside the garage. I checked the back door and front door, then went down the hallway into the bedroom. Linda was closing the box. She held out her left palm. "These," she said. The pills were tiny and yellow. I nodded. I did not ask what they were.

"Do you want me to fix you a drink?" I said. "Manhattan? Kamikaze? Vodka tonic?"

"No," she said, setting the box on the night table and slipping between the sheets. I crawled into bed, dug under the blankets, and made a joke of crawling over her to the other side of the mattress, pretending to get stuck, crashing toward the earth, struggling to rise and defeat a barrier on a nudist obstacle course. By the time I made it to the other side she was giggling, and I had a hard-on like the handle of a buggy whip.

"I'm going to do things to the lower half of your body that are illegal in Paraguay," I whispered in her ear.

Her laughter rang off the rafters, and I don't even have any rafters.

The table lamp was lit by a gentle ivory glow that seemed to rhythmically throb in this steaming moment of unbridled eros. Together we tugged the blanket and sheets down until we were bare-chested. Linda held out her open palm and I took one of the pills. I held it up for just a moment to see it, a meaningless gesture because I had no idea what it was, but meaningless gestures are a thread in the tapestry of life. They can lead to significant results. I placed it on my tongue and worked it around inside my mouth until I had enough saliva to swallow it. I wanted to ask how long it would take to feel the rush, but I didn't. Words are something young people hide behind. In college I would drive friends to distraction asking questions about heart-shaped pink pills, as if I was a scientist examining a new life-form under a microscope. But words were the way I covered up my fear. One night at a party a friend laid out some lines of white powder. When I asked him what it was, he got a look of utter disgust on his face and said, "Just snort it, Quinn." I snorted it. The drug filled me with a sense of elation as the group began playing a game of Risk, my favorite college board game. I later realized the drug was cocaine. It was my first time. I was beaten at Risk right out of the chute. I died in South America.

Linda reached over and switched off the bedside lamp. The image of the entire room remained on my retina like a black-and-white photograph. It was so strong, so vivid, that when I raised my arm to see it, I could not see the arm because the latent image was printed on the background of the lightless room. I felt like the invisible man. I waved my arm back and forth. There was a painting on the far wall. My arm did not cross in front of it. The sensation made me feel ecstatic, and the drug had not yet even kicked into high gear.

Then the white image began to fade, like the light of a flashbulb. The darkness returned to the room.

I moved over and touched Linda's ear with my nose and nibbled at the "leetle hangy-down part," as Festus once said on an episode of *Gunsmoke*. The thin golden earring Linda was wearing felt like a fishhook. "You can tell me anything you want," I whispered. "But if you don't want to, you don't have to."

"I used to live with him," she said quietly. "I met him in Reno. We lived together in his apartment for six months. Then I left him."

I believe it was Mike Wallace who once said that the best way to get people to talk during a news interview was to remain silent. Stick that microphone in their face and wait. There is something about a live mike that makes the average person nervous. Doubtless it is the psychological remnants of teachers, priests, and parents glaring at the inner child and demanding "an explanation, young man." It seemed to work for him, but I waited until it became clear that Linda was not going to elaborate without a bit of investigative prodding. Perhaps if I'd had a microphone to stick in her face, but the only reasonable facsimile was my dick, and the extension cord was not long enough.

"Why did you break up with him?" I said quietly.

She inhaled deeply, she moved, she rustled the sheets. I put my faith in Mike Wallace, and after thirty seconds Linda said, "I found out things about him that were not pleasant." I waited.

"I don't know if he worked for the casino, or if he worked for one of the men who owned the casino, but he was the kind of man they used when they needed to . . ."

I waited.

"To make people pay off their debts."

I turned off the microphone and tossed it aside. "Are you telling me he was muscle?"

"Yes."

"How did you find this out?"

"He told me. But it wasn't until we had been together for three months. He didn't tell me anything about himself really when we first met, but later on I found out."

"How?"

"I asked him."

The picture came into focus instantly. "What do you do for a living?" Which is to say, "How do you earn money and how much money do you have?" Women are like big-game hunters studying the terrain, the flora, the fauna, the high ground, and the watering holes where their quarry might best be cornered. Apparently Linda had bagged a rogue elephant.

"He didn't tell me the details at first," she said. "But I kept asking him. He got mad at me finally. That's partly why we broke up."

"You were dating a violent man," I stated.

"I was living with a violent man. But he never hurt me. He never raised a finger against me."

"But he did things that weren't pleasant," I said. "He did things that violated your sense of ethics."

She twisted her head and looked me right in the eyes. The ambient light of the alley made hers seem like cat's eyes. "Yes," she said. "You have a good way with words. That's exactly how I would say it if . . ."

"If what?"

"If I was good with words."

"You are good with words," I said. "I read your short story. You approach dialogue from a unique angle."

"No, I don't," she said. "'Mister Eight' really happened."

That's all I needed to hear. It put a perfect cap on a perfect day. "I am going to sexual intercourse you." Who talks like that? But I wanted to tell her that "Mister Eight" did not really happen, that this is an affectation of writers and not necessarily beginning writers. "History is bunk" Henry Ford is reputed to have said, and semi-autobiographical fiction is the most egregious bunk of all. But many writers actually believe they are transcribing experiences exactly as they happened, as if words were no different from bugs captured in amber, replicas so exact that no other words could possibly replace them. As I say—bunk. But I did not feel like playing the role of creative-writing asshole right then. I would save my pontification for the classroom. Instead I said, "What's his name?"

Linda slowly rolled, turning her back on me. The rustling of the sheets was like the aural underlining of a silent message. I studied the white flesh of her spine. It looked like the vertebrae of a corpse.

"He once called me a money toilet."

"What?" I said.

"He would get mad at me for spending his money frivolously, even though he had a lot of money. He just said it to make me mad because he would never hit a woman."

He hit men, I assumed. He was a hit man.

"I don't want to talk about him anymore, Charley. Please don't ask me about him again."

Her request was ridiculous. She and I had been followed that day by a man who did unpleasant things for a living. "Muscle." Who has not seen every gangster movie made in Hollywood, starting with Jimmy Cagney and ending with Luca Brasi?

We had to talk about it. But the waters of the Yellow Nile were flooding the bedroom. The pill was entering high gear and I myself did not feel like talking now. I felt like floating to the headwaters if such a thing were possible, which it is if you are riding the electric tide of an illusion. Anything is possible when narcotics meet neural receptors. Already my erection had dissipated. I thanked Mother Nature for our moment in the shower, then I cast a jaundiced eye on the pharmaceutical industry. My body was the crossroad where lust collided with impotence, the worst kind of impotence of all: the kind you create by a bad decision.

I lay on my side and gazed at Linda's back and decided not to take this any further. I felt that she had told me all I really needed to know. A jealous man was following her. A violent man. A mean-spirited man. She did not want to be with him anymore. She was with me. It had the childish quality of a high school spat, a teenage squabble. Following a girl around, watching her from a distance, boiling with jealousy when she goes to the homecoming dance with a jock, writing and burning love poems, listening to Barry Manilow, and entertaining moronic plans to join the French Foreign Legion. Who but a kid would act like that? All boys act like that. Boys—not men. Men wise up, take the pain, and go to a bar.

Chapter 24

"I'm not going with you," Linda said.

"Why not?" I said.

"Why should I? I live with my writing teacher. We can hold class in bed after you get home."

"I'm not teaching you what I know about writing novels when we are in my bed," I said. "You are teaching me what you know about sex, and believe me, I am learning things I never knew existed."

This brought on that charming smile. "I don't want to go to school anymore," she said. "I want to stay home."

Christ—I had said that very thing to my mother when I was six. I kid you not. The very exact words. I hated first grade and all the subsequent grades. I wanted to stay home and watch TV.

"I'll let you stay home if you promise to write something while I'm gone."

She closed her eyes and opened them slowly with that "are you kidding" smile on her clamped lips.

"No, I'm not kidding," I said, beginning to feel like a fool. What was I, a hall monitor? Her father? I was not put here on earth to tell anyone what to do. I could never be a good father. I could never say no to a child. I could never be like my own mother. She made me go to school that day.

"Please?" I said.

This broke the ice that had been forming on the surface of our relationship at that moment. Ice comes and goes. She would not be told what to do any more than I would tolerate bullying.

"Okay," she said. "I'll write you something."

She was naked. Need I mention that? She seemed to have the idea that people who lived behind closed doors had no use for clothes. She apparently did not fully understand the biological mandate of a telephone pole. But I was full-clothed and getting ready to go teach my Monday-night class. Only two weeks left and it would be over. The recent changes in my life were causing me to make a significant attitude adjustment. Did I ever want to teach again? I knew only that I never wanted to lose Linda. Was I falling in love? You got me. I had never been in love before. I did not believe in love. I thought love was a horseshit game thought up by women to corral those recalcitrant telephone poles. But when the lights were on, I could not stop gazing at Linda's face. Of all her body parts, I liked that one the best. Was that love? It felt like love to me.

Linda got up and walked into the living room, made a beeline for my Smith Corona, and sat down. This in turn kicked in the memory of Drew and his phony acceptance slip. I did not doubt that Linda's ex had broken into my apartment, written the letter on my typewriter, and mailed it. How, when, etc., did not matter. It made sense. This was the moment that I realized he had broken into the clinic and filled my wastebaskets with trash. What in the hell kind of person was he? I knew only that he was Nevada muscle. God only knew what kind of demonic skills men like that developed. Maybe he buried deadbeats in the desert.

The point I'm making is that I was afraid to leave Linda alone in a house that was so easily breached by a pro. She said he had never hurt her, and I believed her. I saw no signs of battery on her flawless skin, but pros know how to beat people without leaving bruises. I knew this only from reading crime fiction and watching movies and believing plausible statements written by screenwriters who may or may not have ever met a pro in their lives. But that's what their imaginations are for. To make people like me paranoid.

"I'll be back here by nine thirty," I said. "Do you want me to bring you anything? A hamburger?"

"No thanks, Charley. If I get hungry I'll find something in the fridge."

I started to say that she doesn't keep her pills in the fridge, but something told me to steer clear of that land mine. Good jokes don't always work. I was learning to live with another human being in the same house, and one of my lessons had to do with self-censorship. I did not like it. This brings to mind the subject of Women vs. The Three Stooges.

I left the house reluctantly, as all men do with a good woman waiting for them. The billfold must be fed. I made certain the door was locked, giving the knob a couple of experimental twists before I headed down the sidewalk. I got into my car and started the engine, then looked at my wristwatch. Twenty minutes after seven. I thought about driving away, then coming back again to see if anyone had taken my spot in front of my house. I would recognize the car if I saw it again. A small green sports car. Classy. European. I did not know the model. It was the kind of car I imagined only a young man would drive, a single man on the make. Married men drive sedans, station wagons, married-guy heaps. Young men drive cars with anti-sway bars that take the curves at ninety. There was no use trying to outwit this guy. He would not be back before dark. Muscle works at night, according to the screenwriters. Their bosses work the day shift. I wondered who his boss was. A casino operator? What was this guy doing in Denver anyway? Why wasn't he in Reno acting tough, like Fredo in *Godfather II*, banging cocktail waitresses two at a time. I started the engine and drove toward the less interesting aspect of my life.

When I arrived at the school a few students were standing around outside the front door. I thought something might be wrong. My students always made a beeline for their seats when they arrived for class. Gotta get that knowledge, gotta get that story written, get that talent, get that fifty-thousand-dollar hardback deal from Scribner where Maxwell Perkins is waiting impatiently for another blockbuster!

Then I saw him. He was seated on one of the two low brick walls that border the porch. Drew was smoking a cigarette with a complacent smile on his face. My heart sank. He did not yet know. I knew something though. I knew that I was not going to tell him. His problem was linked to my problems, and as a result I was not going to say anything to him about the fake slip, the man who had typed it, the man who had played that cat-and-mouse game at the cemetery. I would wait until I understood this better, wait until things panned out. I was not going to do anything that might jeopardize my relationship with Linda at this point. Drew was due for a fall, and it did not matter. All writers are due for a fall. I've had writers in my classes who told me demoralizing stories of publication deals that fell through for the strangest of reasons. One man's dream was dashed when a printing plant was destroyed by a flood. Tales of banal woe tied to heartbreak. I walked up to the porch smiling. I would play Drew's game to the hilt, and then commiserate when the truth came out. Give him his moment in the sun. It was artificial sunlight, but it would burn him as badly as the real thing. Writers bathe in thin air.

I greeted my students and made a joke about tempus fugit. They followed me up to the classroom like ducklings and settled in for two hours of in-depth critical response to the stories that were to be read aloud that evening. The classroom air crackled with tension.

The Paradise That Lurks in Female Smiles

I fiddled around with my briefcase in order to give Drew an opening, should he decide to take it. I counted on him to crow, to stand and make the big announcement, but he sat at his desk looking down at a manuscript and did not say a word. This surprised me. Would he wait until the end of class to tell everyone the big news? Maybe he was waiting for me to make an introduction, but I was not about to say a word either. I gave him enough time to hang himself, then I snapped my briefcase closed and started the class.

I sat at my desk at the front of the room and listened to the stories that would never be published. Imitation Hemingway, imitation Carver, imitation Chekhov. Nobody would listen to me. Write in your own voice, I told them. Don't listen to your grade school and high school teachers. Have faith in yourself. I was getting tired of this. The clouds began to part on my own future. I was no longer a janitor, and I was fairly certain that my retirement from the teaching community was coming up as fast as a green sports car with its headlights blaring in the rain. Maybe it was time to get out of Denver. Start over somewhere else. Find out whether Linda would come with me, and if she said yes, ask her where the stalker would be least likely to follow her. I cared about one thing and one thing only: revolving around Linda like a moon around Jupiter, embracing her like a ring around Saturn. Was this love? I would have to take a wait-and-see attitude. I probably still did not believe in love, but as the man said, if you think you are happy, then you are happy. Would I love her if she did not have a Chinese puzzle box and a flawless face? I would have to wait and see.

When the class ended, Drew came up to me with a smile and asked if we could speak. The other students gave us wide berth. A young writer was conferring with his mentor.

"I wrote a follow-up letter to the *New Yorker* asking for more information," Drew said with a grin that made his cheeks bulge like little red apples. I could not have hated Linda's ex-lover more than I did at that moment. "I mailed it today."

I made a quick calculation. Writers do that. Their relationship with the United States Postal Service is unique among desperate Americans. Two days to New York City, two days back, although the time it took for Eustace Tilley's editors to make sense out of an inquiry could last anywhere from five minutes to a week. "We are sorry but . . ." the return letter would begin. It would coincide with the ending of Drew's hopes and dreams.

"Did you include an SASE?" I said.

He stopped smiling. "Omigod. Do you suppose I ought to have done that?"

"Yes."

He grimaced. I knew what he had been thinking: Now that me and Thurber's editor are tight, I no longer have to include a self-addressed stamped envelope. I am a player, am I not? We of the inner circle do not obey the rules written to keep a short leash on the lesser writers, those on the outside looking in. I shrugged and smiled. "Any time you write to a publisher you have to include a SASE, Drew. It's just part of the game. They might not even respond to your inquiry."

"But why wouldn't they?" he said. "I mean, they accepted my story. They know who I am."

I gritted my teeth. Drew had finessed me. If Cheever had broken a rule, Cheever's publisher would have given him a break: "But in the future, lad, remember to include a sassy. This is a business, we are not pen pals."

"You're right," I said. "But don't be disappointed if it takes a week or two before they get around to it. The first person to open your letter might be a secretary who doesn't understand what's going on. It may take a while to get out of her slush pile and into . . . the hands of your editor."

"Damn," Drew said.

"Don't worry about it, Drew," I said. "You have stepped up to a new level of learning. Personally I love mistakes. That's how you learn. You never make the same mistake twice." This was anything but true. But I wanted to make the kid feel good about himself. He was a young pug working his way up in the ring, taking advice from his cornerman. Pace yourself. Watch out for the left hook. Look for an opening.

Drew smiled and nodded. "I guess you're right. I got too eager."

"Listen," I said as I herded him out the door and switched off the lights, "the moment you get word from the *New Yorker* give me a call. I don't care what time of day or night. Leave a message on my machine. We'll go out for another cup of espresso and dissect round two of this battle."

Drew disappeared up the sidewalk toward Colfax, clutching a briefcase that I was certain contained the bogus acceptance. When I received my first acceptance slip, I casually left it on a small table that I had dragged over next to my apartment door so that any of my friends who came in could not help but notice my good fortune. "Oh that? Just an acceptance slip. I got it last week from the *Pinhead Review*. Yeah. No big deal. It's a tri-quarterly published in Butte. They pay in copies, but the prestige is incalculable."

Chapter 25

Things might have turned out differently if I had not decided to go ahead and bring Linda a hamburger. I was glad I had suggested that. There is nothing less motivating than trying to cook food when you are high on drugs and suddenly realize you are also starving. The pizza guy can be called but that could take a half hour, during which time you might succumb to despair. The "hollow feeling" that the graham cracker company nailed so accurately years ago was intolerable when you had better things on your mind than feeding the flesh. It was like all the things you have to do that you would rather not. Drew nailed it down in one of his stories. Shit, piss, fart, sneeze, etcetera, things that interrupt the flow of your cosmic experience as you lie in bed seeking the headwaters. So instead of taking Fourteenth to Washington I stopped off at a Burger King and waited in line with my engine running. That's where my car ran out of gas.

Hell hath no fury like me when my car runs out of gas, partly because I never let it run out and partly because empty gas tanks had been the bête noire of my childhood. To sum it up briefly: my parents were too cheap to top off a gas tank when I was a kid. It seemed I spent half my childhood lugging an empty gallon can of gasoline from a stalled car to a gas station while my father listened to baseball games on the radio. My father had a saying when I was growing up that was a knife in my heart, lungs, and kidney: "Save a couple bucks." Why fill up a gas tank when the money could be better spent on other, more important things, like beer? I will not dwell on this. I was furious and then baffled when my car chugged to a halt in the drive-up lane of the Burger King. A consumer's nightmare.

I dove out of my car and began pushing it backwards along the lane before another customer drove up and blocked me from behind. Having tucked this sour good fortune into my kit bag, I then crossed the lot to a gas station that was open, bought a gas can, filled it, and walked back to the Burger King. I would say that the scope of the entire emergency from beginning to middle to end lasted ten minutes.

I broke the speed limit as I headed down Washington at nine thirty at night. Not much traffic at that time, and it was a straight shot down to south Pearl Street beyond the Valley Highway. Somebody had drained the gasoline from my tank so that I would not get home on time, and I knew who it was. I thought of calling 911 before making it all the way home, but then I might not catch the prick in the act. I knew there would be an act. He wanted me out of the way long enough to perform the act, and an empty gas tank would give him an edge. He had not counted on my stop at the hamburger joint. If my car had broken down on Washington Street halfway to my apartment, there would have been no gas station nearby to refuel. Too residential. I might have lost an hour just getting back up to speed. As it stood now I had lost only ten minutes, which meant I too had an edge. Be it imaginary or not. I had an edge.

It was at this point that I grew embarrassed while alone inside my car. Good God. I was the one who had drained my gas tank. I had not filled up the tank after the flurry and fury of the day before, the Sunday afternoon from hell when Linda's ex had shadowed us. The trivial fact of gasoline had been shoved from my mind by thoughts of assault, death, horseshit races through a cemetery, and our drug party at the end of the day. Who makes practical decisions when swept up in the throes of illegal drugs? What do the AA people say—"First things first"? Those people live by helpful cliches and euphemisms. People whose minds have been destroyed by alcohol need simple road signs. They are not unlike people who have never tasted alcohol. I took my foot off the accelerator and slowed as my car whizzed by the police station near I-25 and University. I had failed to put gas into my car after the trip to the mountains. I had screwed myself. This was not the first time it had happened to me. I was my parents' son. I once ran out of gas on the way to long-term parking at the airport, so excited was I by the prospect of a trip to Los Angeles. Should I mention my reason for going to Los Angeles? I think not. It's the same reason that all writers go to LA. You fill in the blank.

I smiled at myself in the mirror. The ex was not to blame. Someone far more malevolent had not only thrown a monkey wrench into my life but had kick-started the blame game that I live by when feeling particularly put upon. Linda was home writing a short story, and I was racing through Denver whipped by the wet towel of paranoia. Maybe it would be best if I laid off drugs for a while.

I turned south onto Pearl Street, drove down the block, and came to my residence. The lights were on, the home fires were burning, and I knew that if I listened hard I would hear the comforting clique clique clique of my old Smith Corona that I had been lugging around since college. Should I tell Linda what had happened? No. How could I have forgotten that it is best not to give friends and women ammunition to make fun of me when the appropriate situation arises? Telling my buddies stories about the babe that got away never impressed them as much as it amused me. "All of your woman stories end like that," they said more than once, usually in reference to a failed pass made on an airplane. "I once *almost* picked up a stewardess." That was how most of my stories began.

I grabbed my briefcase and hopped out of my car and strode up to the porch wondering how long it would take before I broke down and confessed my foolish story to Linda. The front door was as locked as it had been when I left earlier in the evening, and as I twisted the key I called her name. She did not answer. I opened the door and stepped inside and noted that the Smith Corona was still on the typing table. A sheet of paper lay curled like a fallen flag over the keys.

"Linda?"

No answer. I set my briefcase down and headed for the bedroom of course. It was empty. I checked the bathroom, then the kitchen, switching on lights when necessary. By the time I said "Linda" for the second time, I was feeling uneasy. Was she foolish enough to play a game with me, especially after our encounter at the cemetery? I made the circuit of the entire apartment, then went back to the living room and sat down. Maybe she had gone to The Solid Muldoon, one of the greatest bookstores in Denver—it stayed open until 1 a.m. seven days a week. The ex-hippie who ran the place, Elgie, had nothing else to do. It was a haven for night owls. Maybe I would give him a call.

I began to pretend then. I made myself a sandwich, took a shower, put on new threads, and went into the living room and turned on the TV. I left the sound off. My eyes kept drifting toward the telephone. No messages on the answering machine. I thought about having a beer, then thought about taking a drug. I was not yet willing to write off the trust I had in Linda. Surely she would not play a game with me. She would not pretend to be missing. She would not . . . that's when it occurred to me to go to the typewriter and see if she had left a message. Maybe her mother was ill in Podunk and she had flown home. This is a part of the pretend life, concocting rational explanations that make no sense.

The Boyfriend

By

Linda Hathaway

When we met in Reno I had no idea what sort of man he would turn out to be. I thought he was just a well-dressed barfly like most of the men I picked up on a regular basis. I never dated my customers, but once my G-string was off I went to different bars in Sparks looking for love. Good luck. Asshole.

The End

I stared at the odd beginning. My eyes were then drawn to the odd ending. What sort of last line was that? Linda had already established herself as a peculiar writer, but this was getting into the realm of Dada.

I flipped the page so it again lay over the keys, then went back into the bedroom and looked for the Chinese puzzle box. It was not on the dresser. I looked in the closet and found it on the top shelf where she sometimes stored it for reasons known only to persons who store things in different places for no apparent reason.

I set it on the bed and popped the top open. All of the sex objects were there. I will not delineate them. I then did something I had vowed not to do, which was to break Linda's trust in me. I made a futile attempt to unlock the box by sliding the parquet panels around until I was convinced that it was not possible, something I already believed. If I had a sledgehammer I could have opened it, but that would also have opened a line of inquiry that would embarrass me, destroy her trust, ruin our friendship, and fuck up the best sex-and-drugs deal I had ever gotten involved with. I put the box back in the closet and went into the living room. Even though there were no lights flashing on the answering machine, I replayed the message that had been left over, unerased. Here was Drew asking me to have coffee with him to celebrate his fortune. I shut it off and stood in the middle of the living room nearly ill with unease.

I finally went to my briefcase and dug through my papers until I found the application for my writing class that Linda had filled out. I dialed the telephone number she had given me only to hear the operator say, "I'm sorry this number has been disconnected," which did not surprise me yet it increased my unease. Of course it was disconnected. She did not live there anymore.

I hung up and went to the front door and looked out into the night. I made my decision. I grabbed the piece of paper, put on my coat, and went out to my car. I deliberately left the door unlocked so that Linda could get inside in case she had forgotten her key. It no longer seemed to matter whether my door was locked anyway. I got into my car, turned on the overhead light, and peered at the address where she used to live. It was in Aurora. I shut off the overhead light, started the engine, and pulled away from the curb.

It took me fifteen minutes to arrive at the street where Linda used to live. I drove slowly down the block looking at addresses. When I got to the end of the block, I pulled a U-turn and drove slowly back up the block. Not only did I not see her old address, I did not see anything resembling an apartment building. These were all residential houses.

I stopped the car and turned on the overhead light and looked at the address again, and remembered the moment she had told me the address and how meticulously I had written it down because I had already known that I was going to put the moves on this student. I didn't scribble it quickly. I had written it slowly, as if inscribing it to memory, which I was. I did not need the piece of paper to know the number. I had brought it along as backup. It confirmed that Linda had lied about her old address.

I put the car into gear and drove back toward my side of town in a contemplative daze. I was living with a liar and I knew it, but up until then I couldn't have cared less because she was the best sex-and-drugs etc. She had stayed home from class because she was living with the teacher. But she had not been home when I got back from school, and had not left a note. I recalled how irritated I used to get when my female roommates harped on me to leave them notes when I went out. To phone when I was going to be late. To do this and do that and allow my moves to be monitored like a teenage boy whose parents did not trust him.

Was I now a hypocrite, or was I merely mature? I needed to have a serious talk with Linda when she got home. I was afraid of scaring the unicorn, but this disjointed relationship was leaving me exhausted. I wanted to know where she was at all times. And I wanted to monitor the moves of her ex-boyfriend. I wanted to make it clear to Mister Eight that she was mine now, and not his.

Chapter 26

id I say mine? On the one hand I have no interest in women's lib, on the other hand I am in complete agreement with it: don't take any shit off anybody. Women don't want equality, they want respect. Who says being a CEO is better than being a housewife? Steinem? What a snob. This is the difficulty of being real while at the same time riding herd on a penis. I supposed if I was serious about that I would find a better job, perhaps start a viable career. Broke men make terrible providers. I knew only that my heart was in this. I wanted to know where Linda was and I wanted to know *now*, I didn't want to wait five *years!* he exclaimed.

I turned left onto Pearl Street and glanced at a bar on the corner. It was an old Denver saloon, a landmark of sorts, and I wondered if she might be in there. But I had plenty of booze on hand at home, and why would she interrupt her short story to go to a bar anyway? It made sense that she wouldn't. I continued to drive. I was three houses away when I saw the rectangle of yellow light in the sky. I recognized it because I had seen it when tenants lived in my upstairs apartment. The sky was black, the window was yellow, and my heart was rising to my throat. Could my landlord be showing the place at this time of night?

I pulled up at the curb and turned off the ignition. I sat a moment looking at the upstairs. There was a window at the front of the gabled attic roof but no light was coming from it. The room was a small bedroom with a door. I got out of my car and walked swiftly and silently to my apartment, pushed the door open, and looked in to see if Linda was seated at the typewriter. I walked through my apartment as quietly as I had ever walked, and ascertained that she was not present.

Since I do not own a gun, the only weapon at hand was a small frying pan made of iron, the sort of thing you would cook bacon on during a camping trip. I plucked it from a nail where it hung near the stove and walked back through the living room and out the front door. I did not shut the door. I walked around to the side of the house and looked to the top of the stairs where the cast light from the door window made the upper porch a dull yellow, like dried mustard.

I had never listened to myself walk up the wooden steps, so I did not know if they creaked. I took it slowly, walking along the far right side of the wooden planks. I had seen this technique in a movie. It worked. The dry wood did not creak. When I arrived at the top I kept my head ducked like a man walking beneath the deadly spinning blades of a helicopter prop.

I stood and listened, hoping to hear the voice of my landlord singing the praises of his walk-up, but I heard nothing. I tried to see past the sides of the pull-down shade on the door but they lay flat against the inside frame. A tenant could walk around nude and not worry about people like me.

I hefted the pan in my right hand, squeezed the handle. The pan felt good, like a heavy pistol. It was all I had, but considering the possibilities, it was probably all I needed. If someone was going to shoot at me, a gun in my hand would not stop the bullets. I turned the doorknob slowly, but because it made an annoying click I shoved it open quickly and called out.

"Linda!"

My pan was raised at shoulder level.

From where I stood, the room appeared empty. I did not see it until I took a step inside. I glanced to my left. I did not know what it was at first. I was prepared to encounter virtually anything, and this had the effect of reducing my ability to distinguish particulars, but that lasted only a few seconds. I saw a white shape at the far end of the room, a pale blur. I scanned the thing up and down.

A shiver passed through my body, my pulse doubled, and my grip tightened on the handle. I heard a single knuckle crack.

"Linda?"

I stepped farther into the room. Whatever it was, it was seated on a chair and covered by a white bedsheet, just as Linda herself had sat on my bed when she had sorted through her Chinese box. The only visible article of clothing was the tip of one pink tennis shoe, which protruded from beneath the hem of the sheet.

"Linda?"

My voice was unnatural, shaken, high-pitched. I glanced behind me, listened for the sound of footsteps coming up the stairs. Heard nothing.

"What are you doing, Linda?" I said, then heard my voice say, "Don't do that."

By now I was crossing the room and staring at the rounded top of the sheet, the ghost head. I looked down at the tennis shoe, pink, soiled, inert.

"Linda?"

Should I call the police? Ambulance? Too late now. I grabbed a fistful of cloth and raised it and screamed when I saw the misshapen head, which was made of newspaper.

The sheet fell from my hand. I reached down and touched the blue-jean thigh and heard the crackle of paper. I touched the torso. The mannequin toppled from the chair and landed on its side with the delicate rustle of dry leaves.

Chapter 27

I will admit this. I am not ashamed. When I entered my apartment I began to feel a cold sensation in my pants. I looked down and saw that my bladder had released its load, creating a dark stain on the fly, the crotch, the thighs. My hands were trembling as I reached for the phone.

I tried to dial but my fingers were shaking as if succumbing to frostbite. I slammed the phone onto the cradle, unbuttoned my pants and dragged them down to my ankles, kicked them off as if manhandling a soccer ball with my feet. They flew into the dining room. I picked up the receiver again and reached to the buttons but could not remember what I was doing. My underwear was wet. The bastard had made me scream like a girl. I slammed the receiver back onto the cradle and strode into the bedroom, changed into dry underwear, and walked back to the living room, kicking my soccer pants toward the front door. I sat down on the chair next to my phone and clasped my hands, bit the knuckle of a thumb, and tried to think. What would I tell the police? Where was Linda? Where was this bastard X, this Mister Eight who came and went in my house like a ghost passing through walls?

I sat for a full minute feeling the trembling of my hands like a current of low-voltage electricity, then I got up, walked into the bedroom, grabbed a pair of jeans, and dragged them on over my tennis shoes. Forty years old and still wearing tennis shoes. This passed through my mind. If I met Mister Eight, would I be able to handle him like a twenty-two-year-old jock? Clothes make the man. I felt manly as I reentered the living room. The magic of armor. I remembered how it felt to wear combat boots, fatigues, a helmet in the army. Nineteen and invincible, until the true nature of bullets got through to me. Hand grenades. Mortars. All flesh is onionskin.

I sat down on the chair again and this time felt clearheaded. The passage of a minute plus the magic of pants. Could Linda be in the basement? The backyard? Best to check the area of operations before calling the cops like a frantic old maid screaming at a horse peering through a window. Was that Thurber or *The Russians Are Coming*? I got up and went to the kitchen to find my five-battery flashlight. It weighed a ton and could light up the entire backyard, which was why I had bought it. I used it whenever I heard strange noises in the alley at night, punks painting with spray cans, drunks painting with vomit. You could club a burglar to death with the thing and it would just keep going and going and going . . .

I shined the light through a kitchen window, illuminating the backyard. I aimed the beam toward the lounge chair. Linda was not there. I went back into the living room intending to go outside and around the house instead of walking out the back door into the onslaught of a two-by-four. That was how my mind was working. Ambush. I would circle the block if I had to in order to come at my backyard from . . .

I picked up the phone and dialed The Solid Muldoon. It rang and rang. The place was open until after midnight, but maybe Elgie Troxel hated phones as much as I did.

"Muldoon's," the voice said.

"Elgie, this is Charley Quinn."

"Hey Charley."

"I've lost another woman, Elgie."

"All of your conversations start that way," he said. We had that sort of relationship. Everything was a sex joke. Different friends, different dialogues.

"This is my girlfriend, Elgie. Did she come by the store tonight? A blonde. Tall as me. Large breasts."

He started laughing. I had the sense that he wanted to make any number of wisecracks, but I had warned him away ahead of time: she was a girlfriend. Elgie and I were on the same page.

"There was a woman in here earlier tonight who looked like that," he said.

"Was she wearing pink tennis shoes?" I said.

His silence was like a shrug. I waited to let him sort out the images in his brain. I would define him as a druggie. Pot mostly. "Could be," he said. "I don't have a foot fetish, Quinn."

"That's not what I heard. Is she still there?"

"No, she's gone."

"How long ago did she leave?"

"I don't know, Quinn. It's not my day to watch her."

"Come on, Elgie . . ."

"Maybe forty-five minutes."

"Did she buy anything?"

"One of *your* friends? That'll be the day."

"Was she with anybody?"

"You know something," he said. "She came in alone, but she did leave with a guy."

"What did he look like?"

A brief chuckle. He wanted to crack wise. But . . . "I didn't look that close, Charley. He was wearing a sports coat."

I closed my eyes and made a sound like a deflating balloon. "Thanks Elgie," I said. "Talk to you later."

"See you."

I had never given Elgie Troxel so many straight lines, but he could read me like a book. My girlfriend appeared to be stepping out on me, so he had put a lid on it. This was only the second time in my life that I had called Elgie. The first time was to find out if he had a biography of Oscar Levant. True story.

I hung up the receiver gently in order to avoid slamming it to the cradle.

She had left with him. What the hell was going on? Was I being set up for some kind of rip-off? But what did I own that would motivate them to foment such an elaborate scheme? Christ, Linda had the run of my household. She could steal anything she wanted at any time and hand it over to her secret lover as long as she got naked and came to bed every day and night *in saecula saeculorum amen.*

Should I go ahead and call the police? What would I say? What would they say? The practical things. "Sir, have you ever seen this man before?"

"We played chicken in a graveyard."

"Have you seen him up close? Can you describe his face? Do you know his name?"

Etc.

I stood up and walked through my ground-floor apartment and checked that all the windows were locked. I grabbed the flashlight and walked out into the backyard to take a closer look at the lounge chair. It was empty. I shined the light around the yard, then walked over to the alley and aimed it to the far end. No one in sight. That's when I saw it. A graffiti artist had been at work on the garage wall, but not one of the *West Side Story* punks. The message was crude, simple, to the point. *Good luck, asshole*—in pink paint.

I switched off the flashlight so a sniper with a muscle gun could not take aim. I walked back to the house, reached into my pocket, and pulled out a small ring of keys. I opened the basement door and shined the light downstairs. The sour smell of the basement drifted past me. Without a tenant, the windows were never opened. To me this meant there had been no break-in, no doorjamb jimmied. I closed the door but did not lock it.

Fifteen minutes later I was on the road. I took University up to Twelfth and then over to Clayton. Drew lived not far from the Botanic Gardens. As far as I knew, none of my students knew where I lived, which was how I wanted it. But I knew where all of them lived. Drew had once written a story about a man who befriends a cashier at the Gardens. After "the crime" the cops can't figure the motive. This is the sort of thing Drew wrote about. Mysterious murders. Perfect murders. Motiveless murders. Then a smart cop watches security tapes and begins to note a pattern. A customer spends a lot of time talking to the victim. It's all there on tape. He is caught. Jailed. Executed. Drew's criminals are always executed.

The light was on in his apartment when I pulled up in front of his rental. I had called him just before I left my place. I said I wanted to come by and speak with him about his story. It wouldn't have mattered if he was asleep, or having a party, or was in bed with his own "Leenda." Tell a writer that you want to talk about his prose and you have carte blanche into his house, his life, his heart, his soul, his body of work.

I got out of the car and removed my coat, reached in, and draped the Chinese box so that no passing thieves would see it. It contained God knows how many thousands of dollars' worth of drugs and how many hundreds of hours' worth of pleasure. I tucked it against my side and carried it toward Drew's door like a Fuller Brush man eager to get-rich-kwik.

The smile on Drew's young face was wholesome and depressing when he opened the door. I could see his writing desk across the room. Had he left the rolled sheet of paper in his Smith Corona just to impress me? He welcomed me in and offered me a drink. I declined.

The Paradise That Lurks in Female Smiles

"Drew, I need to talk to you about something important," I said. I held up the xeroxed copy of the acceptance slip from the *New Yorker* and watched the smile become uncertain on his face. The delight in his eyes changed to uneasiness, to worry, to fear. He might have made a smart cop. He seemed to have the sixth sense of which he wrote with such clumsy profusion. All his cops were smart. "Is something wrong?" he said.

"Yes," I said. "Something is wrong."

I looked around the living room, then suggested we sit down at a coffee table where the couch and a chair met at a corner. I placed the coat-wrapped Chinese box on the couch. I set the xeroxed slip on the table next to the sheet of experimental "e's" that I had typed in the hopes that I was wrong about the molecular angle. Drew sat down on the chair.

"I may as well get this over with as quickly as possible," I said. "Prepare yourself for some very bad news, Drew."

All expression fell from his face. No smile, no frown, only the wary inquisitive blue of his searching eyes. I raised the Xerox and held it up for him to examine. "This is not an acceptance slip from the *New Yorker*," I said. "Someone has played a terrible prank on you."

His eyes remained fixed on mine. Had there been color in his cheeks it would have drained. He sat inert, his elbows on his knees, his fists clenched. I continued: "I believe I know who did it. In fact, I am certain I know who did it. It is the same person who has been playing cat-and-mouse games with me for the past few days."

This brought a reaction. His face became infused with color. It was the flush of rage, realization, but also the flush of embarrassment. A large red spot appeared on each cheek with a spidery veined halo surrounding tattoos of sudden, intense emotion. The effect was so startling that I felt a wave of fear pass through me, as if a large dog had snarled at me with teeth the size of cigars.

"I'm sorry to have to deliver this news to you, Drew, but as soon as I realized what was going on, I felt a moral imperative to let you know before you announced to the world that you had become a published author."

The redness faded, the pale pallor returned, and Drew began nodding at me. His lips curled inward, upper and lower touching his teeth as if he had suddenly fallen into a contemplative mode: bad luck, eh what?

I watched his entire body with my peripheral vision. What if he sprang at me? This was the worst news that he would ever receive in his lifetime. I imagined what the past few days had been like, the reception of the letter, the light-headed exhilaration, the dash to the telephone, and the decision on whom to call first? Girlfriend? Mother? Best buddy? Creative-writing teacher? The flip cards of a spun Rolodex, the peculiar inability to even dial a telephone. The dash to the liquor cabinet, the liquor store, any place where liquor can be found because I am now a contemporary of Oates, Updike, Bellow, Cheever.

His lips were pursed so tightly that his cheeks bulged like those of a chipmunk. He looked down at the floor. I set the paper on the table and lifted the sheet of "e's." I decided to play out this scene like a doctor delivering bad news. Emotionless, technical, authoritarian. "I brought this to show to you," I said. "I produced this on my typewriter. Every 'e' on your acceptance slip is an exact match with the 'e' on my Smith Corona at home. This means that the prank acceptance slip was written on my typewriter."

He raised his chin and gazed at me with an expression that struck me as evasive. The wide-eyed defense of the guilty accused. I was so put off by his response that I waved the paper a couple times in front of his face and then set the sheet on the table. "I'm sorry about all this, Drew, and I intend to confront the person whom I believe was responsible, which brings me to the other reason I came over here."

He lowered his clenched fists and sat back in his chair.

"This may sound strange," I said, "and if you do not want to do it, it's quite all right, but I wondered if it would be possible for me to borrow a pistol from you."

"A pistol!"

"Yes, you see—"

"What do you want a pistol for?"

"To be perfectly frank, I don't feel safe in my home. I plan to purchase a weapon of my own tomorrow, but I would like something to have with me tonight. You've told my class many times that you are a member of the NRA and that you have a gun collection, so I was wondering if you might do me this favor."

He looked horrified. Did he equate my request with giving a child a bottle of nitro? Or was he simply astonished that a liberal would want a firearm?

"If you don't want to loan me a weapon, that's quite all right," I said. "My house has been broken into a number of times. As I say, I am going to buy a gun tomorrow but . . ."

"Oh Christ," he said in a voice as soft and weak as that of a man about to faint. He looked at the floor, then looked up at me, his eyes rounded, frog-like, combative, defensive.

"What's the matter, Drew?"

He began to wring his hands. I had never seen a human being do that. It would have been comical but for the painful expression on his face. "I . . . I can't give you . . . listen, Mr. Quinn . . . there's, there's . . ."

I realized my head was cocked at the angle of a dog listening to a megaphone. I straightened up, adjusted my collar at the neck, and frowned. "Is there something you want to tell me?" I said.

It began then, the slow disintegration of a personality. As I say, it would have been comical, a scene in a film, Harold Lloyd perhaps, but he was troubled, I knew that, and it made me uneasy.

"I can't let you have a gun," he said.

"Why not?"

He stood up and crossed the room to his typewriter. He stood looking down at it for a few seconds. I was staring at the back of his head when he said, "Goddamnit."

He turned and looked at me, his face flushed red. He looked around the living room as if searching for an object, a tool, reprieve. "It was just supposed to be a joke."

"What do you mean?"

He gazed at me for a moment, then came back to the chair and sat down hard. He rubbed his mouth with his fist, then looked me in the eye. "Linda . . . oh hell, I can't blame her. I went along with her. But it's my fault." His voice was bitter, filled with disgust, self-loathing, remorse.

"What in the hell are you talking about, Drew?"

He looked up at me. "She asked me to take part in a joke." He stopped and stared as if watching a scenario play out like a movie projected on a screen. "The girl from our class, Linda, she came to me last week and asked me if I would go along with her on a prank she wanted to play on you."

He paused then. He did this frequently during his revelations. He kept rubbing at his nose with his fist, like a cartoon pug taking cheap shots at an opponent's schnozz. I felt a tingle in my spine, felt the hairs on the back of my head twitching. I remained silent. I did not want to break the delicate thread of Drew's confession. It was obvious that this was difficult for him. Almost as difficult as it was for me.

"She gave me this so-called acceptance slip and asked me if I would meet with you at the Oceania for espresso and tell you that I had received an acceptance slip from the *New Yorker*."

He looked up at me quickly, as if the speed of his rising chin would erase the past, the truth, the moment he had fucked up.

"I didn't really want to do it," he said. "I've been in so many of your classes, I've known you for so long, that it didn't feel right."

"Then why did you do it?"

He turned his head this way and that, swayed from side to side, unable to say it. He reminded me of an elephant in a zoo with one leg chained to a stake embedded in the earth, swaying, tugging, trying to break out of an incomprehensible trap.

"I went along with her scheme," he said quietly, "because she . . . she . . . gave me some drugs . . . and . . . you know."

"Drugs?" I said. "Wait a minute. Did she bring a box of drugs over here? A gadget like a Chinese puzzle box?"

His eyes widened even as he nodded yes. We were connecting. I knew something he knew.

I unwrapped the coat from the box.

"Recognize this?"

He nodded. I was not surprised.

"Did Linda bring this over here?" I said.

Another nod.

I opened the lid displaying the douche bag, the condoms, the jazz of jiz that women encounter on their road to find a penis with a billfold.

"Did she open this in front of you?" I said.

"Yes," he said, gazing with a peculiar kind of horror at all the items pertaining to the human crotch. The armaments of love. To what lengths will a man and woman go to achieve the ultimate pleasure without experiencing the ultimate bummer.

I nodded at Drew's reply and raised my hands, splayed my fingers, and shook my head. "You have seen the drugs that are in here, correct?"

"Yes. She let me have . . . my pick."

"If I knew how to open this thing, I would let you have your pick right now. She used you, Drew. I don't know why or what's going on, but she used you."

"I know. I felt bad about the whole thing. But I went along with it . . . because of the drugs . . . and stuff."

I finally heard it. "And stuff." It matched a previous phrase: "She . . . gave me some drugs . . . and . . . you know."

"Did you have sex with her?" I said.

A big-shot Raymond Chandler mimic was I. The kid squirmed, then nodded. I might as well have been his father: "What's this—you got your girlfriend pregnant? What's the matter with you, boy? Who's going to pay for that child's upbringing?"

At any rate I tried not to react. I concluded that he did not realize she was living with me. For perhaps a minute I felt disjointed, dislocated, I touched the box, moved it around so that the open lid was facing me squarely. I was trying to get my head together.

"Why do you have this box?" he said quietly.

I had been staring at the douche bag, but I suddenly looked up at him. "Listen, Drew. There's something strange going on here, and that's why I came over. I was afraid you were going to be deeply hurt by my announcement, but I also wanted to borrow a gun. I'm afraid that someone might break into my house tonight and I want a firearm for protection."

It was peculiar. It was as if my words were pulling away the sticky stuff of a mask utilized by an actor in a play, a rubbery mass revealing the real face underneath—and underneath this embarrassed face was a young man who knew all about guns.

"Were you kidding everyone when you told the writing class that you were a member of the NRA?" I said.

"Oh, no, I wasn't kidding, Mr. Quinn. I never kid about the Second Amendment."

"I'm not talking about the Second Amendment," I said. I gathered that all roads lead to the Constitution at NRA meetings. I was in uncharted territory, but I'm a fast learner. "I just want to know if you, as a gun owner and believer in self-protection, would lend me a pistol until tomorrow when I can go out and buy one of my own."

His demeanor was changing before my eyes, in much the way that a girl possessed by a devil will change from Lucifer to Linda Blair. "I don't know if I can do that, Mr. Quinn."

"Why not?" I said. "Who is going to stop you? The government? Would you be violating some law or other?"

A dark shadow crossed his face. But I had meant to be melodramatic here. I had beckoned forth the boogeyman: Big Government.

"No, it's not against the law, Mr. Quinn, but I don't feel comfortable loaning you a gun. If you got injured, I would be responsible. If you killed someone, the police would of course end up questioning me and finding out why I had loaned a registered weapon to a friend. It could get complicated."

I nodded and closed the lid on the box. "I see," I said. "You are afraid of big government. Well, I don't blame you. The Constitution isn't worth a whole hell of a lot nowadays. When the corporations finally take control, they'll use that sacred document to wipe their asses."

It was inside him now, a fire beginning to burn bright, a spark in the belly of a boiler used to run an entire factory, conveyor belts, auto frames dangling from chains, five o'clock whistles bellowing their message of cessation.

"I'll wait until tomorrow and hope nobody breaks into my house tonight," I said. Was this wrong of me—to bait this gun owner? But I was not lying about anything. I was afraid Mister Eight might come for me in the night. He was obviously a total asshole, and while he might or might not kill me with his gambler's muscle, he might injure me. "Maybe I'll just go to a motel tonight and hope I'm not followed," I said. "I guess it's better to get driven out of your own home rather than risk personal injury."

He was seething now. His glasses were fogging up. Again hyperbole, but I had struck a sensitive nerve in this lover of freedom.

"Okay, I will loan you a pistol," he said, standing up. "Do you know how to handle a weapon?"

"I served in the army," I replied. "I was trained on the .45, the M14, the M16, the M79 grenade launcher, and the M60 machine gun." True story. A light began twinkling in his eyes as I recited my litany of killing machines. He was a changed man when he led me into the back of his house to show me his museum of classic firearms.

Chapter 28

The pistol rode shotgun. It was a civilian version of the .45-caliber semiautomatic. Smaller than the military version which, according to James Jones, stopped native warriors during the war in the Philippines. The warriors tied their balls in a knot with a breechcloth so the pain would drive them toward the American soldiers in a state of madness. It's amazing some of the things red-blooded patriots will do for their tribe. I was willing to pull triggers for my tribe when I was drafted, but I didn't want a staff sergeant messing with the family jewels. Saving the world from communism was motivation enough without incurring battle rupture.

When I came to Pearl Street I did not turn down toward my house, but rather drove past the inn on the corner and whipped my Ford into the parking lot. It was crowded. This was a good location, a residential saloon with no competition for miles. A bar, a dance floor, a pool room, it was not unlike the Sunset Lounge where Linda and I had our first date.

I pocketed the .45 before climbing out. I walked around to the front door, which faced Pearl Street. I entered and passed through the smoky gloom, passed the pool tables, passed the men's, and quietly stepped out the back door. I waited until the light from the door disappeared with the soft slam and click of a lock. I began walking down the alley toward my house. Although the .45 was smaller than the standard issue that I had been trained on, the magazine packed with bullets made it one of the heaviest objects I had ever carried in my life, heavier even than the M16 that I never got around to using on any commies. To my knowledge, there weren't any commies in or around Fort Polk.

The ground floor of my house was as lit as I had left it. I stood in the darkness of the alley for a while, listening and watching, then took the necessary first step into the backyard. I stayed as close to the bushes as possible without touching, rattling, or shaking them. When I came adjacent to the house I crossed over to the wall, went to the basement door, silently shoved it open, and stepped inside.

Did he see me? This was the question I asked myself. I had never sneaked anywhere since I was a boy. I felt as if a spotlight was on me, the prison break, the crosshairs of a sniper rifle. But I made it inside without being accosted physically or verbally. I quietly made my way down into the bowels of the house, where the hippie had lived, where the enticing odor of pot used to rise through the vents into my own staid alcohol-riddled rooms. I missed the hippie. He moved out one day while I was not at home. My landlord told me he had gone to Portland. I had always thought of the affable hippie as a kind of wall between myself and a less appealing tenant. My great fear was that a little old lady would rent the place, the kind of elderly woman who would make smiling requests for help from the nice young man who lives above her.

I did not turn on any lights. I made my way through the total darkness with my left hand caressing the wall and my right hand clutching the .45 for ballast. When I came to the area I judged to be directly below the dining room, I leaned back against the plastered wall and slowly slid down to a sitting position where I immediately realized I ought to have left a drink of some sort down here earlier, hard or soft, for my guard duty. The pillbox was in the trunk of my car. I was not worried about it. My car was safer in the parking lot of a well-lighted inn than it would be anywhere else in Denver. To paraphrase Jack Nicholson: the bartender kept a "horsecock" under the bar.

The Paradise That Lurks in Female Smiles

I waited.

What was I waiting for? The deluge. I began to think about the peculiar relationship between men and women and the things it leads to, like sitting in a black basement with a .45 clutched in my fist. I was now a telephone pole with a pistol. My billfold wasn't worth mentioning. As I stared into the darkness I began to hallucinate, in the sense that certain memories came back to me involving a woman, and money, and disappointment. Her name was Sheila.

She was sitting in a coffee shop working at a laptop, something I had never seen close up. I asked her to show me how it functioned. She was cute, dark-haired, very young. We talked for ten minutes. I thanked her for demonstrating how to use a laptop, then shook her hand, and as we were shaking I said, "Do you come here often?" and her demeanor changed. I read it: this guy is just hitting on me—he doesn't care about laptops. She pursed her lips. She grimaced. She gave me a dour stare and said, "No," with as much derision in her voice as I had ever heard from any woman. I picked up on it instantly. It was almost frightening. I stood up and thanked her again and said I had a decision now, laptop or desktop. I was not hitting on her. But this is how women are wired: he's after me, he just wants what's in my pants. I saw her again the following night. I went in for coffee and there she was. My heart soared like an eagle. She was cute, sweet, but twenty years too young. Maybe she had entertained second thoughts. She smiled and said hello, and asked if I came here often. "Three or four times a week," I said. And then she articulated the relationship-destroyer: "What do you do for a living?" I was unemployed at the time. My world crashed down around my shoulders. She just wanted what was in my pants. Specifically, my back pocket where I kept my billfold. I told her I was between jobs, then I got out of there as quickly and politely as possible. I recognized a dead-end alley when I saw one. But I never forgot her. Cute, sweet, dark-haired Sheila who wanted to know what I had in my pants. The irony is that while I did not fall in love with Sheila during those ten minutes, I have never stopped loving her. Sheila, Linda—who are these human beings who succeeded in twisting my heart into a pleased pretzel?

The single creak of a floorboard made me forget Sheila. I returned to the world of darkness. Someone was in my apartment.

I held my breath as if afraid the person upstairs could actually hear my shallow breathing through the wooden floor, through the support beams, through the dank air of the basement. I listened to the silence, and assumed that he was doing the same. I assumed it was a he, not Linda. Linda would not have crept. My reason was intuitive. A woman bent on pranks would act innocent, come home filled with beans, calling my name, making the floorboards bounce. I closed my eyes the way all people do to increase their ability to hear: the caveman crouches to pounce, the troglodyte sniffs the breeze, claws curled, nostrils flared. I heard the tinkle of ice cubes.

The chimes of my childhood, the music of my mother, moved slowly around the house. What was the intruder doing? Searching for me? There was a long pause, a long silence, and the next sound I heard was soft and rhythmic, and it took a few moments—the time it would take to type two sentences on a typewriter—for me to realize it was the keys of my Smith Corona beating the platen.

I took advantage of this moment of indiscretion on the part of the stranger trying to be surreptitious. I arose and glided toward the stairwell that would elevate me to the unlocked back door.

In the backyard I could not hear the typewriter, but I could see by the light of the garish alley lamp that the back door was open, violated, unlatched for the quick retreat of the person who had invaded my home. The gods were with me. Green light. I mimicked his passage, touched the back door. It opened without a sound. I slipped in and felt buoyed by a cushion of air, the ease and adrenaline making me irrational insofar as I was moving more quickly than I might have had I not been angry and armed. I felt like a dream-wraith floating three inches above the floor.

The sounds of the Smith Corona increased in volume as I entered the kitchen and moved toward the hallway. It seemed to me that the typist was attempting to keystroke his message softly—as if it mattered in an empty house—perhaps the caution of a pro. A housebreaker never knew when a tenant might come home.

I raised the pistol, aimed it at the ceiling, quickly reviewed in my mind the basic rules of gun safety, not excluding the slow squeeze of the trigger. The vertical edge of the door to the dining room stood between myself and the typist. I bent left from the waist up and brought my eyesight in line with a figure standing hunched over my typewriter. I did not recognize his back.

The typing continued. I watched, fascinated, as the oblivious man worked the keys, one-fingered, like someone who had better things to do than earn an honest living.

My floorboard creaked. His head swiveled as on a pivot and his fingers froze above the keyboard. His eyes fixed on my pistol. "Linda wouldn't like for you to shoot me," he said.

What was the first thought that went through my mind? It was this: Was his syntax correct?—"*like for you.*" Was that a proper construct?

"This is Denver, Colorado," I replied. "I can kill you and get away with it."

"The 'Make My Day' law, I know," he said, splaying his fingers, spreading his arms, raising his torso erect, all in slow motion, like a well-practiced maneuver. "You caught me," he said. "Good work."

"I don't know if I'm going to shoot you or not," I said. "But if I do, I will never find out why you're here."

"You can put that away, but you don't have to," he said. "It's your house."

"You're damned right it's my house," I said. "Are you armed?"

"Let's forget about guns," he said. He was facing me now. He looked not unlike imagined Reno muscle ought to look. He looked the way Reno muscle might think Reno muscle looks in the movies. Slick. Low-rent rich. A gambling man. Oiled hair black and well-combed. A five-hundred-dollar suit. Seventy-five-dollar shoes, leather dyed gray. Which is to say, he was dapper. Nobody in Denver would dress like that on purpose. Good taste ends at the Colorado state line.

"I mean you no harm, friend," he said.

"What's that sack of shit upstairs?" I said.

"Someone's idea of a joke."

"What someone?"

"Linda."

"Where is she?"

"Can we talk?" he said.

"*May* we talk."

"Linda told me you were an English professor. Please point the muzzle away from me, professor."

"I don't think so."

He took a deep breath and exhaled. "Okay," he said. "Okay." He glanced at the typewriter. "I guess it's time to bring this joke to an end. I bet that thing is loaded, isn't it?"

I nodded.

"Okay," he said. "Joke's over." He waited a few moments, then said, "Linda told me you pulled a stretch in the service."

I nodded again.

"Me too," he said. "Be a good guy. Don't point that pistol at my face. I know you're not a pro. But you're not an amateur either. I promise I won't draw on you."

"You're in my house."

"We can change that," he said. "We can turn that into a history lesson."

"What are you typing?"

He looked at the typewriter, then at me. He shrugged. "Let's call it the punch line."

"Read it out loud."

He looked down at the paper and recited the words slowly: "I . . . know that . . . you . . . did . . . not . . . write to . . . the . . . *New . . . Yorker.*"

He looked up at me. "I didn't have time to type her name. You interrupted me."

That's when I eased the muzzle away from his face. I lowered it until the bullets were eyeballing my Smith Corona. As far as I knew I did not do it on purpose. Check with Sigmund Freud.

He smiled. A milestone had been passed. "I'm thirsty and I would like some more scotch and soda," he said. "Would you mind if I made another one for myself? And for you too, unless you're on pills. Linda said she left her stash here with you."

"No," I said.

"I think I'll make one," he said, picking up his empty glass and gliding toward the bar. "It wouldn't do you any good to shoot me. The ramifications would be dire."

Ramifications. The things that sociopaths do not consider.

"Go ahead, make a drink," I said. "You'll need it where

you're going."

"Where am I going?" he said as he proceeded to make the drink.

"Jail."

"Naw," he said.

"I'm calling the cops," I said.

"Very bad idea. Let's talk." He carried his drink into the living room. Glided. No sudden moves. Hypnotic as a snake. He sat down on my easy chair.

"If you shoot me the cops will be annoyed at you for making them come off the road and fill out a lot of bullshit paperwork. If you kill me, my friends will be annoyed at you for making them come all the way from Reno to Denver to exact the toll."

Suddenly the pistol felt like a paperweight. "Why don't you tell me who the hell you are," I said, squeezing the butt of the pistol so hard I could feel the crosshatched metal pattern engraving my palm.

"My name is Pearce," he said. "Linda thinks you're a shit for betraying her. You lied about contacting the magazine. But I know why you did it, Charley. It was the drugs and the pussy. That's what did it for me. Nice tits, huh? As nice as the sky. They're artificial. Filled with wax. But they look great, even if they do feel like rocks."

"How did Linda know I lied about the *New Yorker*?" I said.

"I called the *New Yorker* and talked to some people. I got passed around to a lot of different offices. I even had one editor hang up on me. I called him right back and told him not to hang up on me again because I got friends in New York. It was a shitty thing for me to say to him, but it's true. I got friends who aren't afraid to wait outside the *New Yorker* offices to talk to people who need talking to. New York is a tough town. Anyway, nobody at the *New Yorker* ever heard of you. You never got in touch with anyone at that magazine. When I told this to Linda she got mad. Then she got even. I did a shitload of things for her. She is crazy, you know. She wouldn't hurt you, but she was mad as hell. She wants to be a novelist. You shouldn't have lied, Charley, but I understand why you did it. The drugs and the pussy. And I'll bet it was mostly the pussy, right?"

I couldn't believe it. He and I were on the same wavelength. He understood on a crude level what I had tried to articulate on an academic level: women are insane. They know what they got, and they get what they want. The smart ones anyway. I never understood how any woman could walk around filled with low self-esteem when she possessed something as powerful as the Hiroshima bomb. Men will do anything to get it. They'll even make up stupid, desperate lies about slick magazines.

"Women are born crazy, Charley. So don't hold it against her."

"What did you think of 'Mister Eight' after you rifled my briefcase?"

"Realism bores me."

I stared at him while part of my mind reread the short story that it had read a thousand times. The rest of my brain shook its head with disbelief that this thing had happened. How could any woman be so vindictive? Was Pearce lying? But why would a man lie just because a bullet had his name on it?

"Did you break into the clinic where I worked?" I said.

He took a sip, and the tinkling of ice cubes again brought back memories of my mother. Pearce set the glass on the arm of the chair where it left a nice round wet ring.

"I've never met a window yet I couldn't break," he said. "People are crazy. Do you get it now, Charley? Everybody is

269

crazy. That gun you got there, it makes me nervous. You can kill me, Charley, but that gun won't protect you from being killed by anyone who wants to kill you. I could have killed you any time I wanted since I got to town. I've killed men, Charley. Took them into the desert and buried their bodies. But I'm not here to kill you. Linda asked me to do these things, including the wicker man upstairs. She's mad as hell at you, Charley. You should get her out of this house and out of your life as fast as you can because she hates you. She really does want to be a writer. She's mad as hell at you about that lie. You should never lie to a woman. It doesn't work. I don't lie to women. I didn't lie to her about her writing. What do I know about writing? I told her I didn't like her story. What do you think of her writing?"

"It's all right."

"Publishable?"

"That's a dubious question," I said. "Have you ever read a book that wasn't publishable?"

He laughed and nodded. "I read on airplanes. I read crap. It takes my mind off flying. I've read lots of unpublishable novels. They get published anyway."

"Linda writes better than most people. If I taught her how to go about it, I believe she could write a publishable novel."

He set his drink down and nodded. "That's what I was afraid of."

"What do you mean?" I said.

His legs were crossed. He gazed at his upper knee for a moment, reached out and flicked at a bit of lint. "Before she left she told me she was going to write a novel about me."

"This was after you made fun of her writing."

"Yeah. I couldn't let her do it, of course. That's why I'm taking her back with me. If I let you teach her how to write novels, it would cause problems."

The Paradise That Lurks in Female Smiles

I stared at him as he sat there contemplating his lintless knee. The thing he had just said astounded me. He spoke of writing as if it was tantamount to building a model car. Is this what laymen think of writing, of the novel, of literature? Do they think of it as a "thing" that can be put together with the correct instruction, a "thing" that can be dangerous in the wrong hands? Are there people who live in a world so misinformed that they cannot grasp reality? Or maybe it was just a simple misunderstanding. An exposé of a Reno hit man could cause trouble, I could see that, I could understand that. On the far end of the spectrum it could cause death. At this end it could cause—had caused—a hassle that might be defined as "minor."

He glanced at me with a look that I interpreted in ways that were probably erroneous. He looked as if I possessed the secrets of the Aztecs. He looked as if he was trying to fathom what was inside my head. Would this strange power that I possessed, this knowledge, be worth the ramifications of bumping me off? But I wasn't the only creative-writing teacher in America.

I waited for him to confirm my suspicions, but instead he continued with the chatty informality of someone who was bringing things to a close.

"You better cut Linda loose. You made a lifelong enemy out of her and it ain't gonna be worth it. I'm the only guy she could never control. Any time she tried to make me do something I didn't want to do, I'd go out and get laid to get my mind off her pussy. That was my self-defense. I love that Linda girl, Charley. She's the best woman I ever knew, but she'll kill you, Charley. She'll kill you on the inside. That's what women do. They don't have our kind of muscle. They don't need them. They got internal muscle. It starts and ends between their legs. That's all they need to kill us."

"Stop talking," I said.

"You got it."

"Just shut up and go," I said.

"And . . . ?" he said.

"What do you mean?"

"And . . . ?"

"Why are you saying that?"

"You tell me to just shut up and go back to Reno, right, and . . . ?"

"I don't know what you're getting at."

"Yes you do. You just can't bring yourself to say it. I understand, Charley. Put the forty-five away and go back to teaching people how to write. I'll go back to Reno and take Linda with me. That's the 'and.' It was nice to meet you, Charley. I'm going to shut up now . . . and go back to Reno . . . and take Linda with me. That's the 'and.' She's out of your life, Charley, unless you want to keep her here and get laid every night and let her torment you to death."

I thought this over.

"Will you do me one favor, Pearce?" I said.

"Sure."

"Don't repeat this conversation to her."

"You got my word on that." He picked up the glass, looked at the naked ice cubes, rattled them, and set the glass down. "I'm sorry I pulled all that shit on you, Charley, but I let her pussy make me do it. She is one hell of a lay."

"Did you steal the drugs at the clinic?"

"Let's not get into that. Let's get into something else. Linda told me your sob story. Okay. Yes. I put the trash back in the wastebaskets."

"Jesus guy — why the fuck did you do that? What did I ever do to you?"

He shrugged. "Pussy," he said.

The Paradise That Lurks in Female Smiles

I wanted so badly to shoot him. He had invented a synonym for "Linda."

"That's why you lied to her about the *New Yorker*," he said. "She really does want to be a novelist. I read something she wrote and I laughed at it. I mocked her ambitions to be a writer. I shouldn't have done that. She got mad and split. It took me a while to track her down."

"Did you laugh at 'Mister Eight'?"

He shook his head no. "She wrote that after she got here."

"You're Mister Eight," I said.

"That's how she got back at me. I look like an idiot in that story."

Strange, I thought. The idea that character number two looked like an idiot had not occurred to me. A man picks up a woman in a bar, and that same woman tells me she picked him up, but I never read between the lines. I realized then that this is the penalty for writing "true" stories. The real-life characters see what they want to see, not what you want them to see. We are all touchy bastards.

"She picked you up," I said.

He closed his eyes and nodded. He leaned forward, stood up, and brushed off his hands as if they were covered with crumbs. He walked slowly toward me.

I raised the pistol. "What are you doing?" I said.

"It's time to pack," he said. "Would you please not point that thing at me?"

I backed off to let him cross into the hallway.

"No," I said. "I am going to keep this pistol trained on you until you leave my house, which is now."

"No, not now, Charley. I have to pack Linda's things."

"What do you mean?"

"I'm taking her back to Reno with me tonight, Charley. She's done with Denver. She told me she doesn't want to be around you anymore."

I was speechless. Was it his news, or was it his aplomb? He entered the bedroom and opened the closet, hefted the suitcase from the floor, and spread it out on the bed. He began packing.

He glanced back at me and shook his head. "Damn," he said softly. "You might kill me but you won't get it for free. Please point the muzzle away. I don't want to have to punish you."

I eased the muzzle away but kept it pointed at the bedside lamp.

"How do you know I don't have friends outside?" he said as he picked up colorful bras and carefully folded them. "How do you know I don't got a friend who has a pistol pointed at your back right now as we speak?"

I glanced back. Reflex. He did scare me. I had never seen such aplomb.

"You don't strike me as the kind of man who has friends," I said.

He grinned. He folded panties and tucked them next to the bras.

"Oh, I got friends, professor. Maybe our definition of the word 'friends' differs, but I do got friends."

He glanced at the muzzle and noted that it was not pointed at him. He finished up, closed the suitcase, lifted it, and set it upright on the floor.

"Game's over," he said, adjusting his tie, his collar, craning his neck, shooting his cuffs. I sensed he was sticking it to me. His neck had no need to be craned, his tie was not askew. I raised the pistol and pointed the muzzle at him. "You broke into my house. I'm reporting you to the police."

"Gee-zush," he said in the softest whisper. He meant "Jesus," but he was so disgusted he could not gather enough air to make it worth his while. "Put that away, Charley. You're not shooting me and you're not calling the police." He picked up the suitcase and walked out of the bedroom, went down the hall, and entered the dining room. I was astonished that a man could continue with his life as if a gun were not pointed at him. I meant less to him than a wee bee buzzing around his head. I could have shot him and gotten away with it and he knew it, yet he didn't pause or slow or even acknowledge that I held his life in my hand.

"Where is Linda?" I said.

"Forget Linda, Charley. It's over."

"Is she okay?"

"Of course she's okay."

"Well, where is she?" I said, and this time he did not deign to answer. I was nothing to him. Null set. Nonentity. He was looking around, making sure he had everything he had come for.

"I ought to shoot you just because you're pissing me off," I said.

His shrug was small, noncommittal, confident.

"Where is Linda?" I said.

"Try to forget Linda, Charley. She's okay. She's going back with me."

"Does she want to go with you?"

"Yeah."

A simple unaccented "yeah" that spoke volumes. He was not lying.

"Why?" I said. "Why would she want to be with a jerk like you?"

He looked over at me with a small smile as he diddled with the suitcase. "Because I got her a connection at the *New Yorker*."

"What are you talking about?"

"One of the editors I spoke to said he would read Linda's story if I sent it."

"An editor you threatened?"

"Naw. Just a nice guy I spoke to. I told him I was a creative-writing teacher in Denver and asked if he would look at the story if I sent it along. He said yeah."

There it was. The solution to all my problems. Taken from me by this sack of shit from Reno. It had never occurred to me to actually call the *New Yorker*. Pricks like Pearce knew how to get through to people. Browbeating can be an art form.

I lowered the pistol. I didn't have him fooled. I was not going to shoot him.

"Your fingerprints are all over my apartment," I said. "How do you know I won't get drunk some night and report you to the Reno police? How do you know that I won't make a bad decision and cause you a lot of grief?"

He smiled at me. "I have faith in you, Charley. I have faith in all mankind. Everybody is smart. Nobody is really stupid. They just do stupid things and hope they get away with it."

I began to feel like weeping. Please don't take Linda away from me. But his "yeah" said it all. She did not want to be with me anymore because I had lied to her. Shit! That's all men and women do to each other. What did she expect? Maybe Pearce was wrong. Maybe Linda was the one stupid person in the world.

"After I leave, go take a look in the bathroom," Pearce said. He was putting on a pair of gloves as he said this. Gloves to punch a man in the face and leave no bruises, no evidence, no knuckle-prints? Or just driving gloves? I hadn't gotten close enough to him at the cemetery to see if he had worn gloves when he drove that classy little European job.

"We won't be seeing each other again," he said. "Goodbye, Charley."

The Paradise That Lurks in Female Smiles

He picked up the suitcase and walked out the door. His confidence was infuriating. I slammed the door shut as if it was a guillotine. Cut the link of Time between the moment he was in here and the moment he walked out the door.

Done and done.

I looked down at Drew's gun and felt foolish. Maybe there were men in this world who used guns like tools, but I wasn't one of them. I pressed the clip release with my thumb and caught the heavy bullet-laden rectangle as it slid smoothly from the butt. I set it on the mantelpiece and ejected the final bullet from the chamber. The .45 was just a paperweight now. No more deadly than the average piece of steel that weighed 2.437 pounds.

Chapter 29

Let us allow the story to end here, officially, and by the clock. Even though words will continue to flow, the actual story ends so abruptly that it might be best to ease our way out of here like traitor football fans who leave the stadium before their team loses officially. This occurred during one of the greatest moments in the history of the Denver Broncos. I will try not to bore you—words cannot compete with instant replay: The football game was virtually over. The Broncos were behind by three points. There was one second left on the clock. The other team kicked the ball for the extra point, it was blocked, a Bronco lineman picked it up, ran 105 yards for a touchdown, and won the game.

Half the stadium was empty.

The remaining half went insane.

Traitor fans began filtering back into the stadium to see what the ruckus was all about. But because they had been so eager to get out to their parked cars ahead of everyone else and beat the traffic on the highways, they missed one of the greatest, most adrenaline-pumping, inconceivable, breathtaking victories ever enjoyed by the Denver Broncos. Denver won by three points. The traitor fans missed it.

Yes. The story ends here. But it doesn't end entirely. Stories never end entirely.

My self-esteem was shot to shit. How could a man not have feared even Barney Fife if he was holding a loaded gun? How could anybody be so confident? Had it been an act? But Pearce probably was a killer. You don't get that way with a conscience, compassion, sensitivity. He did seem like a sensitive guy though. Our conversation had not sunk to the level of the gutter. He didn't come right out and insult my manhood. He was Reno muscle, and he was amused by me, a teacher of creative writing in a cow town. But he was wrong. I was an amateur after all. So what if I could pull a trigger? A baboon could pull a trigger.

I went to the bar and set the gun down, fixed a shot of Johnnie Walker, and drank it off. Linda was gone. I looked at the bathroom. Why did he bring that up? Was Linda curled up in the bathtub with her throat slit? I will admit that this mental wisecrack made me a bit afraid. Who knows how amoral Reno muscle can be when it comes to a true showdown? But still . . . I did have the option of calling the police. I wished I had gotten a look at his license plate. He must have driven all the way here, unless the sports car was a rental.

I set the shot glass down and moved toward the bathroom, wiping my hands on the sides of my pants as if they were filthy. I wanted clean hands when I gazed upon his surprise. I opened the bathroom door with what I liked to think of as aplomb, as if prepared to see the thing that sergeants had warned us we would see in war: bloody buddies.

The bathtub was empty. I looked around. Nothing was amiss. I opened the medicine cabinet mirror and looked at the odd vials and orange prescription bottles that everyone has in their cabinets. Nothing. I started to close the door when I opened it again and looked at a plastic bottle that had been placed near the front edge of a metal shelf—all by itself. I looked closely and saw the words "Bayaud Clinic."

I picked up the bottle and peered at the tiny printing. "Dilaudid," it read. I knew what Dilaudid was. A carefully controlled narcotic drug. Higher on the scale of pain relief than morphine. A deadly drug in the wrong hands, especially the hands of an addicted hippie who did not understand that allergies were no joke. I imagine that a lot of hippies died way back when because they did not understand that your heart, your lungs, your kidneys, your anything could cease to function if you swallowed the wrong pharmaceutical. It didn't even have to be an overdose. Just the wrong pill. Pearce was wrong too. Hippies are congenitally stupid.

I carried the bottle into the living room and started to set it on the table next to my telephone. That's when I noticed a strange orange shadowy shape inside the Dilaudid bottle. I popped the lid and saw a folded piece of paper. I pulled it out and read the following words: "Go look in the basement bathroom."

I did as I was told. Without being told, I even went upstairs and looked in the medicine cabinet of the attic apartment. Yes. A third bottle of pills stolen from the Bayaud Clinic sat on a shelf. My house was a nest of stolen narcotics.

Let us end the story here for real. I will not go into detail about my manic search, my ripping up of the floorboards to find the hideous, noisy, thudding plastic bleeding hearts that Pearce had planted all over my house, booty from the Bayaud Clinic.

Oh yes, Charley Quinn. Call the police. Bring them over to search the joint. Tell them that Reno muscle did it, that they could catch him fleeing across the Rockies in a classy European jobby that did a hundred and ten on the curves. Catch him! Make him pay for his crimes! I will be a witness in court! I will nail his ass, send him to Leavenworth, then roll up my sleeves and prepare myself to take down all his friends from New York to Reno. Either that or give my landlord notice and start looking for a new place to live.

No wonder Pearce was filled with confidence. He was so afraid of me that he had arranged to have me kill myself, provided I did something stupid. I have to admit that I felt honored by Pearce's faith in me.

Men and women lie all the time. It is the basis of all relationships. If men and women stopped lying to each other, the divorce rate would clock in at ninety-nine percent. Only the chronic liars would remain together. Which means that to this day I wish Pearce and Linda a long, fulfilled, and argumentative life.

I will never stop loving her.